Shattered 1
The Impact

Thompson Charlie

An Imprint of Sulis International Press
Los Angeles | London

Library of Congress Control Number: 2019920791
ISBN (print): 978-1-946849-66-3
ISBN (eBook): 978-1-946849-67-0

Published by Riversong Books
An Imprint of Sulis International
Los Angeles | London

www.sulisinternational.com

Contents

*To my dear wife
our three lonely sons
and all who bathed in pain
loosened by a vampire regime*

ACKNOWLEDGEMENTS

The work of putting together these incredible experiences will not be complete without paying due respects.

To Fouad Asfour, a great friend who pushed my pen by giving encouragement at a bleak time when I could have given up.

To Dandira Mushangai and Martin Gwete, who in that maze also walked their journeys.

To Menzi Mbonambi, Thobile Disemelo, John Wanjiku, Thotho Mubhenga, Sister Lulu, Charmaine and all the members of the African Writers Forum who gave their wonderful support and constructive criticism of my work which gave me back my voice.

And without reserve I owe this book to my loving wife and our three lonely sons who never lost faith in me under difficult times when everything seemed lost and broken.

PART 1

ONE

The morning arrived. I had exhausted the night snoring on the pavement under the safety of the sky. People stumbling across us, startled, would warily make a detour. Some struck with fear melted away. Casting lofty glances back over their shoulders. Unflustered, we would sleep. Like ghosts from another world, we fused with the city life, transforming the city landscape with our smelling pervasive presence. Other people would scrutinize our emaciated forms for the branding abnormality that would betray to them our sickness in vain – our drab lives which had sneaked out of the bile of an evil tummy that wolfed and vomited the lives and flesh of its own children. The terror and sorrow that etched its familiar road upon us only known to ourselves.

We were running away with our lives from a brutal wicked regime that never saw us as part of the "us" that was the nation. When they spoke about us their blood boiled, calling us "them!" Them who had the mark of death —the flotsam of a revolution.

I did not know that I was stuck somewhere in a crevice of grim war between what had been and the future. A womb of embryonic divide where the grief soiled past was being slaughtered and the fierce probing present unlocked the door that breezed in a new world. Agony, fear, anger, hope and courage squaring up in a collision of knowledge, wisdom and cruel hope! It was a war zone where on one hand raged an inferno where vanquished, the fragmented mind surrenders and the soul is consumed into nothingness, turning cannibal upon itself and erroneously admitting that what one stood up for was actually a pound of flesh and only a preserve for the privileged few. On the other hand, a transformative amalgam where all the joys and horrors of life painfully give birth to a new respect of the self and mankind.

A haughty looking woman, smartly dressed in tight navy blue skirts and a white blouse surged up the street. Making a detour, she cast mystified glances under her drowsy eyelashes as she edged by. I twisted a wry smile into my itchy beard. Reaching into my satchel, I produced a copy of Leo Tolstoy's Anna Karenina that I was reading. Reading and writing snatches of poetry in my uprooted loneliness was the only thing that kept the balance of my disintegrating system under decent robes. A writhing mass of fragrance, pampered skin and sartorial wealth, she rolled like Cleopatra stepping out of Egyptian Poetry.

My mind spun, the shame and dishonour of abrogating my responsibilities as a husband and a father exploded, smothering my consciousness for a split second. And loneliness was a flooding river of iron filings, slashing mercilessly into my broken heart. Yet most of us had to depart so that we could return. Disappear so that we could see our loved ones again! The sun scorched our bodies, reeking with the sweat and grime of several days. There were days when the rain sluiced down at night from bilious skies. Such cold nights stabbing our sleepless forms on the pavement stayed with us forever in our minds. And we wandered around the world like thin smokes, a whole gamut of bad emotions detonating inside us. Largely misunderstood and doing all kinds of dirty jobs.

Her hauteur and stiletto shoes murdered the frail heart of man on the tarmac. One, definitely, could never escape the magical odour of wealth and silk that rustled with the movement of her rippling body. About fifteen paces away, she turned and retraced her steps. Stopping beside me, she fished out of her bag a red lunch box. It was offered to me, in haughty patronizing silence. I just looked back, my eyes inscrutable behind my large thick brown lenses. My pride spoke. I had lost trust in humanity and hated any demeaning charity.

I think the big tinted old eye glasses, awkwardly sitting upon my nose-bridge must have impressed as huge, brown compound eyes. Darkly mysterious! People stopped, stared and laughed at the comic figure before them. I never cared about what they saw or thought. All I cared for was what they served - my precious sight.   Three months ago, two men had accosted me one night, walking in the street near my home. Their wicked fists flourishing in the air, they spewed out of their mouths some political slogans. I never responded. Instead, I spit out saliva on the roadside. One of them, biting his ugly lower lip, had then produced a gun. The evil black thing rose in his trembling hands until its barrel coldly kissed my forehead. I saw a hatred born of the filthiest night flashing in his murderous eyes. His colleague becoming aware of my neighbour watching from his garden, swept away the gun with his right hand, saying that I needed re-education. Brutal kicks and blows rained. A broken tooth jerked out of my mouth and I yelled for help. My neighbours gushed out shouting in anger. One of the thugs lifted his ugly foot as if he were about to march, then it came crashing down upon my glasses which lay fallen on the tarmac.

Dazed like a bat that had fallen out of the moon I found myself on the run. I crossed the border with death yapping at my heels. My near-sighted eyes registering everything in a blur, I was in grave danger of being run over by cars like a rat. Then I bought this comical pair of spectacles for R20 from a vendor on the street. The man sold an assortment of junk items in front of the Market Theatre in Joburg.

I must have appeared a creature of gnawing curiosity to her.

"You don't want it?" She spoke in English, pouting her vanity all over her cherry red lips.

"So you can speak?" I said.

"I thought maybe you didn't want it."

"You can speak to me, too, when you offer me something."

"Wow!"

"I need a job, I don't want to live like this."

"What is your name?"

"Bloggs."

"Are you coloured?"

"Black."

"Do you have a phone?"

"No. I was mugged walking along Bree Street."

"May I see what you are reading?"

I showed her the front cover of the book.

"Is it a good book?" she spoke her eyes sweeping my face.

"To me it's. I really like it."

What more could I say? She looked more like someone who spent most of her time calculating figures and navigating through financial statements. My heart thawed towards her. Yet the echo of her voice jarred in my ears like a siren.

Smiles and snarls! All I saw were luscious lips hiding the colour of intention. I had ceased to trust all people, existing only for myself.

"I will talk to you after work," she said in her raspy soothing voice. "In case you get hold of a phone, here is my business card."

"Thank you," I parroted back, taking both the business card and the lunch box smiling. Confused.

"Keep the lunch box for me," she said as she waltzed away, swinging her imperious bottom in irreverent circles to the rhythm of the merciless explosions detonated by her heels on the tarmac.

I could not remember the last time I had had such a properly cooked meal.

TWO

My clothes were always clean, even though sometimes wrinkled as if they had been pulled out of a cow's mouth. To solve the ironing problem, I went and bought some second hand jean shirts and trousers on the street, throwing away all the rumpled clothes. Some looked at us with a cold nauseated repugnance. The despicable odour of layers of sweat and the destitution we radiated subtracted our humanity in their eyes. Yet stubbornly, undisturbed by their prying eyes, I bore their patronising attitude without even a shred of rancour. Though crumbling into ruins as I was inside, I looked straight ahead with a light hard as granite shining in my eyes from one place I did not understand in the bottom of my soul. Casually, I would stop to look into shop-window displays with a calm poise, cool as a watermelon, appreciating the aroma of breakfast-cooking from Wimpy. Just the way they felt it, too! Yet, in my pain and reasoning, I did not know that transforming in that virulent ugly cocoon, a butterfly was being nourished for birth.

In the multi-layered puddle of the chaotic life of Joburg, we had our own distinguished world. Punctuated by sporadic violence and prejudice. People called us names like Makwerekwere because of our language which they did not understand. Some held their noses as we passed by. Though indigent and living on the street, I still treasured the nuggets of my mind and carried a good book wherever I went—the sole exhibition of value which attracted respect from those who noticed. Once a man driving along Simmons Street stopped his car to interview me:

"Where do you stay?"

"On the street."

"And where are you coming from?"

"The Salvation Army soup kitchen."

Puzzled, he turned to look at the group from which he had picked me up for the talk. He looked back at me and shaking his head, he started his car and drove off without saying another word. Evidently gobsmacked. To be able to look at another man and be able to see a part of yourself in that other man is a simple challenge that mankind still has to learn and overcome. Yet it will be a gross injustice to say that the whole rainbow nation of South Africa treated us with contempt. The majority of people behaved with charity and understanding towards us.

When we didn't know whether it was good for us to live or die we went and poured Joburg Beer down our parched throats at Shanty-Town. With our stomachs bulging like small tanks we perched on rough wooden benches where we explored all philosophical questions about our miserable life. Intoxicated, we thought very hard and talked so eloquently about being alive or dead that those who despised us, had they heard the profundity of our intellectual reasoning, they would have died of envy. We drank copiously, our pain and sorrow melting away. Insouciant, sometimes our life became an exploding adventure beyond an adventure, revealing and unravelling the pain of confused platitudes within and beyond our frugal proximate mortality. Our nearness to being doomed into oblivion. Exploring even into the vast mysterious lands of the unhinged, our life became a river that passed through both rich and famished lands. A multitude of journalists rubbed their shoulders with us for money-spinning articles and the simple poor sat together with us on the table, sipping Joburg Beer. Drinking sometimes as if there were no tomorrow.

We went to bed many a day without food and survived several consecutive days without a drop of water on our bodies. Sometimes we ate from handouts we got on the street from ordinary people and from soup kitchens. When we had money, we would buy pap with some relish to go down with it; pap and chicken skins; pap and beef bones; pap and mogodu (rough tripe); pap and bybles (soft tripe); pap and pork head; sometimes pap and chicken livers or chicken feet. I could give you a long list of all the rough food we savoured! We terribly missed perching on the toilet seat or standing under a shower. Feeling ourselves becoming strangers to our children and wives, some of us lost it with screws becoming loose and voices whispering in their softening heads. We pined for our loved ones, brooded over the poverty and the political repression enveloping their broken lives. Some were slowly dying alive while others were painfully being pulled out of death in the shadows. We were having journeys inside journeys!

Though sometimes I felt drowning in the sweltering sea of depression, I deigned to embrace the dogging battles and the sneering demons as challenges to live with rather than fear and avoid. Starving as I was, I fought the temptation to do crime every day. On the streets of Joburg one can easily make money through crime and also plunge to an early death by crime. Anyone could easily wake up of a morning cradling a gun in his hands. Yet life can be jam-packed and beautiful in that sprawling metropolis where the multitude strove to be caught in the explosion of its success and happiness.

One Saturday, late afternoon coming from Mashona Bar, near Park Station, I was crossing Bree Street into Von Brandis when two young thugs swooping from nowhere flanked me left and right. They strutted forward with distended chests and an air of exaggerated ferocity. I was carrying my most reckless and buoyant humour on that day. My eyes bloodshot with Joburg beer scanned all over their faces, hands and feet. I knit my brow and smiled at the borrowed fearsome gait they exhibited. Both of them bounced dramatically in their stride as if they had swallowed some tennis balls.

"Hi maSpecs, today you meet with big brother Kays."

"Big brother Kays?"

"Big brother Kays the original from Mfombi!"

"Kays never walked on tennis balls or half-inflated football bladders."

"You don't speak to Kays like that!"

"The last time I met Kays he opened the trunk of his car and gave me a thick wad of cash for beer."

"Who are you to speak to me like that?"

"Someone who knew Kays, smoked weed and played with him."

"I will cut your tongue and feed it to the dogs maSpecs."

"The last time I checked Kays never robbed a poor man on the street."

"You must be kidding maSpecs, I will shoot you."

"Go and shoot your father, he sired a demon into the world."

He dipped his hand behind the belt into the crotch of his trousers. My hands shot out like a couple of rattlesnakes, grabbing him from behind by the belt and dragged him into the middle of the street. Caught by surprise, he tottered twisted an ankle, lashed out with his other flailing hand and flipped about like a fish on a hook. Right in the middle of the street. There we were. Entangled in a chilling macabre dance. Bree Street is a wide one-way thoroughfare with three traffic lanes. The approaching cars and taxi minibuses, hooting madly, screeched to a halt. I nearly burst out my lungs trumpeting:

"Help! Muggers! Help! Muggers! Help!"

I weaved my right leg into his left leg and we both fell. A taxi driver came out of his vehicle wielding a whip. The thug rolled onto his feet and grabbing his foot, I dangled after him. The looping whip was a gigantic stitch of lightning in the air as it came down striking in an embracing wrap around his back and stomach. He shot up like a rocket and twisting, the shoe came off. It was left docking like an abandoned ship in my hands. I hurled my arm backwards and sent it dashing against the back of his head. He staggered, his arms flailing in the air like a drunken man who had taken a drum of skokian.

A car with its brakes screaming rammed into his buttocks and he leaped into the air like a cat, landing on top of a dust bin as a pistol fell out of the leg-end of his trousers. Rolling over onto the sidewalk, he had no time to pick it up. A confused mass in motion, he rammed and melted into the flow of human traffic swamping the street! An explosion of hysterical screams and curses chasing after him. The taxi driver casually picked up the gun and went back to his vehicle laughing. I picked up my pair of spectacles which had slid off my nose-bridge and fallen on the tarmac during the scuffle. I put them back where they belonged. The traffic surged forward. Instead of crossing over into von Brandis, I floated down Bree Street. Scenes of scuffle randomly exploded, defused and melted into thin air! As if nothing ever happened! Such is Joburg inner-city!

Bree Street is one of the busiest thoroughfares in Johannesburg. It is, like Smal Street, most popular for its clothing shops selling an assortment of affordable merchandise. On the different side, Bree Street is always a maze ranging from pedestrians, cars, metro and South African police on patrol to vendors pushing trolleys selling fruit and criminals of all types.

Different music tunes thundered out of these shops and people stood in the doorways accosting customers. Some stood on street corners trading and handing out fliers to passers-by. Fliers advertising backstreet doctors, abortionists, private colleges, driving schools and shopping specials. Women who did braids on the street, most of them foreigners from Mozambique and Zimbabwe, stood alongside the street holding boards with pictures of women's heads showing a variety of different hair-styles. Shoppers weaved in and out of shops. Nervous women firmly clutched their purses against their voluptuous and lean bodies.

Occasionally, the metro-police or the South African police assisted by members of the community policing forum came by patrolling in groups. The vendors selling all sorts of wares, fruits and stolen phones would scatter away together with people who had no papers. Tramps walked around foraging through the dust bins for food. Half-eaten chicken bones, fruit and anything! Pickpockets roamed the street with their magnetic hands, bumping into people and dispossessing them of their wallets and cell-phones. A pickpocket bumped into a middle-aged man and started talking very fast, furiously gesticulating with his hands.

"How would you feel if someone bumped into you and didn't apologise?"

He faked limping in front of the unfortunate man, grabbed his trousers in the front by the buckle of his belt. Up and down he vigorously shook the man's trousers. Another man appeared behind the victim and fished out his cell-phone and wallet. The shaken man's eyes bulged out, glistening like ostrich eggs broken into a pan. In a very thin reedy voice he stuttered an apology, reduced into a confused terrified toddler.

"It is always good to apologise when you hurt other people," the robber growled like a bear, limping away. And so relieved was the man. Feeling that he had just had a very narrow escape, he hastened away. Only too late to discover what actually had been played on him. Both his wallet and cell-phone had dissolved from his pockets! In disbelief, he pushed himself away bracing himself for the long walk back home to Alexandra.

It was an explosive playground for spinning deals and crime. Yet like a drug, the city that never sleeps never ceased to attract those who have been robbed back to it. I carried with me my global heart and the whole town was my home. Every God's day I plodded on. Dreading and not dreading. Gripping on. And sometimes just going with the flow. Every night I emptied my sleep on the pavement lying on cardboard and wrapped in plastic paper without a blanket. I had not known what it was like before not to have the protection of a roof. To be vulnerable. To live the conscious definition of destitution in the absolute. Leaving a beautiful home behind, a pretty wife, and three beautiful babes had not been an easy decision to make. Disillusioned and tired of running around in the shadow of death, life became a dream most possible in a foreign land.

I carried the rucksack of my past in the back of my mind, where with the rising sun it burned the lethargy of my constricted life like a furnace. Then at night, with the spilling out of the soft moonlight the guilt clawed out ripping my conscience. It spread a nameless fear over my heart, choking what was left of my frugal masculinity and hope! It roared with the anguish of flesh roasted on plastic fire, petrol bombs and the napalm that had eaten the lives of the children buried in shallow mass graves. The fire that had burned my arms, legs and back. The fire that had burned Nkosi's hands and face leaving contours of gnarled ugly flesh. The fire that burned our freedom.

*

Nkosi snored his pain and drunken sleep away beside me. A couple of months ago, my new friend and a former member of the military police, coming out of a bar in Noord Street, he had been attacked by unknown thugs, and was left with a badly crippled leg. Opening my bleary eyes to a sensed intrusion, suddenly, I espied him sitting and rolling a cigarette beside me. He had been discharged from the Johannesburg Charlotte Maxeke hospital. Back home his hand committed heinous crimes whilst on duty. He even murdered! Forced by the ruling party. Until he decided to become AWOL. Now he had nightmares and he slept holding his crutch in his hand like a gun. Because of these dramatic sleep-acts, we changed his name to AK47. Scenes of a horrific massacre exploding in his mind he would sit up in his sleep, shouting and brandishing his AK47 at unseen enemies.

"I am back," he had spoken through his beard like an indestructible reality.

"Good to have you back, pal."

Silence. Twitching burn scar muscles just beneath bloodshot eyes and a scraggy beard. An open and shut case, for all political crimes against the opposition were never prosecuted. If one ever tried to seek justice, then, death was near at hand. Just that! No prosecution but persecution.

"How did you find me?"

"Zulu told me I would see you here and I came straight."

"When did you come out of hospital?"

"Yesterday afternoon."

I looked at the crutches lying beside him and he discerned the question in my eyes. He looked at them too and nodded. His bearded square face cracking into a smile.

In silence, I glimpsed him in my mind cutting across the streets, through clogged traffic and hordes of people. I thought this was not a good place for him to sleep. Not for both of us. The sunlight filtered through the top and gaps between the skyscrapers of Johannesburg. I woke up my friend so that we could share my meal.

When I finished eating, I gathered the cardboard paper that had been my bed for the night, carefully folded and deposited it into the rubbish bin. There was nothing to throw away from the meal, even the chicken bones, we obliterated them all and wiped clean every morsel of rice that was in the lunch box. Then I put the plastic in my satchel. We did not need blankets. They were a huge encumbrance to carry around, frequently got dirty and needed washing. Cardboard paper and plastic sheets were the best. We picked them up free on the street at nightfall. Best of all there was no need to wash them! Sometimes feeling light at heart of a morning, I would, laughing at myself, trace with my finger the lines of my scrawny ribs indented overnight on that cardboard.

I went and perched on the roadside curb, waiting for my friend to finish. My satchel which I also used as a pillow when I slept lay beside me. That satchel was my precious wardrobe. All my clothes in there, soap, toothpaste, Vaseline, toothbrush, towel, books and certificates. All possessions that made me human. Me, a father on the street! A school teacher learning life on the street! I sorely missed my wife and my children. I even missed opening and closing the doors of my house. I burst out laughing. It was a real good laugh!

THREE

Every morning we washed our faces with water from a broken pipe in the street and then walked to Powerhouse where buses from Zimbabwe arrived and departed. We would stand in a queue and someone would come to hand out numbered tickets. There were so many people around, mostly Zimbabweans, then other foreigners and South Africans themselves. I espied how Joburg was a melting pot of exotic and local cultures, wealth and poverty. One had to wake up very early to get a cup of tea and six slices of bread. Sometimes we joined the line again for a second share which we shoved into our bags. Then we would go looking for jobs. And there were no bad jobs! The criteria for good or bad, normal or abnormal became a matter of personal conscience. The queue of hungry stomachs and anguished lives wound round the double storey building.

The police frequently patrolled the area, hunting for those who had no papers. If they caught you, they would load you onto the van and drive around until you paid them a bribe, R10 or R20 or something. Those who could not raise the bribe would be taken to Lindela Detention Camp where they awaited deportation. By early 2008, South Africa was deporting hundreds of Zimbabweans every day. But people kept streaming back, one deportation after another.

Everyone was a billionaire in Zimbabwe and those who still could get petrol on the black market drove around with stacks of cash in the trunks of their cars. I remember being attacked by some robbers in a restaurant. I had the bearer checks bulging in my back pockets. I fought them and fell on my buttocks, kicking in the air like a mad grasshopper and yelling for the security. The security guard came and they fled. People asked me if I had lost anything to the robbers. I said that they had made off with my purse. No sooner had I finished revealing my loss than I noticed two men float out of the crowd, following the robbers. I guessed they were part of the gang and now were following their colleagues to share the spoils. Yet, I knew I had not lost anything. I still wonder what bloody act happened when their colleague told them he had gotten away with nothing.

The government had suspended the conventional banknotes and was printing bearer cheques. Some worthless tender that soon went to par with toilet paper! Overnight, we became a country without a currency. The government blamed the opposition for all its failures. Even for the drought. Inflation passed the 1000% mark and prices were going up every minute. Madness sprouted in our midst. Business people no longer wrote down quotations for their customers.

There was no food in the shops. People waited, wrestled and fought in queues for the whole day. Anticipating deliveries that all the time never came. People knew that they were being diverted to the black market by corrupt politicians yet to say a word was to court the wrath of the mighty. Weak from hunger, some people collapsed in the queues. Others sustained serious injuries and left for their homes empty-handed. Bank coffers ran dry! With the economy in the hands of the black market the cogwheels of industry ground to a halt. Everyone had to be corrupt to survive. The newspapers reported that there was no fuel in the petrol stations. The president, on one of his trips abroad, had literary responded that anyone who doubted the availability of fuel in the country should go lie down on the street and see if they were not run over by a car. When asked about the food shortages, he had ejaculated that Zimbabweans were choosy people and did not like potatoes; that was why they were going hungry. I remember that is how the big hole began to grow and spread like a devastating cancer.

The South African government could hardly cope with the influx of the political and economic refugees from Zimbabwe. The exodus rendered the border porous with people risking their lives by wading through the crocodile-rife Limpopo River. Some of these illegal immigrants had their fates piteously decided by being mauled to death by the alligators. Relics of bodies mangled beyond recognition, were picked up and given a pauper's burial. Others were swept away and never seen by the ruthless river's current whilst some were robbed, raped and killed by the Gumagumas. Gumagumas are ruthless criminals who wait for the people in the bushes around the border post and perpetrate all sorts of crime against them.

The South African government noticed that most of the people came to South Africa to sell their wares, work and buy groceries but with the economic situation in their country, Zimbabweans were finding it difficult to raise money for the visa. They decided to scrap it, which saved a lot of lives from impending death by starvation and hunger. Still some could not even raise the money to obtain a passport which normally took between six months and a year to land into one's hands. Thus we found ourselves broken, battered, bruised, trapped and in near despair in a foreign country. A multitude of us without papers and wanted back home by the fascist police for speaking in defence of our political and social rights.

*

The other day we went to the Home Affairs offices at Marabastad to apply for asylum permits. We joined the other men in a gigantic python of a queue winding on the dusty ground outside the offices. The line lurched forwards and backwards, retching sideways like a tormented serpent. We held tightly and pressed into each other. Our ribs ached and our stomachs growled with hunger. The dust rose into our nostrils and mouths. We swallowed it with the wind. It painted our faces with the colour of desperation and tinted our hair. The sun burned our skins, our scalps, our brains. We sweated wetting our clothes whilst the government officers regarded us like madmen acting a stupid movie. Here and there, we ploughed our feet into the soil. Pressure came from behind and we scattered, some falling. People cursed. Fighting, I slithered back into the queue. The man in front of me spun out, stretched backwards and fell dizzily landing on his buttocks. He rolled in the dust and became the colour of dust. His eyes red as chillies! He came back fight-ing like a demon, wedging himself back into position, inch by inch. I felt him like a flat sheet of human flesh between me and the next person and his bones creaked. Then some-thing happened. He groaned, his eyes bulging out, spun around showing the reddened whites only. Like one who had swallowed a fish-bone. He vomited. Only a trickle of bile spewed out of his flat belly. Again the line lurched forward and he was violently catapulted out, falling hard on his back. He lay blinking at the frowning sky, clawing and twitching like an overturned cockroach. His large deformed boots scribbling supplications of his suffering to his creator in the heavens.

The whole day we battled an indifferent force that ran on the blood of corruption, arrogance and spite. We had ar-rived there just before seven o'clock in the morning yet by close of business at five o'clock I had moved no more than thirty paces ahead. Frustrated, we hung around soaked in disbelief. We heard that some people had been there for more than five days. They bought chicken heads or chicken livers from the shops and cooked their meals in tins on naked fires speckling and wretchedly burning in the open space. Sometimes the wind rose like an evil spirit swirling and slapping dust in people's faces, inside the cooking pots and on the food dished out on the plates. There were no toi-lets or bathrooms. People released themselves in the nearby bush where sometimes they were robbed with their pants down. They fetched water for cooking and bathing from the river cutting through the same bush. Women bathed from small containers under the cover of their blankets. Some-times they went into the cemetery where they could bath freely under the cover of darkness and the guard of their men. The men bathed in another section of the same river. The same river into which drains deposited the industrial and commercial effluence from the city of Tswane (Pretoria).

I bought half a loaf of bread and a tin of baked beans. I had no tin opener, so I ground its top hard against the tarmac in circles until it came off. A spiteful wind sprung up, leaving grains of dirt in my beans and on my bread. Wincing upon every single bite, I had to philosophize that at least it was better than supping from the dust bin. Other people had no meal at all. That night we slept under the safety of the open sky. We slept on cardboard and wrapped ourselves with plastic against a very thin interminable drizzle.

When daylight peeled the darkness away, we were already standing in the queue. This time I counted less than twenty-five people in front of me. My heart vibrated with hope. Yet no sooner had we taken position than the thugs burst upon the scene. People paid the thugs money who planted them in the front part of the queue. In anger we flew at those people clawing them out and the thugs whipped out knives. They charged and we fled. Then we returned to reclaim our positions. When they started serving, I saw that we kept on being swallowed further down the gut of the retching python that was the queue. The much dreaded torture of the previous day erupted again. The rain came and we got wet. We wrestled, slithered and fell in the mud, rolling like poor sumo wrestlers and nobody cared. The writhing queue broke and the security whipped us away like undesirable skunk.

It ignited the truth that getting papers without bribing the thugs or some kind of foul play was a pipe dream. They had the security and some unscrupulous home affairs officers in their pockets. We quietly deliberated among ourselves and connived to take one of the thugs out. I approached him:

"How much to get in the front?"

"Give me R200."

"Only R200?"

"Don't waste my time."

"I just came from home chief, do you know where I can sell some of my diamonds?"

His facial expression came alive with greed.

"You have diamonds?"

"Yes, don't talk so loud."

"I know of someone who runs a jewellery shop. Can you show me?"

"Perfect!"

I made as if to produce something then abruptly stopped.

"I need where no one can see us. This is real big money we are talking about."

"Let's go to the river."

We found the river deserted since all people were busy trying their luck at the Home Affairs offices. My heart beating, I fumbled with my bag. My partners in crime seemed never in coming. When fear and uncertainty had just begun bruiting in my mind and the thug had begun to grow horns, five apparitions loomed large and menacing out of the bushes. They built a solid human wall around us. Two men jumped the thug. They twisted his arm. He leaned forward in pain. The locked arm moved over his back. The two men pressed him downwards and soon he lay flat on his stomach the twisted arm still on his back, the other arm on his side. I took a handkerchief out of his pocket tying it around his mouth. I never anticipated what happened next. One of the men grabbing the twisted arm suddenly jerked, brutally wrenching it outwards with inexpressible force. There was a cracking sound and the arm broke in two places. It had never spread in my mind that we were going to punish him with so much violence and cruelty! Appalled, I did not wish to be part of it anymore! I picked up my bag and immediately fled to the train station. It was a dull and cheerless ride back to Joburg.

There is a time when the good fight is sullied and debased by senseless revenge, a kind of revenge that drags one into the low league of one's enemies—an act that does not differentiate one from the evil that one is fighting against! Such an act is the beginning of all feuds, leading to senseless bloodshed and absolute loss of reason in a cause! Sadly, I felt such an act as one I had just witnessed and undeniably partaken of.

I returned to Marabastad the following day hell-bent on getting my papers sorted out. I had no money to bribe the security but my will spurred me on. I did not stand in the line. I went straight to the front where I joined those managing the writhing column.

"Who're you?" someone barked.

"What're you doing here?" another one challenged me.

"You can't see what I'm doing? I'm controlling the line! Stopping anyone who came here after me from getting in before I do!" I snapped back. While we wrangled the security instructed the people in the front to move forward, through the gate into the yard. I sprang forward and before anyone could stop me, I had gone through, marching with the others into the reception where I claimed my seat. Victory in that place only came the way of those who dared. The cunning and the fittest!

I saw people who walked with a limp of something that had been taken away from them. People who walked vast distances to save their skin until their feet burst into blisters. Stories of loss and losses that bespoke of blood, humiliation, sweat and tears. Dark stories of a pain that ripped their ruptured souls with anger, shame, guilt and fear. I saw in their eyes the bombs that may have killed their loved ones which now roasted their hearts like a microwave. And their faces groaned a shouting silence of grief on sagging shoulders. A big sneering hole was eating into the whole community, threatening to swallow their humanity like a mass grave. And now they sought to rise out of their warrior blood, flesh, bones and souls the last fight of their redemption.

Holding a cup of black tea in my hand, I searched for a quiet free spot under a tree where I could drink in peace. I had only taken a couple of sips when I felt someone lightly rapping my shoulder.

"What! Rob, you are here, too!" I exclaimed. Rob was an old friend I last saw several years ago in high school and he was the first person I knew to meet since my coming to Johannesburg. He was one of those civil servants who had been doing well.

"As you can see my friend," he grinned back.

"Wonderful. How did you get here?"

"I came by bus a month ago,"

Before I could say anything he added:

"I came with Pete but he is in hospital now." Pete was an old friend and we had played football together in high school.

"Pete? What happened?"

"He suffered a stroke. He burst a vein in the head and he had to undergo surgery," his sombre tone told me it was a grave matter.

"Seems not good,"

"Not good," he nodded, sipping his tea.

"How long has he been in there?"

"Two weeks."

Rob gave me the ward number and finished his tea. I knew I would never go to the hospital. Figuratively, I was already dying inside! Then Rob left. Pete had his sister with him in Joburg and I had no one, what if it happened to me, too? And what if I would not be able to recover? I felt a tearing stabbing pain around the right-hand side hairline of the forehead. Swaying I rose from where I was crouching. My contorted face collided with the bright sunlight and my vision swam. A labyrinth sea of lightning burst in my mind, sending shock waves through my body. I bent forward, my head in my hands and staggered, vigorously rubbing the spot at the same time. Sweat poured out. Saliva drooled. I urinated in my pants!

"Bloggs! Bloggs! Are you ok?" Nkosi was hobbling on his crutches in front of me.

I just shrieked in pain, unable to answer him. After about thirty seconds, it swept over. I was surfacing out of it, straightening up and taking my hands off my head when another huge wave struck.

"Aaaaghhhhh! Aaaaghhhhh!," I shrieked several times, twisting and turning in agony. Then barely half a minute again, it was over. Yet the severity of the agony I felt was something I would feel for the rest of my life. It was the ineluctable pain of blood and flesh poisoned by wretched loneliness and a mind become self-destruct. The pain of being hounded by a cold usurping force that callously wrenched a part of my life out of me and whispered in my ear:

"I've got you! I am inside you and you will never escape. I've got you!"

I was on medication for depression and sometimes I must have felt like a zombie. A moving chunk of useless flesh and broken bones. I thought very hard what it meant for me to be alive and because I did so without limit my thoughts would twist and subsequently conjure ghastly images of my death. One day it was good to feel alive and on the next day it would be good to feel numb and dead! For three weeks, I had been fermenting like that. Sometimes my throat would run dry and my tongue would scrape against the roof of my mouth like a claustrophobic crocodile trapped in a tiny rock cave. I would feel a lump of a croak slowly rising in my gut and as it burst, its poison would burn like sulphur, pulling at my gut walls. My stomach heaved and convulsing I would throw, drenching everything in front of me with the excrement of this monster which usurped my inner self. Then, only then, would I be temporarily delivered from the arrogant demon. A couple of days ago I had been thrust out of sleep in pain and that was the first time I had ever urinated in my pants. And that is what happened again on that day! I spewed my vomit all over Nkosi's plaster and we had to do a job cleaning it. Something was wrong! I was more than a broken man. I felt like DYING!

We left Braamfontein and Nkosi was speechless. But I smiled at him, trying to reassure him that I was all right. I had only known him for a couple of months before he got clobbered by some thugs, landing in Johannesburg hospital. This dark side of my health was something he had never known. I searched for my tablets in the satchel, stared at them and tossed them back inside without slipping any in my mouth. Then I asked Nkosi to give me time alone for I wanted to go and rest awhile in Joubert Park. I said he could come back and fetch me after an hour which he did but found me gone. I had made up my mind.

I got up and went in search of those vilest areas of Joburg where soulless men of darkest blood and deeds frequented. Suddenly a young couple spewed out of McDonalds Restaurant in front of me. The young lady, her rippling legs bare, stamped on the tarmac in gleaming black heels. She wore shorts of tight fitting blue jeans that strapped around her like a bikini and a tight fitting leopard vest that half-ejected her large breasts as she leaped up and down. Shrieking with anger she pummelled her boyfriend with impotent blows using her handbag. A small purse flew out of the bag landing right in my path. Both of them did not notice it. They continued with their fight, the young man hitching up his black leotard jeans which he wore below his small buttocks. Heavy silver chains dangled in the buckles of his jeans and around his neck. I picked up the purse and followed them.

"Do you love her?"

No one answered her.

"Tell me! Do you love that bitch?"

The man fumbled with his chains. She pummelled him again with the bag and her fists which were ineffective like two small buns.

"Yes, you love her more than you love me! But you know that I love you more than she does."

Frustrated, hurt and hopeless, tears streamed out of her eyes washing away the make-up on her cheeks. The boyfriend flung his hands with a ring on every finger and hunched around her small frame. He mumbled something and stroked her dishevelled long hair. She trembled with emotion. Defeated!

I walked to them and holding out the purse I said:

"I think you dropped this."

The lady raised her head from his chest leaving a thick smear of rouge on his white T-shirt. A ghostly smudged face. She grabbed the purse with her long fingers and quickly checked its contents. Then she said:

"Thanks."

"Only that? Aren't you going to give him something?"

"Does it look like he needs something?"

"Honestly, I don't need anything from you. I'm tired of this thankless world. You could even do well if you could kill me."

I turned to continue on my quest for death. I felt a careless light-heartedness I never experienced before. I looked upwards and saw crowds of praying people in the clouds doing various processions, dances and rituals about the end of the world. Cold, weird dances which touched my soul as beautiful and enchanting, in the shimmering bluish black sunlight, with a whiteness that dazzled, dimmed and stirred me into a drunken stupor. I greeted these menacing men where I saw them but no one minded me. Darkness fell and still I went further courting evil to befall me. Goading the devil to come out of hell and incur my wrath, too.

I teased one I thought was the weirdest and most foul, one I thought harboured a legion of demons. He struck me with the foul palm of his open hand leaving an imprint of five fingers on my cheek. Blood trickled out of the corner of my mouth in a rivulet. He let out of his mouth an avalanche of the cruellest angry venom I have ever heard, before suddenly shutting down into a sneering silence. Veins throbbed in his forehead as if he wore his heart in that place. Biting his ugly lower lip, he stared at me, his nostrils dilating like a roused rhinoceros. I crouched in his lair, my dirty shoes soiling his blankets and urging him to kill me. Ugly and towering, he stood. Clenching and unclenching his scarred massive pumpkin fists. So hard he stared and with a frenzied elation I anticipated his charge. Harder, I stared back. Poised for the charge with all his demons he tensed. Silhouetted against the entrance. Swaying like gorilla! I waited, molten lava tearing through my veins and playing heavy metallic drums in my ears. Then shaking, he raised the hand that had struck my face and smelled it. Still harder I stared back, the rage in my eyes not of this world. Suddenly, his demeanour altogether altered and I saw in his eyes the confused soul of a frightened hare. His head dropped as if an electric switch had been flipped down somewhere inside his body. Immensely puzzled, I saw him shift a couple of steps backwards, turn and dash out of his lair. A howling, scuttling rabbit he forsook his only home.

Seeing him take flight threw me into a nameless rage. I had wanted to feel the pain of death meted upon my miserable body yet he could not do it. My chest and throat burned. Incoherent words crackled out in chocking flames that burned my lips. I grabbed all his possessions and heaped them together. A crumpled handkerchief tumbled out from somewhere amongst his linen. I took and thrust it into my mouth where it was reduced to shreds by grinding teeth. Then, I struck a match setting everything ablaze. The sound of exploding bottles and empty aerosol spray cans blocked my ears. A terrible whirl of wind wrapped around the bridge. I felt its hulking violence burst inside my body and many times I exploded, too. Death had to come! But one way or another, it had to.

My head roared with terrible sounds whilst my body grew tense and burst in sweating fits. Digging into my satchel, I extricated my antidepressant tablets, my passport, my plastic identity card and tossed them into the inferno. I hated that state in which one day I woke up with a new identity. After I had been mugged walking on the street, I went to replace my lost identity card and was blown out of my mind to hear that I had lost my valued citizenship as well. I scratched my eyes like a wild cat coming out of sleep where it dreamed it were a rich king in a palace. When my eyes slapped again on the new document, it still screamed the new status: ALIEN! ALIEN in my own country! How? A stranger and despised in the country of my birth. What a shocking metamorphosis, from CITIZEN to ALIEN. The meaning of this betrayal kicked in. I was STATELESS! And I could be deported out of my own country. The only country I had ever known. Where could I go? The only option was to seek asylum with another country.

I watched with a barbaric gratification while the pile was reduced to ashes. I flung the business card the lady gave me and every piece of paper except my books and clothes into the fire. Gallons of glistening sweat poured out as I towered above the hungry flames that licked my trembling body. And as the sweat fell in drops into the fire, its scalding tongue of flame leaped up in hissing curses that spiralled up in the middle of thick black smoke and died into the darkness. No one could see me. I became part of the smoke! Marijuana-like seeds cascaded in my mind, They burst in a myriad of shocking explosions escaping through the roof of my scalp like a tree with a million roots being pulled out. I heard a howling whose monstrous decibels seemed not to come out of my mouth but the top of my head. Yet it did spread from the depths of my oratory caverns. From the mysterious dark secret place every man finds hard to believe he has. That carnal bestial resource given a place over reason diminishes and hideously corrupts the soul! That night, I paraded all my potential brutish madness.

When I finally tossed out of that den, all the man's property smouldered before me in a pungent heap. I stood there, my face black, plastered with soot. My colossal spirit towered above, gaping at the destruction my hand had wrought. The man had not returned and the advent of dawn streaked the eastern sky. The cold morning wind plunged up my spine like an injection and I surged away from the scene. I wanted to mark my callous deed in the old testament of my life. I felt something anew creeping up my inner self and challenging the outer world. I passed by my bedroom but I did not go to bed, for the time I got there, the sun was up and people in smart clothes and pointed shoes were already walking all over my premises like small gods. My body hurt as if I had traded blows with Mike Tyson. Nkosi had already left for breakfast. My feet plodded the other road, to the Library Park where we went to read newspapers every day.

Selecting a lonely spot where the sun's rays dappled through the buildings and shone softly with a shimmering tussle of light, I dropped the sore body I had borrowed on the lawn and was immediately snoring. While there, I dreamed of Jesus roaming the wilderness for forty days, wrestling with the devil on the cliffs and hurling it over the precipice. When the devil had been vanquished, I saw him kneel down in prayer. Dawn was coming and I came out of the clouds to kneel before him. Then he stretched out his hand which I held, feeling the hole in his palm. Coming down the cliff, holding his holed hand in my hand, I felt the hole inside me closing and swelling with a strength I never knew could rear up within my body.

My eyes flipped open and I saw the twitching, bearded face scarred with burns smiling down at me. In one hand AK held a plastic paper bag with bread and some black tea in a plastic bottle that had been disfigured by the heat. It was in the middle of the day and the tea was now cold. Nevertheless, I enjoyed it and fed ravenously, feeling my strength streaming back.

"I'm not going to sleep on the street today," I told AK.

"Where're you going?"

"I'm going to the church."

"I thought you never wanted to go there," he said.

"I've done something terrible."

"What've you done?

"I nearly killed a man last night! A homeless man!"

"What happened?"

"I attacked him in his home under the bridge. I wanted my blood on his hands. He could not bring himself to do it. Because of that, I wanted to break his scalp. He ran. Left me to take away everything he had. I do not like the man I have become!"

"Oh, God!"

"I was not quite myself. I was evil charged with what every man would condemn. Yet it is a condition that society turns people into, prosecuting, judging and executing them in the end. I saw how it turns people into what they're not and how it sets them against each other. How it condemns people into outsiders and breaks them into prisoners of worthless illusion, leaving them shadows to live and die ignominious deaths in the dark shadows of the truth."

"That was terrible!"

"Terrible beyond measure. It was madness in the heart of madness. I looked into the depths of his eyes and instead of him being the murderer I wanted him to be, I saw his broken soul. I saw myself! My broken soul! My cruel shadow! I suppose he saw himself in me, too. Yes, that's why he would never attack me. Where my lens were failing his were sharp and clear. When I could not acknowledge and appreciate his humanity he could mine! He would not stoop low so low as I had done. In every one of us all lies a piece of everyone. Whatever we can see in other people—good, bad, success or failure—we're capable of becoming it too."

"Even our enemies?"

"Even our sworn enemies! When we love our enemies, we liberate ourselves from hatred and its poison. We therefore love them for our sake, not for their sake."

"I have done worse things, too, Bloggs. Things that have left me with a lot of enemies. Yet the people who made me do those things will never feel their terrible weight either."

"That's the problem. There must be a system in place to protect all people. When the system fails other people, they are tossed out onto the fringes of existence where their lives are not only vulnerable but treated like worthless animals. Their senses become affected and begin lying to them. Distortion reigns! Their value eroded and believing their condition unalterable, life turns into something else than what it really is. That's the cruelty society is guilty of. That's why we've been tossed miles away from the fringes of our own yard where nobody knows us. And when we die here, we'll all be buried just like crickets that made noise in the darkness. No one wants to see us now, who'll want to see our corpses? If they can't see a piece of them in us while we live how could they when we are dead?"

"I guess you're right."

"Sometimes the old that once seemed right ceases to be and one has to stick by the truth in order to do what is best. Now's the time to make a move!"

"We'll go together, then."

Something shifted in the balance between my inner world and the outer world. Fundamentally, my situation of displacement, degradation and depression uncoiled into a budding flower that springs out of the charred debris after a forest fire. The horrid flood of that night tore away all the baggage of my idiosyncrasies! Between those beastly blows delivered and not delivered, those callous words said and never said; in the silence of the despicable murder that never happened, I walked out of a corridor whose darkness washes either your sanity or your insanity. I strode into a new philosophical reality about how people lose their selves due to cruel pressures in life.

New dimensions of living emerged. How many times we die every day in our nature so that we can have a chance to be reborn into better new capacities. Yet in our vast denial we refuse to acknowledge the truth and shift. The biggest tragedy is that we fail to take the chance, not that the things are broken in our lives; that in our consciousness we lack the fluid spark to make the shift; that we do not see the truth. The truth will eternally confront us; it is our responsibility to make a choice and see it for what it is. The battery of our idiosyncrasies will continue to inject poison into our troubled lives and unless we take the chance to become cognisant and progressively independent of them, the condition of our lives will stay the same. But real significant chances for self-redemption in one's lifetime may happen only once or a couple of times.

The emptiness that had been tiptoeing into my mind like a foggy thief evaporated. My life yanked into an immutable trajectory whose master was none other than the self. A door had swung open! Out of a shattering darkness! An invitation to surf the daring wave of life.

FOUR

Unbar the doors! Throw open the doors!

I will not have the house of prayer, the church of Christ,

The sanctuary turned into a fortress...

The church shall be open, even to our enemies.

Open the door!

—T.S. Eliot

The Central Methodist Church, a five-storey building is located along Pritchard Street, corner Smal Street. Pritchard Street is a wide conventional two-way thoroughfare with single lanes, wide pavements and shops on both sides. Smal Street cuts across Johannesburg from the north to the south and as its name sells it out is a narrow thoroughfare with no traffic lanes for cars. Yet one must not be deceived for it is one of the busiest streets in Joburg. Shops loaded with clothing merchandise line both sides of the street. Because of the frequently heavy human traffic on this street, it is also infested with marauding pickpockets and gangs waiting to dispossess shoppers and passers-by of their wallets and cell-phones. Only delivery vehicles are allowed in some sections of that street. Otherwise it is human traffic, only.

Just after 6:00pm, we walked through two broken glass doors which served as the entrance to the church, into the foyer. There was no need to open or close the door behind, you just walked through the frame where the glass once stood. Here we paused in the middle of a bustling scene. Women with the help of men were setting up their trading stalls, small tables upon which various foodstuffs were on display . There was pap, meat, fish, rice and vegetables as favourite dishes on one side. The other side had tea, coffee, snacks and cigarettes.

"The Bishop can't see you now," one of the security guards told us.

"Why?"

"He is having a meeting with some journalists,"

"Do you think he can see us today?"

Someone passed by, his foul breath hurling a barrage of obscenities at a sickly looking man who stood eyeing with bulging globes of eyes a dish of fat-cakes across the room. He ran up the stairs onto the first floor. The security guard turned and shouted at the cursing man:

"I could beat your mother for that! She should have done better raising you!"

AK repeated our question to the guard.

"After the meeting with the journalists, he's going out to meet with the evicted residents of some building in Jeppes Town. You will have to wait for him in the reception of his office."

We walked to one of the stalls. I could not believe it that pap started from as little as R5 a plate; served with beans, boiled cabbage or chicken skins and chicken livers or chicken heads. Pap and chicken, beef or fish was R10. I had R7 in my pocket. Enough for a plate of pap with a pig's snout drowning in an ocean of soup, obstinately sniffing at the small heap of spinach in one corner. AK chose a dish of pap and horse-shoe mackerel fish. There was nowhere to sit. People shovelled around, ghosts lost outside the yards of heaven. Looking for the door to a new life. Talking. Patient and impatient with their lives. There were newcomers like us who wanted to see the bishop for a roof over their heads. Others who seemed to exist but not living at all.

Men and women beholding neither joy nor hope in life. People whose better scripts of life had once been written but now erased lingered in the blank twilight of existence— waiting for proximate mortality to bring its curtains down!

Then there were visitors, journalists and other people who needed some kind of help or another. It was like a social service department, a kind of station for different kinds of broken people under a thousand strains of challenges and adversities.

I followed AK, his crutches sounding like muffled gunshots on the tiles leading to the steps by the right side of the front door. These steps led to the first floor where the sanctuary was located. We found space and sat down to our meal. There was a man sitting at the top of the stairs. He had just begun to eat his supper of pap and chicken skins. Another man with a dent in the side of his forehead and dressed in oversized shorts over his tight undersized trousers approached. He wore slippers of different colours on his feet and he had no shirt on. Slowly, he came and stood towering above the man's meal. Staring lifelessly like a corpse! Scratching his scabby belly that peeled off bloody particles into the man's meal. The man roared and shook in anger with the energy of a giant. The filthy scratching man rolled his glazed eyes towards the vast ceiling. Smiling! Glistening saliva toppling down his rough dry lower lip and seeping into a scrawny beard. Scratching and scratching!

"You puss bleeding bastard!"

No one answered him. Livid, the man grabbed the plate and flung it into the scratcher's hideously beaming face. He stopped scratching and started smiling. Quickly, he wiped his long repugnant face, licking the remnants of the meal, blood, puss and scabs with his tongue. Then he started eating from what was littering the floor.

"Wait until I bleed death and then you will all leave me your food!" the scratching man spit out the words between a mouthful of food. "I am Chimwene! God's whip! Sent to punish all mad and greedy people like you." Laughing, he continued to wipe the floor with his hands and licking them. Grabbing and thrusting morsels of pap and chicken skins into his mouth. Ravenously.

One of the security hulks came and ordered us to go and eat outside. Preventing us from potentially messing up the stairs. I was relieved to move my legs away from this gruesomely creature. We saw more entrepreneurs busy setting up stalls and some already selling pap and rice dishes. The street was jammed with people checking and buying the foodstuffs on display. There was a man doing brisk business, selling in a colourful heap some expired cakes. The price started from R2 a piece. People swarmed around him like flies. They sold like hot cakes.

Everywhere, people jostled for the best buys. People whose existence dangled at loose ends of life. A man in front of me was pushed by someone. Leaning in the wind, he stretched out backwards, the lapel of his dirty jacket dipping into my soup. I stumbled, kept my meal and balance. Saying nothing and imagining nothing wrong with his jacket, I just let it go. We crossed the street and continued to search for space along the pavement until we turned into Kruis Street where we sat against the barricaded windows of a shop that had closed for the day.

We ate with our fingers. When we were full, we licked our hands clean with our tongues and dried them up using newspapers. We threw away our pig and fish bones into the dust bin. Others who no longer had a care in the world threw their chicken bones and plastic plates into the street. A youthful man came along picking up the plates. He took them to one of the women selling pap who dished out a plate of food for him.

The sanctuary occupied the entire first floor, vaulting into the second floor which formed its gallery. We stepped onto the green carpet and walked five rows in. There were only men and every seat was taken. Some sat staring vacantly in front of them listening to the yowling poverty inside them. The Molotov cocktail of sadness, loneliness and devastation spookily galloping in dark flames across their faces. Tired, haggard, happy, resilient and sad broken faces rippled in the aisle and every available space! Flowing in various shades like a mixture of dirty oil and water! Those who had seen better days and those who would say they had never seen one in their lives, mixed, chatted, grouped and re-grouped, making conversation and in search of information. And there were those who sat mute, starring and stunned by the shock and awe of their situation. They all carried, sat or lay on flattened cardboard paper which they used for their bedding. My eyes strayed upwards into the gallery. I noticed that only women, some with babies crying, were its occupants. The gallery, its folding seats arranged in a semi-circle claimed a significant portion of the second floor, too.

Despite getting ready for bed under lice infested blankets, both men and women could be heard laughing and throwing jokes at each other across the floor and the great void between the two floors of the sanctuary. STRESS and RE-SILIENCE reigned the building like two powers littered in one day. Yet the positive and more appreciative in spirit won with an awesome authority—RESILIENCE!

"We better go outside," advised AK and I agreed.

Halfway down the stairs I said:

"Why don't we go and find the bishop's office?"

Up the stairs again we went, AK's crutches striking against the tiles. From the second floor the stairs were in darkness and The Bishop's office was on the third floor. We sat on the cold tiles in the corridor, joining the queue of people who had no appointments already waiting for him. One or some other kind of disquiet painted on their faces! Two hours later he breezed in and I saw every face lift and brighten up. IT WAS HOPE THAT I SAW! He smiled and greeted us as he walked up to his office. I felt curious to know more about this ever busy man who made it so simple for everyone to approach him. He never turned a soul away. And one thing he never failed to see in everyone was their HUMANITY.

Our turn came and we presented our request. He called a man who wrote our details down so that we could be issued with plastic discs for identity cards. Then we were supplied with a couple of blankets each and we left.

Just outside the corridor, we found people preparing to sleep. We had to step over them, some of them already in their blankets. Gliding down the stairs, we noticed that every step had an occupant and we had to ask people, with some cursing us, to give way to AK and his crutches. When we got to the second floor which housed the gallery, we found it covered with a confused mass of human bodies. The door leading from the gallery to the stairs going up to the third floor hung heavily on its hinges, leaning on the floor. We simply walked through the wooden frames that swung on their hinges. The gallery was loaded with women getting ready to sleep. They folded the seats and spread their blankets on the carpet. Nobody was allowed to sleep on the seats. The security moved around their eyes glowing like luminous marbles, checking on the women's safety and thrashing the trouble makers with whips and baton sticks.

Outside the gallery men and women spread their blankets, too. It would have been stupid to ask for space. Absolutely, there was no room for us on that floor, so down the dark stairs, we floated to the first floor. Again we found every step taken. The wooden door connecting the first floor to the stairs going up to the second floor stood swaying to the touch. Again there was no need for us to open or close it. We just glided like ghosts through the space where glass once stood in the frame. I tried opening the door into the sanctuary and found bodies blocking its movement. Every nook and space in the church was already taken. And everyone practically owned the space they slept on. Whatever time of the day, one could accurately show the tiles one slept on. Fierce fights could erupt for sleeping space. With difficulty finding space to place our feet, we slowly negotiated our way. Voices cursed us as we awkwardly manoeuvred and fell sprawling on bodies of people lying on the floor. Saying our apologies, we clambered to our feet. Like hesitating chameleons, we groped our way in the semi-darkness.

Once more, down we floated. Our feet still groped for space among the bodies lining the steps to the thriving humming foyer. The stalls were still operating. I smelled the aroma of fat-cakes and coffee flooding my nostrils.

A man dressed in an overcoat, came in flying and immediately rammed into a brick wall formed by the guards manning the entrance. He had stolen a cell-phone from someone outside. The security opened the door into the chapel and bundled him inside. Another one hunched in a hug staggered in but was prodded backwards by a baton stick. He was trying to smuggle alcohol into the building. He tried bulldozing his way through. There were cries of pain from the bundle of flesh, bones and crumpled clothing inside the chapel. Then the sound of curling and lashing whips escaping through the half-closed door!

Later I learned that even though people slept in the foyer, this was one place of the church that never really slept. This was undeniably the heartbeat of life in that place. One could get food at any time of the night. During the day charity organizations served lunch in the Robertsons' Room adjoining the foyer. It was also in this space that some of the stall owners prepared their meals. A considerable number of people of an entrepreneurial spirit from the neighbourhood prepared dishes in their homes which they came to sell at the church every evening, too. It all unfurled like a settlement fable of careless humour and gentle chaos practically fallen out of the murky depths of a magical Gypsy sky! Here we saw there was no space for us, too. We bought two fat-cakes and stepped outside through the broken glass doors into the refreshingly cool night.

We found space on the pavement outside the church and across the road in the various stages of people preparing to sleep. The same activities were happening corner Pritchard and part of Kruis Street, corner Pritchard and part of Von Brandis Street, corner Pritchard and part of Von Weilleigh Street. In the whole vicinity around the Central Methodist Church bodies of people lying down covered the pavements like a carpet. Their slow heaving presence spewed out of the bowels of the church powerfully like a blocked river. Finally we got a spot in the middle of Smal Street in front of a noisy bar. The street was effectively blocked by bodies of sleeping people. Smal Street is a narrow street built like an arcade with shops on both sides and roof sections on some parts. It cuts right across the centre of Johannesburg's Central Business District from The Bridge to the Carlton Centre Hotel.

No one seemed in a hurry to sleep. There were those who brazenly moved in gangs looking for people to rob. If one slept soundly, they ran their forked hands through one's blankets and pockets without any shame. We wrapped ourselves with our blankets so that the thieves could not steal them away, Then like packed sardines, we lay on our cardboard mattresses tossing as if we were trapped worms and quietly talking to one another. With a burning survival interest, people were discussing their day's exploratory activities around Joburg.

An empty bottle of beer hurtled through the night's breeze. It landed breaking on the paving next to my head, spilling dregs of beer in my face. Luckily I was not hurt and I wiped my face clean. A man sat upon by a horrid drunken spirit staggered out of the bar raving mad and howling obscenities. A bottle of beer grasped in his right hand. A woman followed him out, shouting too:

"I don't need your money, you idiot! Just go and leave me alone."

"Now your stomach is full of my money and you talk shit!" His speech slurred out, staggering like a giant out of a comic magazine. Struggling, his legs twisted, hands stretching out as if he were looking for a wall in the air, staggered, tripped and fell knocking his big head on the paving. When he rose the bottle in his hand had broken. He firmly held it by its neck and took a couple of sips from it.

"They put drugs in his beer," AK whispered to me.

"This is Joburg! Go back home to your mama, country boy." Someone shouted.

A group of thugs glided towards him. They grabbed him, ran through his pockets and slapped him in the face. Dazed and staggering, he melted away into the darkness.

"You don't go where your mother isn't!" One of the thugs shouted.

I got up and went to pass some water by the roadside. Coming from there a young man followed me. He spoke to me. I did not answer. In Joburg you do not just open your mouth to strangers.

"Hey, I am talking to you. Why do you keep quiet?"

I reached my blankets and slipped myself under them. But he violently grabbed and pulled them away from me.

"I don't know you! What do you want from me?"

"Don't you know the space you were walking on belongs to me?"

I saw three more arrive. I was not going to allow them attack me while I lay on the paving, so I stood up. They pulled away AKs blankets, too, tossing them on top of a neighbouring snoring man. When an ugly scene like this happens, nobody wants to be near. One can get mixed up. People around us woke up and pushed away leaving us in the open. They could only push back a little as there were other people sleeping. In fact they only stood up to create some space.

"Who do you think you are?" he hissed.

"You think you are walking in your house?"

"Give me my money!"

"I don't owe you any money!"

"Hey! That's my space you were walking on, I said let me have my money right now!"

"I said I don't owe you any money!"

"Fuck you! Bastard," and he slapped me on the cheek.

Caught by surprise, I recoiled, disappearing into the confused crowd behind. My spirit dipped into that macabre arsenal inside me which often puzzles me and in a blur, I erupted back at him in a flying kick that squarely landed on his advancing chest. And backwards he went flying with arms and legs thrashing in the wind like a doll. Dazed, he landed on top of some sleeping men. Feebly trying to get up without much success, his hands groped for support among the sleeping figures.

"Thief! Thief," someone yelled.

The men he had fallen on top of all rose, the confusion of sleep in their eyes and minds. A hand flashed up and curved downwards like a comet. There was a cracking sound and the sound of a breaking bottle on the man's head. That incident taught me to go to bed with a weapon. Blood poured out of his wound onto the blankets and people around him. He swayed back to his jelled feet, bulldozing his way like a blind buffalo. Reeling, trembling and thrust in all directions by angry hands, he fell on top of waking figures. He was a pirouetting scarecrow in the middle of a storm. Rising from sleep along the way, people blindly meted out more punishment until he came to the corner of Smal and Jeppe Streets. No-one saw his friends melt away into the darkness like ghosts. And long after they were gone did I stay awake, afraid that they might return with reinforcement. No one ever came back!

Dawn was breaking when sleep came. Yet no sooner had I fallen asleep than my senses were re-awakened by screams and the noise of stampeding feet. I rose holding my blankets and my satchel in my hands. A gripping shock chased all sleep out of my eyes when I saw a bloody man writhing in pain on the paving. Screaming and clutching his stomach. Nobody knew what had happened. His innards bloating out like a glistening pink tube! Somebody lit a fire using newspaper and waved it around the gaping wound and the innards seemed to be shrinking back into the vault of his sagging tummy. Two men quickly tied his shirt around him like a bandage.

While we were busy trying to figure out who had done this, the police, heavily armed with guns arrived. With eagle eyes they did not talk to anyone, they just combed our section of the street from both sides. Very soon two policemen grabbed a man and put handcuffs around his wrists. He fought them. They tightened the handcuffs. He howled in pain. Again they tightened them. The man protested:

"Hey! What do you think you're doing?"

No one replied. They punitively dragged him like an obstinate circus bull to the place where the man with the slit belly lay.

"I didn't do it!" he shouted

"Shut up!" One of the policemen roared. "We saw you. You can't hide."

"It's not me!"

"It's not him, you are making a mistake." his friends joined in.

"Stop the nonsense, the camera doesn't lie. Now you have the right to remain silent or every word you say will be used against you in the court of law."

The ambulance came and the man whose belly had been slit open was taken away to the hospital whilst the criminal was pushed into the back of the police van.

There was both surprise and relief among the people. Thanks to the hidden camera on the street and the alert police who were manning it.

We did not go to sleep again. We talked in grateful tones about how the incident had come to an end. After his arrest we heard the criminal got eight years for attempted murder. Yet, having read about how convicted criminals were frequently returning from jails without having served their sentences, people were just sceptical.

By half-past five o'clock in the morning we were all awake, folding our blankets. We had to vacate the street so that the shop owners could prepare and open their businesses. We put our blankets into the sacks and took them to the storeroom in the church where we piled them one upon the other up to the roof. Then the rule was that everyone left to look for work. Only the sick and mothers with newly born babies remained behind.

I looked where I had been sleeping. The "Pikit Up" cleaners, armed with their brooms were coming to work. Like nurses they would take care of the bruised street. Everywhere the street resembled a rubbish dump of cardboard, trampled newspapers, plastics, empty water and beer bottles, some filled up with urine (I now saw why people never left their places to urinate), lice infested clothing and abandoned filthy blankets. Some young men were moving around, picking up the cardboard and loading it onto small carts which they pulled behind them. Others picked up the empty plastic bottles. They would empty the urine on the tarmac and throw the bottles into their trolleys.

"What do you do with it?" I asked.

"We sell it at the scrap yard," one of them said.

"How much do they pay?"

"Five cents per kilo."

A City of Joburg truck pulled up. Workers in black gumboots poured out clutching hard brooms and unrolling a thick hose pipe. They located a water terminal on the sidewalk and connected the hose. One of them effusively sprayed some detergent all over the pavement and the tarmac. Then, they sprayed and vigorously brushed the whole street, turning it into a black foaming river heavily laden with litter, human excrement, urine, rotting perishables, chicken and fish bones. All the detached grime was eagerly guzzled by the yawning drains along the street. What shocking bothersome refuse! I wondered if people would ever want to come and shop on this street again, if they saw what I had witnessed. As I walked away, unaware of it, my foot kicked a wallet which was lying idle on the paving and it flew open like a sliced fish. There were some particulars inside but I did not bend to pick it up. In Joburg you don't just pick up things like that. It could be a trap by thieves waiting to rob you. I proceeded on my way to wash my face in the toilet, letters skating like kites into words for the dark poem I would write, The Cardboard People:

the fury of slighted pride

spilled lust from sweating hips

in clouds of dust they glide

FIVE

We had a survival plan.

From Monday to Friday we had two options for breakfast. Either we directed our footsteps to Powerhouse in Braamfontein or to the Roman Catholic Church in Jeppes Town where we were served by very mature serene nuns with a lot of biblical love. I was born and raised in a Roman Catholic Church and this bode well with me. It was no surprise that the morning following my bizarre experiences, there my heart chose to go.

We stood in a queue and prayed before anything else. Unlike at Powerhouse, here an atmosphere of reverence, peace and respect prevailed. The conditions were strictly no pushing, swearing or violence. There was a prayer before we received our bread dressed with jam, margarine and peanut butter. Then one would choose between tea and coffee.

Some people would return later in the afternoon to solicit for assistance with money for various problems. The nuns usually assisted, but it had to be a genuine problem. A lot of people told lies to get the money and they would squander it on drink and cigarettes. I felt this was reverent help which people needed not to abuse and there was no need for me to do like-wise. Even though I had no income, I desisted from asking for such help.

There were a lot of unscrupulous herbalist doctors operating in the Joburg Central Business District. They wanted people to work for them handing out fliers advertising their services to the people. They paid us R30 per day working from 7:00am to 6:30pm. We would stand on street corners and hand out the papers. If one got a client which one took to the doctor's rooms and the client paid well, there was a bonus of R10. Lunch was served, plain bread and Drink O Pop. Drink O Pop was a highly concentrated cold drink sold in a small packet. A single small packet diluted with water made an unbelievable two litres! My stomach utterly rebelled against its after-taste in my mouth.

One Saturday morning a young girl about seventeen years of age approached me. I handed her the flier and she stopped to read it. There was no problem without a solution for Dr Kirimani! He called himself an international psychic who could tell your life from past, present and into the future. His mission was to make people's life better, his pamphlet declared. To those who had financial problems, his Magic Ring or Lucky Stick would provide boundless financial breakthrough. He could bring back your lost lover. He could give you the magic to drive people insane by casting beauty and sex appeal spells. He solved all sexual problems and transformed people into tigers in bed. Gamblers could get rich overnight at the casino. You could hire small boys from him that would go into banks and bring you money while you slept at home. Or one could get sandawana oil from him to rub on one's body and attract good luck and business with very rich people. He could fight and defeat full moon spells from witches which drove people mad whenever there was a full moon. Dr Kirimani had the panacea for all problems in life and could give you absolute power over everyone!

"Is this a good doctor?"

"An excellent doctor," I lied. I had only given out fliers for two days and I knew not even a single customer of his.

"Is he good at abortion?" she asked.

"He is the best I ever saw, do you want me to take you to him?"

Soon we were in the doctor's office and to my joy she paid in cash. I bounced out of the office with R10 in my pocket. It wasn't much but it could buy me a plate of pap at the church.   About fifteen minutes later, she came back past my post on her way home. Again she stopped to chat. She carried the concoctions for the abortion in a carefully concealed black plastic bag.

"Hi!" She greeted me.

"Hi!"

"Are you sure this will work?" there was a shade of doubt in her voice.

"I told you he is the best. How old is your pregnancy?"

"Two months."

"I promise you, it will work," I reassured her.

We stood in awkward silence. She did not make a move to go.

"Why do you want to abort the pregnancy?"

"I don't want it. I did a stupid thing. I went to a party together with my boyfriend. We had lots to drink and we ended up having unprotected sex. But, since I told him of the pregnancy, he has been avoiding me. He is very angry and accuses me of wanting to ruin his life. How could he say that? I thought he loved me." She was nearly in tears as she spoke.

I felt pity for her and said:

"I am very sorry to hear that."

"Tell me how am I going to raise the child alone if I keep it? Besides, I have to do one more year in school to finish my Matric. Why did he have to run away?"

"That was cruel," I said.

Then she spoke in Sotho language and I did not understand.

"Which language do you speak? Where do you come from?"

I hesitated and then the words toppled from my lips:

"I come from Zim."

"I have heard you guys treat your women well, I wish I had a foreigner for a boyfriend."

"There are some who are cruel, too," I said.

"Oh! No! Not like our South African men," she protested and then added. "What's your name?"

"Bloggs!"

"I'm Lebo. You're very kind."

"How do you know?"

"I can see by the way you speak and listen to me," she said, her beautiful grave face cracking into a dimpled smile. A white line of bewitching milky teeth glinting in the sun.

"God, what have I done?" I thought, reprimanding myself.

"Yes I can feel it. I have only one year to complete my Matric. Will you, please, wait and marry me?"

Shocked and not thinking clearly, I promised I would wait and do exactly as she had requested. I could not keep this conversation. She was young, beautiful and tempting. A packaged meal every man would secretly open and savour in the shameless chambers of his imagination. I struggled with reason. Knowing she was a nuclear bomb waiting to explode, I wanted her gone.

"Give me your contact telephone number so that I can call you."

I wrote her cell-phone number on one of the fliers and then she said:

"Give me your cell-phone number too."

I gave her my stolen cell-phone number. She tried dialling it on her cell but it went to the voice mail box.

"I need to put my phone on the charger, the battery died," I lied. I knew I would never use that number again.

"I will come and see you again on Saturday."

"Sunday will be the best. We can have all the time to ourselves." I was now getting distressed with my own lies.

"Ok my darling," she said. Smiling and hugging me.

She clung to me as if she were someone drowning. Like someone who did not want to go. She burned my heart with her warm body and her growing tummy nudged a reproachful appeal against my conscience. Like people who have known each other for a long time, slowly we drew apart. Then she waltzed away leaving me drenched in misery. Feeling irrevocably complicit in a terrible crime. Being a Christian and not given to telling such despicable lies, I was shaking as if I had been missed by a bolt of lightning. Sweat poured out of my body with anticipated retribution.

We got paid on Saturdays and often the payment was half. The doctor would complain of business not doing well and then promise to pay the balance on the following Saturday. Another Saturday would come and again we would get half pay. I guessed this was a trick all those bogey doctors used to retain labour. The balances would pile up until one, tired and frustrated with the job would decide to quit. To chase after the balances was normally a waste of time since one seldom got them after all.

On that Saturday I met my client and prospective wishing sweetheart, I quit. My simmering consciousness told me I had boarded the wrong boat.

"What if that child she wanted to abort was the only gift of her womb from God? What if she died too? God! What have I done…? What have I done…?" It gnawed my heart with nameless guilt and I called myself a shameless reprobate. I saw how desperate people, struggling to survive, changed themselves into contemptible characters living on the street. I witnessed, too, how people, uprooted and perplexed lost themselves in their wandering and died miserable deaths. I saw their lonely bodies stretched out on the streets without anybody pausing to shed even a drop of care, love and understanding towards them.

"Why did it have to be me?" Little did I know that in the near future I would sit with more sinister issues.

With shame and regret burning like a furnace in my heart, I thought of something else I could do to earn money with a safe conscience. I had to fight. I had to do things differently if I were to preserve my own essential deeper self. If my self-respect and celebrated spirit were to be restored. Like a forgotten prisoner who gropes the dark walls of his cell for a hidden fissure that might lead a narrow way out, I set out on my quest.

I went to a supermarket in Bree Street and bought a pack of frozen Cool Time drink. There were ten 200ml plastic tubes of guava juice in a pack. I bought the pack for R10 and then resold the refreshments for R2 each on the street. It turned out to be better business than handing out fliers. I became my own boss and it was a good feeling. Not to be dependant. The only problem occurred when it got cold. In Joburg sometimes the weather is difficult to predict. Without a television set or a radio, I had no means of getting weather forecasts. But it was in February and I had to worry mostly when winter arrived, that is, if I still could not secure a job. I would walk up and down the streets dodging the Johannesburg Metro Police. If they caught you selling on the street, they confiscated all your stock. I did not mind that. My business posed no danger to anybody. My only crime was that I was not trading in a designated place. At first I met them so often and ended up running away like a criminal. I would rather do that than lose my stock. I learned to be more alert and streetwise.

After a good day's work, I took Nkosi and Ncube, who always mumbled in his sleep that he should have made his wife pregnant before she left, to a bar that sold Joburg Beer. A local cheap opaque brew made from sorghum and maize. It is a very potent improved version of a traditional brew that comes packed in a rectangular prism paper packaging. The packaging is popularly known as the "shake-shake." One could easily notice and read the warning inscribed on the shake-shake in bold letters:

"Do Not Walk on the Road, You May Get Killed!"

My pocket was full of jingling coins. We drank and our tongues loosened and oiled by the beer, slid and lost control like tortured worms in our mouths. Things we never spoke about before which made us connect and resonate with our experiences took us into deeper private lands. Baring our miserable souls to each other! I was their hero on that day and they ended up borrowing money to start selling the juice too. Then chattering we weaved our way home. Our broken shoes creaking. Sometimes staggering and stumbling over each other's heels along the pavement. Ak's crutch crackling like muffled gunshots against the paving bricks. We did not walk in the middle of the road. And we never got killed.

When we got to the church, we went to the scores of Zimbabwean women who lined the street selling pap and checked their menu. I bought a plate of pap with beef rough tripe and casings (intestines) mixed with vegetables. Nkosi and Ncube each ordered a plate of pap and cow-heels for relish. We washed our hands by the roadside with water pouring out of a cup. Then we all asked for hot chillies which we tore with our fingers and mixed them with the relish. Oblivious of the cars going by and the fearful belated travellers hurrying to their homes on the street, we could not dream of any better meal than we had. After eating, we picked up newspapers littering the street and cleaned our greasy hands.

SIX

I lay that night with the others littering the street. Littering the town! That is what the police had said at one time when they came to arrest us sleeping in the middle of the night. When they failed to catch criminals, we were always their consolation prize. They charged us with LITTERING THE STREETS! Human litter charged with littering the streets! They pulled us out of our blankets and squashed us together in truckloads to the police station where we were not allowed to see anyone. Even the Lawyers for Human Rights and the Doctors Without Borders who were our friends. How they strove to make us non-entities and non-accessible to any nurturing jurisprudence. Some people had been injured during the raid after they were assaulted by the police and needed medical attention. Yet they were denied. All reduced to an undeserving existential argument. For three days they locked us up demanding a fine of R100 from each one of us. We had our papers and we decided we were not going to pay. Then someone had a plan:

"We will block the toilets!" he said.

We used to dress in many clothes because we carried with us our wardrobe everywhere. On our bodies and in our satchels! So he pulled one pair of trousers off his legs, wrapped it into a thick ball and flushed it down the toilet. It got stuck in the entrance! Someone took off his shoe and we used it push the blockade deeper into the toilet pipe. Then we flushed again. The toilets blocked. We flushed! And flushed. And flushed. The sewage spewed out. It was a mess. The offices became suffocated with the reeking effluence. The police came:

"Who blocked the toilets?"

Silence.

"I said who blocked the toilets? You, answer me!"

"I don't know!"

"You tell me, who blocked the toilets?"

"I don't know!"

"I will ask you for the last time! Who blocked the toilet?"

"We don't know!"

"Don't tell me you all don't know who did it. We are not going to release you then. All of you."

The police officer roared and called for the plumbers who came about an hour later. It took them thirty minutes to remove the blockage. They left.

"We'll block it again," again someone said.

"This time we'll wrap a shoe inside the pair of trousers and tie the package with some shoe lace," someone suggested.

"Brilliant." We all agreed, laughing.

Again, someone peeled a pair of dirty trousers off his legs. Then we shoved the package as planned into the back of the toilet. Again, we flushed and flushed until the smell of human excrement fouled the corridors.

"It is done!"

"It is done!"

"It is done!"

"Whoop! Whoop! Hooray!"

The words boomed out laced with derisive laughter and we clapped hands for ourselves. We had a good feeling that we were fighting back. We were not rubbish on the street. We were PEOPLE!

*

My childhood flashed through my restless mind. I saw myself in blue shorts, white T-shirt and bare feet. I was playing with this girl from next door and we were both about five years old. Her name was Muna. We walked until we got to the outskirts of the compound, past the rubbish dump into the bush of thick elephant grass that grew far high above our heads. Her small hand in mine! We followed the small path until we got to the big pond in the middle of the bush. My elder brothers once took me to that pond where I had watched them swim and play in the water. Its brown muddy waters glistened in the sun. It had rained the previous day and everywhere the ground was wet, muddy and slippery. We took off our clothes and started playing on the edge of the pool. We splashed our hands in the cold water and felt it sting our bodies. We stood facing each other and splashed water with our palms into each other's face. I loved the way it smelled and tasted in my mouth and laughed at Muna's small nimble body ducking and staggering away from my blows. Enchanted, our small gleeful voices leapt into the sky and we waded deeper into the pool. We felt the mud shifting under our small feet, curl up between our miniature toes and cover our legs well up above the knees. We lay on the water and splashed the water with our hands trying to swim. We went nowhere and sinking in the water we struggled back to our feet.

We must have been there for more than an hour before we came out of the pond, put on our clothes and went home. The muddy water left our skin white as tomato-less fish soup. Our eyes were bloodshot. They looked as if somebody had rubbed some bird's-eye chilli in them. Our feet and clothes dirty with mud, people curiously looked and laughed at the sight we made. When we arrived home, everybody had been looking for us. Mum was an angry hornet. She grabbed one of her shoes and beat all the mischief out of my small body. She asked me where I had left my white vest and I led her to the great pond where she picked it up brown like chocolate with the mud. Her anger dissolving, she cried at the pond and thanked the ancestors that we had not been drowned. But I did not care. I just failed to understand what the fuss was all about.

Two months after this incident, Muna's parents got a new house somewhere and they left. I missed her dimpled face and the tiny knot of pleasure I felt in the chest when we played together. Strange how I first collected my feelings of emptiness in life! I refused to play with other children in the neighbourhood. I played alone until my parents put me in school.

*

I started going to the cinema when I was eight years old. Every Friday there were two shows screened at the cinema. The first one for young kids was at two o'clock in the afternoon. The second show mostly attended by adults was at seven o'clock in the evening. The afternoon show did not have an excellent clear picture. The hall had big windows which allowed too much sunlight inside. People erected boards against the windows. But like a stubborn spirit still it sneaked in through the edges. The evening show had the best picture and my brothers liked to watch that one. Whenever they went, I would cry for them to take me along. I used to fall asleep during the movies so my brothers normally sneaked out without my knowledge. This happened for some time until I learned to be alert every Friday. I would tug along one of them like a trailer all the time to avoid being duped. They would try to send me on an emergency errand somewhere but I would stubbornly refuse. In the end we often went together. And I would fall asleep again.

As I grew up, I began to watch the film to its end. We watched Bruce Lee and I dreamed of going to see him in England for I thought China was in England. I loved the wild western movies and balked in the imagination of the tough land of underdogs who turned heroes. I whooped with ecstasy when they fought in the dust or mud imitating every blow. I had a list of my favourites including Charles Bronson, Clint Eastwood, Lee van Cliff, Terrence Hill and Buddy Spencer. Their daredevilry thrilled me to the bone.

One day we took to the cinema a visiting cousin who was older than us. We watched Lee van Cliff's film entitled 'Man to Man.' When the movie finished, we went home chattering bundles of bouncing energy. Now, my father used to keep some benzene in the house for cleaning his police tunic and John, our cousin, saw it. He opened the bottle and sprinkled some on a piece of cloth and started sniffing it. This use of benzene was an absolute novelty to me and my brothers. John passed the cloth to us and at first we could not stomach the dazzling punch in the nose and throat. Then we got used as it penetrated our senses. I sniffed it until there was a buzz in my head and my vision became corrupted. The movie began playing out itself again in front of me. I saw Lee van Cliff leaping, shooting and rolling in the dust. Then I became Lee van Cliff and exploded into action against the robbers who had robbed the bank in town. I was diving, ducking, leaping onto the table, somersaulting over the sofas and chairs whilst my gun went bang-bang all the time. The two small fingers of my right hand curled into my palm pressed down by the thumb while the other two pointed out like a barrel. I shot at unseen gun-wielding thugs behind curtains and win-dows! I shot at my brothers! I shot at my cousin! They all nearly died of irrepressible laughter whilst I turned the lounge into a broken saloon. After that experience, I stole father's benzene a few more times and then stopped. My body constitution could not fully savour the horrible taste and the buzzing kick it gave my brain.

The best movies were screened at the Cyril Jennings (CJ) Hall in Highfield and we were staying in Rugare Township. To get to Highfield, we had to use a direct road that passed through Lochinvar. This was a beautiful suburb reserved for white people only employed by the National Railways of Zimbabwe. Rugare was actually a compound reserved for its black workers and their families. We were never welcome to use that direct road. We often had to go round via Green Trees Road outside the Lochinvar compound fence. We had to leave home two-and-half hours before movie time, yet using the direct path it took us just an hour. Now it happened that on one particular day, we were behind time and we had to take the short-cut. We knew what we were up to, so we took our catapults with us. Half-way through Lochinvar, far ahead of us a group of white kids appeared out of a side road, riding on their shiny bicycles. We were so close to going out of the suburb that we could clearly see the traffic on Willowvale Road. Going back and going round to Green Trees Road, definitely, was not an option for us.

"How many are they?" Simba asked.

"Six," Taurai counted.

"What do we do?" I was not sure about our capacity to deal with the situation.

"We go forward," Taurai ordered.

Meanwhile they had seen us too and they were chattering wildly among themselves. Ostensibly, there was promise of some sport to them. They stood and barred our way with their bicycles, we kept moving forward, our hands in our pockets where they wrapped over the catapults and the stones. We had to be quick before they had time to call their elders, so we increased our speed.

"Kaffirs! Where do you think you are going?"

We kept quiet and advanced. Resolute.

"Go back! This is not your territory."

"Don't be afraid," said Taurai. "Today we will teach them a lesson."

Less than fifteen metres away, Simba took out his catapult. It was already loaded. In one deft movement, he raised his hands in a graceful arc, pulled backwards and released his missile. The stone hummed a dangerous potent song and struck one of our enemies' bicycles. We saw their eyes painted with fear, confusion and surprise. The great wall of steel and flesh collapsed as they collided into each other. Two fell in a grating and howling heap of metal and flesh on top of their bicycles. I saw some buttock flesh peel out of torn pants and laughed. One of them left his bicycle behind and ran with the wind. We did not touch it, we only dashed around it and flew towards Willowvale Road. In no time we were out of the boundary fence surrounding the compound and by the time we crossed the road we were choking with laughter and delight. That was our first defeat of the enemy. On that day they screened James Bond in 'For Your Eyes Only.'

We took the longest route back home, but we did not mind at all. We just loved James Bond, the man with the licence to kill.

The following day we woke up with the James Bond euphoria blazing in our blood. Simba whose mind was that of a mechanical nature and given to doing experiments all the time had secret work to do. He hid himself behind the sugarcane patch immersed in a design of warfare. Then suddenly in the afternoon, he sprouted in front of us with one of his amazing inventions, a pistol made of wire with bullets of ball-point pen barrel pieces. He used the spring from a Parker pen he had stolen from our sister. He used a trigger system whereby the wire trigger pulled back the barrel pellet against the spring. Upon releasing the trigger, the pellet would shoot out like a miniature missile. We marvelled at his invention and very soon we had a gun manufacturing workshop behind the sugarcane patch. By the end of the day we all had guns and holsters in our belts and Stetson hats made from plastic. The guns could shoot from a distance of almost six metres.

We were a cool rowdy bunch in the neighbourhood, affectionately known as 'The Terrible Triplets,' for that we looked! Though all born a year apart from the other! We moved around with our hands drooping on our sides imitating tough hombres, eyes squinted and fore-heads creased. We shot at each other in dangerous clashes where we all died several times. We hunted down another group of kids from the neighbourhood who admired our skill and wanted to come and play with us. We told them they could never be our friends because they were not sophisticated like us.

"Go and make bows and arrows and shoot mice," Simba told them.

"Go and shoot mice," I scoffed at them, too.

"You are just good for nothing," Taurai rubbed it in.

We shot them with our stinging pistols and they fled for their lives like robbers. The following day we saw them with bows made of curved sticks and rubber bands. For the arrows they used elephant grass stems fitted with sharp wire tips on the stabbing end. They came boasting their invention.

"Move your bandy legs before I blow them under you," Simba growled.

"No! You can't!" Jongwe, their leader replied.

"Your technology is too primitive!"

"Nonsense!"

"You haven't fought the oppressor like us! We are not in the same league."

"Liars!"

"We'll show you!"

Then, without warning, we fell upon them, shooting at close range with our guns. Taken by surprise and humiliated by our arrogance, they melted away. Yet they were determined to prove themselves a force worth reckoning. They went to practice at shooting with their weapons amongst themselves. Two hours later Ponde, who was Jongwe's younger brother, was heard howling in the street. People flowed out and saw Jack kneeling in a ball of anguish, grinding his forehead on the tarmac. His brother held him up and what we saw shocked us all. He covered his left eye with his hand. Blood mixed with some sticky glistening fluid streamed down his face. Bits and pieces of torn flesh dangled through his fingers. Simba said it was the vitreous humour but to me it was absolutely tragic! I saw no humour at all! Ponde had been shot in the eye by his brother. Thus their technology had come to a sad end. And our armed group was disbanded, too. Our holsters and Stetsons burned! When the boy returned from the hospital, he had a big hole in the place of his left eye. It made me realise how fragile human life was. Yes, life can be one big hole. And full of shattering explosions.

*

We lay in the blankets on our backs and whispering to each other in the dark because it was past bedtime. Old Popa had a cluster of banana trees in his yard where we had chopped off a bunch of fat green bananas and hidden them in the middle of that cluster to ripen. We wrapped them with thick khaki paper and thoroughly covered them with a layer of dry banana leaves.

"When did we cut them?" Simba asked.

"Five days ago," I replied.

"We will go and check them tomorrow."

"If you sneak away from me like you did last time I'll tell on you." I threatened.

"To whom?"

"The policeman!"

Dad's other job was a policeman and he often went on duty from six o'clock in the evening to twelve o'clock midnight or from twelve o'clock midnight to six o'clock in the morning. Despite his two jobs, he had nothing much to show about it. The salaries were pitifully small and a mockery to the valuable work he did. In his other job he worked for the National Railways of Rhodesia as a foreman. However, we always referred to him as The Policeman because he was always policing us for crime and when he beat us he did so like we were real criminals.

Our deliberations for the following day were suddenly cut by a series of high pitched crackling sounds followed by heavy explosions. Kkrrrrrrrrrr-krrrrrrr B-O-O-M! Kr-rrrrrr-krrrrr B-O-O-M! The walls of the house shook and the roof rattled. A strong light spread into the room. The explosions came again and I felt the bed shaking. A couple of cockroaches tumbled down the wall on top of my blankets, did a jig in confused circles and then sped off in different directions. I was terrified like a mouse. Mother called from her bedroom. Shaking and excited, Revai flew in from outside where he was keeping warm by the fire.

"What was it?" Mother was asking.

"Fire! A big fire. Sounds like guns," Revai shrieked.

We all streamed outside. People squeezed each other through the doorways of their houses to get a look. And there it was! The biggest ball of fire I had ever seen appeared to have sprouted on the edge of the compound. Yet my eyes were deceived. Everyone's eyes were deceived for even some people whose houses were on the edge of the compound fled towards into the interior. I wanted to run away, too. We could feel the heat in our faces. Yet it was happening far away in the heavy industrial area. Those were the fuel tanks at the Petroleum Depot. The guerrillas had sneaked into the city and blown them with their deadly rocket fire. It was the first sound of rocket fire I ever heard. Things were never going to be the same again for the liberation war had come to the capital city.

SEVEN

I stood in the middle of the road, the mirage in the distance beckoning to my stinking unwashed body. I had not washed in a month—a month of aimless search, watching dreams fly-by like blind bats, dwindling self-esteem and sickly coughing. I was lost in a darkness I could not fathom; my spirit trapped in the vast privacy of my inward wilderness.

Death trailed me like a chameleon stalking a fly. But there was nothing it would celebrate upon. I was not worth a kill. Not at all! Transformed to utmost loathsome measure. Bemused, weary and tragically comic, I stood in my greasy tattered outfit. Licking and caressing sponge-like lips, my dry rough tongue turned to sandpaper…I had stood in the way of death, but it smacked and shamed my wish. My blazing tongue acrid as an apprentice baker's ginger biscuit, there I stood in the middle of nowhere. Nowhere because death never came. Nowhere because I was stuck in a place where my precious life had become the value of nothing.

"One…t-w-o…t-h-r-e-e…"I stood there, trying to count the senses left in that numb derelict skull of mine. Servant to HARD TIMES and slowly becoming her slave. Dominated and rendered powerless by absolute need! Broken and in utter desperation I tried to make sense of my spiralling odd life. Unable to see that I could be master and dominate HARD TIMES, too. Sometimes I did not know whose head I carried on my shoulders. My mind scattered all over the place. My blurred shimmering vision captured my ex-future dreams stuck in mirages. Cold and deserted of company, I pushed my step in a corpse-like trance. Not knowing what to make or break out of my experience. Giving up power over my destiny?

From the other side of the road, full of unrequited love, my wife called out my name. Telling me to cross over to her side. Roots of blazing steel grew under my feet, deep into the tarmac. Paralysed! A river of shame, guilt, failure and regret washing all over me. My soul darkened. Lost!

I looked down and saw this scrawny puppy looking up at me. Staring right in my face. Two balls of sapped energy speaking to me. Pleading! Four crippled legs planted in the dust. I stared back, struggling hard to get the story. A spear ripped into the back of my brain scattering bolts of wicked lightning through my spinal code. Stiffly, I bent forward to pick it up and saw it was my son's face sitting on its shoulders. Broken! Tears rushing down his ashen ill-fed cheeks whose skin had the blinking tousled colour of boiled tomato-less fish soup. Owls hooted in my ears. Jackals yelped. Voices wailed. Broken voices I marked belonging to my children. Stabbing into my cold lonely heart like hot pitchforks!

The wind sucked me backwards. I struggled. The air I breathed out ejecting in fiery white puffs. I summoned all my remaining energy to keep on my wobbly bootless feet. Stumbling! And stumbling. Suddenly, I did not want to die. Not anymore! Yet, I kept on falling. Falling into an endless pit like a scarecrow whose feet had been eaten by termites. Stiffly. Ungainly.

The road spun like a giant black ribbon and I caught the sound of an approaching helicopter, the thunder of its guns spitting molten anger that shook me like a termite in a frying pan. Voices yelled and gigantic trumpet-blasts that seemed to tear from the heavens hurled me to the merciless ribbon that pricked my body in a million places. The ground rippled all around me as if it were a rag ripping apart. I felt the wrath of the storm straddling over my miserable body. Sensing the lightning strikes. Rolling in its thunder. I lay there on the tarmac, my cracked bulging lips smiling for the first time in I did-not-know-how-many months. Happy in a dark and white explosion of the mind, that death in its merciful roaring beauty to the tortured despairing wretched I was had finally come! And I opened my torn heart for it to enter!

The storm passed quickly and as its tail receded in the distance, I felt its warm thick rain in my face. Blood! It was blood! For moments I lay there licking the warm sticky rain on my torn cauliflower lips. Enveloped in a storm of life and death my ex-future was nailed on the cross! Then, a cloud of faces burst above my head! Someone sat me up and cried:

"He's alive! He's still alive."

I looked all around the tarmac yet there was no dog at all. I wanted to get up but a thousand hands pinned me down. My shoulder blades were shovels digging into the tarmac.

And as they lifted me onto the stretcher, I could not help but notice a squashed loaf of shaggy hairs spread like marmalade on the road…My body a writhing jelly of flesh fastened by belts, I struggled to get off the stretcher. I wanted to go and lift the poor flattened life off the ground and see what its face looked like. To confirm what my eyes had seen! And as they put me away, I felt my eyes being pulled out towards the dead dog. Its fur then extricated itself from the body of broken bones and minced flesh. It rose in the wind and roaring like a jet fighter, flew crashing into my face. My head turned. The stretcher spun. And my fingers twitched. There was the cracking sound of a gun and the world exploded in a rushing whirl of sirens…

Then I was lost in a swimming darkness. My spirit, floating in that blackness was watching friends and family at a funeral. My three sons staggered out of the crowd, their features twisted and torn by grief. One of them picked up a derelict suit from the ground. My suit! The eldest two started slugging each other over it. Brutally. The third one sat naked. Watching. Passively. Weirdly not the gentle that I know, my brother violently prised open the coffin and I saw my undernourished body lying in there. My own funeral underlined by the anger of those who loved me…

*

I woke up in a river of sweat. An iron hand of fear gripped me by the throat choking the air out of my lungs. Dazed like one who had fallen out of a rocket, I looked all around. Scattered figures of men slept under dog-blankets teeming with lice and bed bugs. The cool glare of street lamps spoke to me and my confusion ebbed into its hideout. I felt as if a bottle of brandy had been broken and spilled all its contents inside my chest. Burning! Unable to breathe. I sucked in huge bags of air and slowly released it from my tortured lungs. It calmed me down. Yet my forehead continued to burn like a furnace.

A grisly figure with a dent in the side of the upper forehead and naked from waist to the top came up the street with long exaggerated strides. It was Chimwene, shouting in a half strangled hoarse voice:

"The President's wife is the fly in your soup!"

Someone raised his head and said:

"Shut up Chimwene!"

Chimwene walked to where the man was lying. He looked into the man's eyes words toppling from his huge lips:

"You are full of faeces and flies in your eyes."

"What!"

"Like your president, you are full of faeces and flies in your eyes."

"Why don't you find a place to sleep?"

"They threw me out of the Robertson's room. They threw me out of the sanctuary. They threw me out of the Minor Hall. And they threw me out of the foyer. They even threw me out of the toilet! Everywhere I went they took pleasure in throwing me out like a piece of excrement. Crazy how they snore, sleeping on top of each other like mice. Parents and children! Lovers wriggling on top of each other in the street! Shame!"

"Shut up and just get some sleep." someone shouted.

"You think all's well when you sleep in the street like dog pooh? The day you shall wake up from your cruel dream you'll then know how much responsible you're for deceiving yourself. Tomorrow I will make you sleep on top of fish bones, maybe that should take the faeces out of your mind and make you think."

All the people who were awake and listening started laughing. Then, a passionate comic ridicule of The President's wild dissolute sons and his wife's unending debauched escapades, conceit and looting broke out. From that moment till dawn. A penchant for Gucci fashion-wear saw her being christened Gucci Gee. Their eldest son was a liability. Always in the newspapers for the wrong reasons. Drugs. Lechery. Abusing state property. Prostitution. And folly. Like a chest of indispensable medicine the president and his wife went everywhere with their retarded moron of a son to keep an eye on him. Even overseas. Lest they be shamed.

What exactness and truth sometimes lies in the irony of madness. Chimwene was attacking us for our deceptive optimism and how it drove us on with a cruelty that had become normal to us all. I craved sleep no more for the night was almost gone. And the nightmare lingered into the daylight like a terrible hangover. Grabbing me by the front collar. My ex-future gawking at me from the depths of the subconscious.

*

When we saw the newspapers that morning, the president's wife had struck again. This time visiting a neighbouring country. The front page of the newspaper screamed her assault of someone with an electric cord. A lady she had found in her children's room. Her crime, being in that room. And now she was asking for diplomatic immunity from prosecution. Or, maybe for diplomatic impunity? Coming from a country where she and her family had a licence to fix people with impunity. Meanwhile, at the hotel, her son was busy pouring champagne over his expensive US$800 000,00 Rolex watch. They always had a knack of letting the cat out of their bag of crimes. Where did our diamonds worth US15 billion go? And here we were! Doomed to spend our lives in exile. Destitute. Sleeping under bridges and on street pavements, next to rubbish bins and rotting garbage. Scoundrels without a name, they were.

*

Every day I rose to face life and every day, rising from the shadows of my being the nightmare would not leave me. Its dreadful content and meaning was all that was me and what was falling apart! The deepest fears I had always suppressed or denied! The guilt! The shame! The illusion! The rage! It was the reflection of my shadow—my other being I had always sought to hide behind the untroubled mask paraded every day on the street. I had to acknowledge its existence—its pulsing darkness—if I wanted to transcend it by any light and return to my original being. It was a chance for me to die and be re-born. Indeed we fear dying yet if we do not confront death every day to become better men never will we be able to live our lives free. Neither can we own our lives, too! Nor can we stop our shadows from owning us! Which is worse than death itself!

the light we shine in our face

comes from the deepest darkness within us

and the beauty flowing out of us is strong

for our pain and past teach us along

EIGHT

Elections 2008

I sat in that place alone. I sat fearful of my own country-men. I sat afraid because of what they had done to me. I spoke to No One because they had sewn up my lips with the needle of violence. And told No One to speak to me! I spoke to No One because they had come to my house and told my wife that if they ever lost the elections in that con-stituency my house would be the first to burn. My children paying for my sins with their death! Neither did I ever look for anyone to speak to nor did I care! I was alone! Afflicted by nervousness! Terrified! And lost!

News coming from home was frustrating, infuriating and depressing. Wherever we went we put on a cloak of sad-ness. We commiserated, yet we never lost hope. We hurt inside! And we ranted! The devil in control had painted its repressive masterpiece in our lives! They had perfected the art of using fear as a weapon to silence their own people. The same tactics that we had been subjected to at the hands of the colonialists prevailed. And they found an audience willing to be misled in the African Union (AU) and Southern African Development Community (SADC). And collusion from big brother South Africa's quiet diplomacy! Regrettably!

Because they could not get hold of us in the diaspora, they inflicted pain to us through our loved ones at home. Hit and run accidents sprang up like a curse on the narrow streets of our famished ghettos. They denied our children, wives and relatives medication at the government hospitals. Instead, they used massive amounts of money buying arms to suppress the citizenry. The Star reported of a ship heavily laden with cruel weapons of war being refused by officials to dock at the Durban Port. They found an alternative route through another ally. The police, the army and the militia, popularly known as the Green Bombers raised their filthy hands against blameless souls. In a rabid madness, they slaughtered the guiltless. Tortured the defenceless! And brutally silenced the voices of reason! They sought to obliterate our existence and only legitimise their right to a livelihood! The country was prescribed only to the success and wellbeing of their selves. And their own kith and kin.

*

"Who do you think you are?"
　"I'm a journalist."
　"Why are you here?"
　"I'm doing my job."
　"Who invited you here?"
　"I'm a news reporter!"
　"A news reporter?"
　"An accredited news reporter."

"No! You are a sell-out!"

"I only write about what is happening. The truth."

"Who gave you the permission to take pictures?"

Then one of them arbitrarily pronounced:

"Don't waste your time with him! He's a criminal! Just like all the others!"

"No! No!"

"You have the right to remain silent. Otherwise whatever you say will be used against you in the court of law."

Despite his protests, they confiscated his camera and bundled him into the police van like a goat. Only when they were at the police station did they give him the chance to verify his accreditation. Then the charges became schizophrenic:

"Why did you do it?"

"Do what?"

"The bus! Why did you burn the bus?"

"I didn't burn any bus!

"Yes you did!"

"I only took pictures for my story! A camera doesn't burn things!"

"Shut up! You think I am joking?"

"How can I shut up when you ask me questions?"

"You'll die for your morsel of stupid news like a rat. You'll see!"

And so the charge sheet was changed from arson to causing public disorder and acting in contempt of the law.

*

"Why are you spreading lies about our country?"

"I don't understand."

"You do! Why are you writing bad things about our president?"

"I am not writing anything at all about your country or the president."

"You are lying. You think I am a fool?"

"No, I don't."

"You think you are smart?"

"Smart about what?"

"You don't ask questions! I'm the one who asks the questions here. Do you understand?"

"Okay! But I don't know why I am here."

"What do you need to understand?"

"About the writing. I'm not a writer and I'm not a journalist at all."

"Tell us what you know about Sky News and BBC."

"I said I'm not a journalist at all!"

Even though he was proved as having no ties with any of the two news organs and not being a journalist, the man had to languish in jail for five days.

*

"Comrade Member in Charge, who do you work for?"

"The government."

"Then why do you arrest people supporting the government?"

"I am only arresting people who are committing crimes."

"Who told you that people supporting the government by re-educating sell-outs are committing crimes?"

"When any victim reports a crime of assault, it is common practice that we institute an investigation into the matter. It is their constitutional right!"

"I see you need re-education, too!"

And so the surprise visit by the high-ranking officer to that police station was expressed and highlighted. Callous bruising slaps roasted his baby-clean face. Baton sticks converged on his buttocks, legs, arms and back. Ages after they were gone he was still squealing for mercy. His face swollen blind. When he entered his home a mere shadow devoid of his lively confident gait, his family knew he had to niftily dissolve away before the belly of the earth swallowed him. The fire for his braai had been lit. And they had just come to marinade his wretched flesh.

When he woke up the following morning, the Member in Charge's sore distended body was an ungainly dinosaur tottering on chicken legs. He could not report for work. But while he slept at home, two men in black suits and dark glasses came to see him. One of them sneered:

"We came to inform you that the First Lady is visiting your precinct right now. There are some changes that you need to know and not to interfere with. All the Mazoe Citrus Estates now belong to her, including the Mazoe Dam. From today nobody must be seen within its vicinity and no one fishes in that dam."

"What about those who hold permits from the Department of National Parks?"

"I said the dam now belongs to the First Lady! What language do you understand?"

The Member in Charge had to save his skin by keeping his silence.

"You are therefore required to arrest and have all trespassers prosecuted. And remember, yours is not to question anything but to take orders!"

*

Meanwhile the Joint Operations Command (JOC) made up of the Zimbabwe Republic Police (ZRP), the Central Intelligence Organisation (CIO), the Zimbabwe Defence Forces (ZDF) and the Zimbabwe Prison Service (ZPS) wreaked havoc, stealing and confiscating goods in an effort to control prices. The goods ironically ended up being sold on the black market at insane prices above those stipulated by the price control. The JOC's secret true mandate was to intimidate the people and make sure that the ruling party regained power.

The torture and disappearance of political activists continued. The government was prepared to unleash another Gukurahundi like they did in Matabeleland where thousands of the Ndebele people were raped, tortured and massacred. The whole country will now have to confront one another for crimes against humanity perpetrated by a handful power-hungry politicians. Yet when that day arrives, we all will be called upon to take part in telling the truth and in taking responsibility of what happened.

NINE

My head was spinning again. A heavy load pivoted on a long invisible dagger embedded in the back of my shoulder. A merciless pain clawed into the chest pricking my heart. Flies played around my head. I lifted my hand to strike them away. A bolt of pain that darkened my eyesight shot through from the shoulder to the fingers. They shook like a bolt of lightning branching out in five famished streams. The flies sensing that my life was coming apart, called more of their callous clan. They settled on my back. They hummed the story of my life. In an insulting buzz!

People were busy waking up and wrapping their blankets. I had not written poetry in a long time. And chunks of jabbering verses rattled like bones in my creaking head. My breath came in small compressed spurts. Like a man who had fish bones in his chest. I licked my lips but no saliva came. They felt like a sponge. Slowly I spread out one blanket on the paving and placed the other folded blankets in its centre. I placed the plastic bag with my jeans on top of the folded blankets. I held two opposite angles of the spread out blanket tying them together. Over my meagre property heaped in the centre! My shocking momentous history! For such moments define and separate the heroic from the cowardly. Those who want to live from those who simply want to exist! I repeated the same action with the two remaining opposite corners. Then, struggling, I straightened my back. Staggering on numb limbs! The paving looking like an infinite distance beneath my feet. Figures of people waking up swam and danced without rhyme or reason. I closed my eyes. Releasing bad air from my loose bowels! And felt the swimming darkness in my eyes burn with half formed meteors of thoughts landing nowhere.

My stubborn spirit lifted up the baggage from the street. Like a drunken man I weaved through the throng of my weary, broken but hopeful fellows. The load swayed on my shoulders. Bowed like a man with a crippled spine. I floated into the church, the skin of my head gleaming with sweat. I kept a bald head because I did not want my hair to be a breeding ground for lice. We had an oversupply of this in the church. Going up the stairs from the foyer to the sanctuary, I felt a stunning cool tap upon my burning pate. I did not know what it was. Yet I appreciated the frigid comfort it diffused to my laden heart. I had both hands occupied with the load on my shoulders. Hence I did not feel compelled to check of what nature it was. I simply walked on towards the storeroom. The cool balm caressing down my head. Into my eyes. Down the steps on the other end of the sanctuary I floated. Ignorant of the source of my placid blessing. Nobody noticing. For the storeroom was sunk in a dark corner of the building. So dark that light was needed every hour of the day. And somebody had stolen the globe.

It would just happen like that. All the time! We had become used to it. The darkness that permeated every aspect of our lives.

I stood in a queue. My turn came. I handed over my belongings for safe keeping. I would collect them back at eight o'clock in the evening. This was a key routine to a free day. After six o'clock the store-room was locked. Then you missed it! Meaning having to go round the city carrying your pack of blankets, wardrobe, lice and bed bugs wherever you went. And one had always to be there when the bundles were brought out. Once you missed the time you would surely miss your bundle, too. Thieves floated around, waiting to pounce on unclaimed baggage. In those miserable packages there was always a shred of value.

As I walked away from the dark storeroom, I wiped the salve off my head with the palm of my hand. I saw it was bird pooh. Bird pooh on my pate in the house of God! A scream of surprise! Silence. Panic! And a calmness. Then the sound of whispering angels caressed my ears. Gurgling rivers rising and falling in my head. My bones creaked. I thought out loudly to myself:

"That's good luck my boy."

Things moved. Voices sang. In my creaking head. I followed the path I had come in. At the base of the stairs I flashed my eyes upwards. There it was! Perched on the trusses! Eyes gleaming with a mysterious brightness from the calm dimness in the lofty realms of the sanctuary, the dove looked down upon me. Its luminous eyes pouring out arrows of molten light into the sucking depths of my probing eyes. Bathing my still body with a mystic radiance. Sealing all the inveterate scars sprawling across my broken heart. The light surged through my veins like an electric current. I must have gulped beyond measure for when again I looked, I found the dove gone. I did not know where. What was this? A sign? An optic illusion? Yet what a positive one. They say a drowning man may clutch at straw. That vision infused a straw of light where there had been darkness. And it burned with a power that made my heart kick wildly in my chest.

My feet did not take me as usual to Powerhouse for tea. I bought some fat-cakes on the street. Then I went to the Roman Catholic Church in Jeppe's Town where we had tea or coffee and bread with peanut butter. I chose tea because I discovered that coffee had become a catalyst for my depressive state. That morning I felt my heart urgently craved intimacy with the Lord. I hungered for the word and thirsted for his blessing. I wanted prayer to liberate me that I should be his instrument in my life and that I should be able to forgive all those who had caused me pain. I prayed with the nun before breakfast. I prayed with her humble voice and her words lifted up my spirits. I drank from the energy of her voice and the timbre of her mellowness. I sent my searching voice inside of myself, deeper into the caverns of my sub-consciousness where God's mission and purpose is ensconced waiting to germinate in my life. In that place, waiting to be tapped resides a capacity inexhaustible as the sea for ourselves and even for our enemies that we may help to free them from the bondage of their evil deeds against us. A capacity that sets us all free and pulls us all together!

Something grows when you plant it. How it develops will depend on the soil you plant it. On that day I planted a new crop of love. I carefully chose to grow out of the mud and dirt of experience. Dirt is good. How would we know cleanliness without dirt? Dirt is there so that we can know how to value and appreciate cleanliness! I purchased free of charge a can of laughter to fan the growth of my new garden. Determining to grasp and exalt that hidden light always difficult to fathom, I made an oath to bide by positive thought patterns and stir myself out of the corrosive reactive state. A war had started in my mind. A struggle for liberation which I dared not linger. I had to do this for myself. My children. And my wife. Thus in that moment of lucidity I found my pen dancing in my note book:

i will only have peace

when i return to you

i will only have joy

when i laugh with you

i rise each day

your image moulding life

in my murky thoughts

softly caressing my heart

with distant defying love

o! my hour will only come

nestled in your arms

when peace finds home

in the comfort of your zone

I downed my cup of tea and saw her face smiling up at me from the bottom of the cup. Then the birds flitting across the sky were reflected in the place of her image. I rose with my eyes in the sky and noticed how the sun mercilessly scorched my skin. Setting my bald pate on fire! I no longer grew my hair because of the head lice which had turned it into their colony. A flock of doves deftly cut across the sky with an ease that defied the power of words. I wondered if ever I could pass through life with such ease and infinite grace.

I felt the sweat gushing out of my pores and I sniffed my armpits. They reeked with the sweat of five days; the last time I washed. Something tickled my neck. I plucked it off with my fingers and saw that it was a louse. The sun's heat always flushed them out of their hiding places. Mostly they hid in the seams of clothing and in the lining of underwear. In those places they laid their glittering roe. They stole out of their hiding places and sucked our blood. I pressed it between the fingernails of my both thumbs and ground them together. There was a small popping sound and it burst. Blood splashed out leaving small red streaks on the fingernails. Their hard roe was harder to deal with. The best way to destroy them was to dip the clothes in boiling water.

My feet followed the snaking black ribbon that led to the Rand Dam. My sore eyes swept like lightning on dancing skyscrapers of Joburg. I saw trees with their leaves and branches planted in the ground and their roots flourishing like arms in the air. The arms had small heads on them celebrating their emancipation from the bondage of the earth. Their stupid mouths spit glistening saliva drenching my skin and my jeans. I scratched without end around my neck, waist, stomach, back, legs and arms. There was a black belt of bumpy flesh lining my waist like a black mamba. This came from the lice sucking my blood. They liked to hide in the waist line of our trousers and underwear. I scratched the abominable girdle until small sores burst all over the midriff. My fingertips choked with black dirt and blood between my long un-kept fingernails. I licked my lips and they felt like a rasp. They did not belong to me. Even the tongue did not belong to my mouth. It felt like a broken sheet of metal. The sweat in my armpits and between my buttocks was like hot chilli sauce. I shivered and gyrated obscenely in my walk. I did not know whether I walked or danced. I only knew that my feet carried me forward.

The cool waters of the Rand Dam gleamed with beckoning waves in front of me. The smell of water and assortment of vegetation in different forms of life soaking into my nostrils. An anticipation of freshness and rejuvenation creeping into my bones. A group of the Apostolic Faith Mission (AFM) congregation was gathered in an open space on the left. I avoided them making a detour further to the right and as I took the bend I espied another group of men standing demurely and talking in hushed tones. They faced the bush far right of the dam. I approached them.

"What is it?"

"It's Rasta," someone said.

"What happened?"

"Can't you see?"

"Who has done that to him?"

No answer! The stiff lean body of Rasta hanged from a branch on one of the trees overlooking the dam. The thick shoelaces of his Haix army combat boots dug mercilessly into the flesh of his neck to the bone. He was dead. The police were examining his shack by the side of the dam and all the surrounding area. The forensic team took his body down and placed it in a steel coffin. The police asked us whether we knew Rasta. Someone answered in the affirmative. He said Rasta had been his friend and just a few days ago he had looked depressed and given him his brother's contact details to keep.

"Greetings Jah Man," Rasta had come to him smoking weed.

"Greetings Rasta."

"This world is not our home, Jah Man."

Rasta was looking at the affluent restaurant far across the dam. People resplendent with the musty smell of money sat around round tables, drinking and talking animatedly. Some were puffing at cigarettes with the coils of their smoke spiralling up in rings of a burning joy. George saw that Rasta spoke with a voice whose soul no longer looked at life as a celebration. And a heart whose zest for life was fast trickling into a dry riverbed.

"I have a brother who is a professor."

"In Joburg?"

"No! In Zimbabwe!"

"A rich brother?"

"Yes! May you save his cell-phone number on your phone? I have it on a piece of paper and I don't want to lose it."

"Alright Rasta."

George gave the cell-phone number to the police. We all stood in silence as the police convoy slowly drove away with the corpse that smelled of fish and marijuana. In a confused reverie, I walked to the edge of the dam. My eyes fixed on Rasta's shack, the tins that were his pots and his wooden stool faithfully waiting for him. An empty washing line could be seen erected behind the shack. A lizard fell off the nearside post hitting its head against a rock supporting the post. Dazed it lay on its side in pain. The loss in that place was just beginning to settle in.

*

Just a week ago Rasta had sat on his stool smoking his weed. He was inseparable with his weed. He sat there, talking to me, Dan and Matt while we were bathing in the dam.

"I had a dream." He was saying.

"A dream?" Dan echoed.

"A dream that nearly broke my heart when I woke up!"

"Let's hear it Rasta."

"I was driving my Jeep Sahara," he began, stopped and drew heavily from his weed. I watched his chest billowing out whilst he held the smoke prisoner inside. Then he slowly let it escape in compressed trumpet-like gusts that left a thousand stinging blows in his mind. The blows shook his mind and reverberated throughout his lean hairy body."

"I was driving my Jeep Sahara. I had my wife and two children. We were travelling along a dirt road in a remote rural area. It had been raining and still dark clouds lingered with the promise of a returning storm. The road was slippery and wound like a huge serpent trying to escape. I could feel the tyres spinning, clawing and skidding in the mud as we went up and down the treacherous slopes. The Jeep became the colour of mud all over."

"Suddenly there appeared a heavy laden bus in the front. It travelled in the same direction as we did. Then a long narrow bridge sprouted ahead of the bus. It could only accommodate one vehicle at a time. The bus trundled along like a gigantic beetle. It rattled and coughed with a tail of smoke waving behind it. Then something strange happened. The giant beetle weaved from one side to another, seemed to break the front right leg and hobbled as if an invisible magnet tugged at it. It struck the flimsy rails alongside the bridge tossing it into the river below. Then it followed after the rails. The passengers wailed, stampeded and collided with each other as the bus flew fifteen metres down. It landed on the muddy brown waters and sank like a paralysed silly goose. The tail of smoke rose and continued to rise wailing silently out of the river where it had fallen."

"I drove past where the bus had fallen and stopped right at the end of the bridge. I made a 105 degrees from that spot to face the sinking point. Then I leaped out and rushed to the back of the Jeep where I retrieved a very strong long rope. I tied it to the towing hook and grabbing the loose end of the rope I ran like the wind towards a tree that stood boldly by the roadside with a very stout trunk. A group of villagers had sprung from nowhere. I gave the men the instruction to hold the rope around the tree and be ready to pull like in a tug-of-war with the Jeep at my command."

"My next activity blew me to the front of the vehicle. I grabbed the hook of the winch fastening it to my belt and with the same miracle of movement tore down the side of the hill towards the river. I became a miniature of a storm myself breaking and uprooting small bushes. Their surprised roots clutched at heavy rocks that powerlessly followed us down the way. I heard them splash in the river long after I had disappeared under the water. I groped against the torrential brown screen with my hands, feet and eyes until I bumped against the front of the sunken bus. I located the towing hook and my fingers working like a machine soon had the winch's hook in. out of the river depths I shot like a canon. With my hands I hung on the taut winch's wire. The muscles of my body quivered with a nameless energy and I was Tarzan swiftly swinging and propelling my feet on the side of the hill."

"My wife and my children had fled from the car and were watching my madness as they cried and wrung their hands and prayed. I leaped into the Jeep, started the engine and engaged the reverse gear. I felt the vehicle tug against the weight of the sunken bus and at that moment shouted at the uncertain villagers to pull. The Jeep pulled! The men pulled! Both ropes became taut with tension! I stepped on the accelerator and again shouted at the men. They pulled. The Sahara pulled, the roar in its throat becoming a deafening roar. There was an inch of movement! The men sensed it and were encouraged. I sensed it too and my foot dipped more on the accelerator. The movement slowly picked up and soon the bus nosed out. With a flourish I yelled at the men. I saw them plant their heavy bootless feet into the mud and straining like yoked beasts of burden, their tortured muscles rippled with a power never seen in a human body. And I heard the Jeep growling in defiance of the evil spirits that had thrown the bus into the river. Miraculously, the bus emerged, crawling over the river bank."

"Suddenly I felt the wheels slipping and spinning with futile grip, throwing out a volley of mud like canons. Realising that I had come to the edge of the bridge's concrete slab, I bellowed at the men to move round and round the tree trunk. I could see their feet digging into the mud. Round and round they went at an acute angle. Then they tied the remaining piece in several knots on the stretched out rope. I pulled up the handbrake and a brief look showed as if a deep plough had gone round and round in the soil surrounding the tree. Only the back of the bus kissed the river. People with distended tummies tumbled out of the bus onto the small patch that was the river bank. Water flew out of their mouths as if they had swallowed water cannons. A lot of them still gripped with shock floundered in the water that gushed out of the bus through the windows and the door. The men flew down the hill pulling those who had totally lost their faculties and were slipping back into the river. We managed to save sixty-six bodies. Six however were swallowed into the stomach of the river and when I looked hard into the water, I saw their ghosts emerge. Carrying between them an ivory coffin, their cursing eyes were gleaming twelve balls of fire whose rays shot in search of my body like the spider-man's yarn. Straight for me they came. My feet dragged, knees turned into jelly and my body ached and became stone cold with the anticipation of death. My whole body reeked of death! I reached out to the surviving crowd, but they all covered their faces with their hands and turned their backs on me, the handwriting on their backs screaming DEATH and the figure 666. Even when I woke up, the stench of death still hung upon my body!"

When he finished recounting his dream, Rasta had strikingly become pensive and sad. A sudden immutable gloom seemed to descend upon his spirits.

"What do you say of my dream?"

None of us could interpret dreams. We remained silent.

"What do you think of the handwriting on their backs and the figure 666? Do you know that I was born on the sixth of June 1966?"

"You could try visiting the Apostolic Faith prophets," Dan said. "They could help."

Rasta, smelling of fresh fish and marijuana, just shook his mane of dreadlocks. He had reached an unalterable present where the past and the future could never be reconciled, even in the world of dreams. The bleak domain of the shattered soul!

I checked the date. It was the sixth of June! Rasta's birthday! That afternoon, I went through all my jeans crushing the lice between my thumbs' fingernails. Their fat round bodies burst and the blood they sucked out of my body looked like red fingernail paint on my fingers. How I wished to kill that life and bury it in a past that I wished I could kill, too. I washed my jeans and hung them in the hot sun over the small bushes to dry. Thrice I rubbed soap all over my body and scrubbed myself with a piece of rough stone. When I scooped water with my hands and sent it cascading down my body I felt a myriad stabs of mint coolness penetrating into the skin. The itchiness around my neck and waist died. For long and twice did I apply soap before it foamed and showed its efficacy upon my dirty skin. For long did I scrub the itching rash until the sores opened to the healing magic of a bath. Then, naked, I leisurely took possession of that small portion of the dam as I waited for my underwear and jeans to dry. Rasta's dream and death playing out in my mind.

Water is a great medicine! After bathing my mind cleared and the vitality that had vanished returned. I rubbed some petroleum jelly on my skin. My clothes were half dry and no longer dripping with water. I carefully lifted them off the bushes neatly folding them into a plastic bag. Besides the books I carefully picked up at The Salvation Army, they were the only thing left that defended my dignity and gave me an appearance of sanity. I respected them for they preserved an essential part of my identity.

*

Dan was smoking a cigarette when I arrived. As usual he had his bag slung over his shoulder. In it he carried his high school certificates and his degree in Economic History. Both our bags ensconced more books and literature than clothes. He was discussing politics with Matt. Nkosi was sitting on the stairs talking to Ncube in hushed tones. The two ex-servicemen both now grew long beards and long hair to disguise themselves. Something unusual hung in the air. Looking around, I noticed that for the first time, we had soldiers, members of The South African National Defence

Forces in the building. A number of them planted in the crowd. Why they had come amongst us was going to be a mystery to everybody as they stayed with us for the following two weeks. To this day I still wonder why! There were rumours of some particular people being the regime's informers at the church who passed information on police and army deserters to the regime's intelligence. As I went to Dan and Matt with the news, the two men's body postures and serious expressions made me wonder what the two were talking about.

"Rasta is dead."

"What happened?"

"He committed suicide."

"I told him to visit the Apostolic Faith prophets. They could have helped."

I nodded my head. Religion and faith suddenly became a very important thing to many people at the church. Most people became born again Christians several times at the different churches they visited.

It was Friday and the day of the week when we had the Refugee Meeting. Every Friday of the week we had this meeting. We came in early so that we could have seats either in the sanctuary or the gallery. The gallery was always full of women and children. When the kids cried it was difficult to hear anything. Thus the sanctuary became our first choice. We met poet Nya who also had been an educator back home. We found seats in the front half.

"On Monday we must go to the Library at Khanya College," Nya was saying.

"Good idea." I said.

"We need to pursue the idea of forming a writers' organization," Dan added.

"I like Khanya College," Nya said.

"I like it, too!" Dan responded.

"I took to books the way a duck takes to water!" Said Matt.

Khanya College was our newest find. It was located in the central business district of Johannesburg, along Pritchard Street in the House of Movements building. Khanya College was a house of movements itself! There was a free library where we read books and newspapers and a theatre open to the community on the fifth floor. We determined to approach Ras Menzi who worked in that library.

Three quarters of an hour later, the Bishop floated in. The refugee meeting started. Bubbly Liz who was the school secretary was also the secretary for the refugee meeting. She moved in an agile graceful body, briskly distributing the minutes of the previous refugee meeting. Like all busy men, I presume The Bishop had no time to stand in front of the mirror holding a shaving machine. I bet he used a barber to trim his side-whiskers and beard. Yet I think his beards clothed his benign smile most becomingly. A clean shave could have done no better!

The minutes were read and passed as a correct record. The school principal presented the school report on the progress on various fronts of education and getting the school registered. He could have patted himself on the back for the work he was doing. The school had almost a year in operation. Interesting corridors of learning for both children and adults were developing and literally, almost in the blink of an eye, it propitiously asserted its place as a reputable institution in the city. The Bishop announced that volunteers were needed to assist the children with their homework and act as care-givers. I put my name down. Dan put his name down too. There were reports from the crèche, the sewing club, the karate club, the chess club, the football team, computer lessons, the hotel and catering training. Cleo reported on job placements. Some people had been placed with some farms in the Eastern Cape. People were asked to be careful with people who came from nowhere to give them jobs as some unwittingly ended up doing criminal jobs. We were asked to register our skills with Cleo. More farm workers were also needed. People were free to join any of the clubs mentioned. Anybody could initiate a project if they wished. The Bishop said that the Book Club needed someone to run it. After the meeting, I went to his office and volunteered to run it. I would start reporting the following week.

We fetched our blankets from the storeroom and went to our bedroom out on the street. We decided to find a better sleeping place than Smal Street. We crossed to the other side of Pritchard Street and found space in front of the First National Bank (FNB) branch. We slept a stone's throw away from the bank's automated teller machines. Normally they did not allow people to sleep there but on that day the guard on duty seemed to have a soft heart for refugees. He asked us to make a list of all people who slept there and organise ourselves to make sure we always left the place clean in the morning. With our heads resting on our bags which were our pillows, I mused over my first Refugee Meeting. Like slow dashing sea water stealing in and out of crab holes on a beach I drifted in and out of sleep. It felt like my clock had started ticking again. I only needed to reset the time accurately.

Nkosi fitfully dozed beside me. He held his crutch in his arms as usual. Like a rifle he was ready to fire. I smiled to myself and in the middle of that contented smile, a miniature star flew over my head. Hitting against the wall, it burst scattering its liquid contents all over us. Nkosi, breaking out of sleep swung his crutch dangerously. We all erupted to our feet in time to see the three thugs we had given a hiding on Small Street laughing and casually strutting away. It was a small plastic bag full of urine which they had dashed against the wall just above our heads. We cursed them, their wives, their children, their mothers, their fathers and their tribes. They only laughed derisively. Challenging us and creating rings of fire with their knives as they scrapped the blades against the tarmac.

It was good to know that our enemies were still around before they took us by surprise. It re-engaged us into a state of perpetual mindfulness, ready for any war! A long way away from home the lessons we learned from the regime were following us without fail. A survivor of traumatic visitations will always be stuck to certain routines. Instantly, there appeared a police van on patrol and the thugs melted into the darkness.

TEN

The following morning Nkosi threw a bombshell,

"I am leaving this place."

"What!"

"I am leaving this place."

"When?"

"Today."

"What's wrong?"

"I don't feel safe here."

"What happened?"

"That Chiku guy."

"What did he do?"

"He is an informer."

"What?"

"He is passing information to the intelligence."

"Oh! Really?"

"I heard some army and police deserters have disappeared from the church and Chiku's involvement is highly suspected. Yesterday, after he addressed us suspiciously, we followed him to a building in Kruis Street. Coming out of that building, I saw and recognised someone who works for the intelligence"

I was shocked. To think that the intelligence could be brazen enough to kidnap people from the church. What were they doing with those people? There were rumours of the South African Police arresting and organizing the rendition of prisoners who were wanted for political crimes in Zimbabwe. I determined to make an investigation and my shocking discovery was that all ex-policemen and ex-soldiers never stayed for long at the church because they found it not safe. Two ex-service men had gone missing, later resurfacing in police stations back home where their relatives collected them dead. The third man had his ancestors to thank for escaping from death with broken bones and deep lacerations.

It was sad to see AK47 leave and go back to the street.

*

The morning came with a bristling ravishing breeze that swept out the dead leaves in my broken heart. I felt my soul take a buoyant leap upwards and my feet were pumping pistons going up the steps on the ground floor. Passing the drab figures on their way to the storeroom, I strode the length of the first floor with a flourishing alacrity until then I never felt possible. Light and buoyant of spirit, I floated. Refusing to be corrupted by the pervading human stress spreading through every space and nook of the building, I moved, determined to be in my own way the best I could live. The battle loomed hulking and I advanced like David before Goliath. I smiled and greeted almost everyone. Taken aback with my sudden resurrection, some people raised their eyebrows at me. I flashed my gracious regards at the store-man as I deposited my sack of clothes and blankets for the day's upkeep. From that moment my internal world flowed in a steady peaceful acceptance of things I could not change. I noticed how my manifestation of these beautiful feelings touched the external world and how everything combined and blossomed. I found laughter! I found joy! I found purpose! And I found love of all humanity! I was convinced that I did not need any material possessions in order to enjoy life. Panic and fear evaporated. An irrevocable force stirred and seized my entire faculties, the mind, the spirit and the body.

Back in the foyer I approached a crippled man in a wheelchair. He sat alone with dark shades of dejection in his deeply lined face. I greeted him warmly crouching in front of his vehicle. I saw there were rings around his eyes and they spoke of a desperation bordering on helplessness and resignation.

"Are you well?"

"Not at all."

"I may not be the right person to speak to but you can tell me what is bothering you."

"And then what will you do?"

"I won't know until you tell me."

"I am such a burden," he commiserated his voice disappearing under the flow of tears.

I touched him on the sleeve and waited in silence.

"Do you stay here?"

"No! I stay at The Chambers."

"Are you here with someone?"

"No!"

"Then, why are you here?"

"I need help."

"What kind of help?"

"I have not properly eaten for three days and I am on medication."

I slipped outside and bought some fat-cakes on the street which I brought back to him. I waited for him to eat and finish. Then I gave him some water to take his tablets. Shadows appeared and disappeared in his ashen face. His cheeks quivered, bulging and vomiting, he stretched out his weak neck like a starving drake. I helped him clean himself.

"What is your name?"

"Mutawo."

"Do you stay alone?"

"Yes."

"How do you manage?"

"I have a nephew. He has a room in The Chambers, too."

"And you have your own room?"

"Yes. But now, I can't go back there, I have not paid the rent."

"You pay your own rent?"

"Yes."

"How do you do that?"

"My nephew takes me to the robots on William Nicole Road near Four Ways Mall where I beg."

"So, why are you here?"

"He has deserted me."

"Can't someone else help you?"

"I don't know of anyone."

"That is sad."

"May you please help me?"

"Me! How?"

"Take me to the robots. Please! I beg you!"

When we took the taxi to Four Ways, near Park Central Mall in Noord Street, he was exceedingly happy and I was terribly confused. I had no idea how this was going to work out. I did not know how I was going to lift him alone into the taxi. Yet, when with doubt I tried to lift him out of his wheelchair, I was shocked by his very feathery weight. Expecting to struggle and call for help from the next man, I had put my hand under his thighs and summoned all my power, sweeping him up in a single jerking movement. I must have looked like a gentle hulk, surprisingly hauling him up like a doll without any effort. People looked at me in disbelief as I carried him into the taxi like a baby. Astounded I thought it must have been "The Hand of God" at work. The man's weight seemed trapped in the wind. Light as a chicken! I placed him down on the seat, folded the wheelchair and loaded it onto the taxi. Then I took my place beside him. My arm which I had placed under his buttocks when I carried him smelt of urine. I did not let this affect me at all. Floating down the stairs, I had blown into him, quietly commiserating in his dark corner. He had not imposed himself on me, something which took me back to my child hood when a deranged distant relative popped up at our house with a sick child. I took the child full of excrement in his napkins. I cleaned and bathed him with my bare hands, feeding him with my lunch. My grandmother smiled and said:

"You are a special person, Bloggs! In the old days gone by, when our tradition was unsullied and debased by the coming of the white people, before becoming a king, one was asked to hold the vulnerable of all ages and wipe their dirty bottoms with his bare hands. Then he had to taste all their faeces in his mouth!" I nearly vomited when I heard that.

We dropped off at a service station near the curios market along William Nicole. Mutawo was already tired and hungry. I t was already lunch time. We went into the service station shop and bought some refreshments. I fetched water for his tablets. I noticed that he was shielding the medication away from me which made me curious. It was then I noticed that he was taking anti-retroviral and tuberculosis tablets. I said to him:

"You can trust me, too!"

"With what?"

"Your life."

"My life?"

"And whatever!"

I let him feed in silence. When his stomach was full, I took him to the toilet where I lifted him onto the toilet seat and said:

"Call me when you are done."

He called. I went to him. Wiped his bottom. And placed him back into the wheelchair. He thanked me gratefully. It was not a huge task for me to hoist his straw-weight. The petrol attendants hailed him and asked him where his nephew was. He told them he had dumped him. And they all spoke like prophets:

"We all knew it!"

Then they said to me:

"You could help this man!"

I did not know what to do at the robots, so he instructed me to push him in his wheel chair to and fro between the traffic, when the traffic lights turned red. Uneasily, I drove the wheelchair slowly along the road, between the stationary cars with the motorists dropping some coins and notes into the cup which he held out in his hands. A beautiful woman with long black hair drove up. Espying us, lustre dropped out of her eyes. Shook her head like one upset. Her slender arms two white rods glued on the steering wheel. Tears brimmed up in her eyes. Tormented by God-knows-what! She remained shaking her shimmering long black hair. Staring straight ahead. Tortured! We passed by her car. The robot turned green. She drove away. Another elderly lady came up. She handed Mutawo a plastic bag of groceries which I believe could have been meant for her household. Coins and notes rained into Mutawo's cup. Backwards and forth we moved. Meandering in and out of the lines of motionless vehicles. Making business! Big begging business! Another man hooted in his vehicle. When we got to where he was, he harshly berated me. Accusing me of using a crippled man to make money for myself. My ego bled! Mutawo thanked him for the insult meekly saying:

"God bless you!"

Four hours passed and Mutawo showed signs of exhaustion. He was exceedingly frail and looked like a doll. I took him to the roadside where I let him eat some more and I saw a sick, hungry man on a rare painful journey. A journey I had never fully given myself to explore and understand.

To be disabled and dependent for the rest of one's life! As I sat there, trying to connect the dots to the universal feelings of that world, a motorist hooted to us. I rose. Saw a slender hand holding out a new blanket to us. I ran towards the car. And discovered the tortured brunette. Her harrowing passions quelled by her act of philanthropy. Smiling graciously, I received the blanket. Uttering:

"God bless you!"

Again, tears rose in her eyes. She deflated in a long whispering exhalation. Ghosts of words sweeping into my ear in an unforgettable cascade:

"I'm sorry!"

Then she wiped her eyes with her slender hand. And drove away. First she had passed us. Then she drove back. Shedding tears. In the challenges of other people around us – in the countless forms of deformity and misfortunes of man – God speaks to us. Showing us our vulnerability and the reason to love one another. To unite as the human race! The value of life of a child dying of hunger in Ethiopia is the same as that of a child punching at a play-station elsewhere in the first world! I truly feel that it is because of our open awareness and honest understanding of our vulnerability that we are able to offer other people random acts of kindness without their solicitation.

We perched on the lawn and counted the donations. I was amazed with the figure. We had R985.68 in cash. One blanket. And a variety of food-stuffs. Mutawo paid me R450.00 for my work. Four times as much I ever earned in a day all the days I stayed on the street and at the church. What a lucrative business! With the money I could buy a cell-phone which I sorely needed. For a long time I had been off air! But I knew I was not cut out for this kind of survival. Yet necessity, being a ruthless constant, sometimes catches up with us under absurd states. Then we are obliged to eke out an irreverent existence on the margins of society.

We took the taxi back to Joburg and by the time we arrived, darkness had fully asserted itself. Mutawo directed me to The Chambers building near Ellis Park on the periphery of Johannesburg Central Business District. When I got there, I saw the picture of a huge derelict building without electricity and with more broken windows than fixed. I wondered what broken souls must be languishing in there. I had no doubt that most of the tenants eked out a precarious existence on the streets. Some of them broken beyond repair. That whole part of Joburg was a block of rolling darkness. Against its interior rich pulsating rhythm of night life, human caprices and street lights. It felt like entering a zone of perpetual dread and human vice.

I rolled Mutawo inside, into the candle-lit foyer where confused and blinded by the darkness, I stood not trusting its entire confines. Despite such darkness the tenants seemed not disturbed by that fact at all. My mind flashed through John Milton's Paradise Lost where he says "the mind is its own place, it can make a heaven of hell or hell of heaven of itself." These people had adapted to their environment and moved with ease in that place, seeing with a cat's eyes. They could easily spot that I was a foreigner in that building. I became relaxed when I noted that a greater portion of the people spoke my language. We had all run away from our own country, either for political or economic reasons! Another slouching figure quickly approached us and greeted Mutawo heartily whilst he scrutinised my face.

Apprehensive, I approached the stairs. I turned, then with my back to the stairs I began pulling Mutawo's wheel-chair up as his room was on the fifth floor. A sudden terror flew into my mind like an army of bats. What if I slipped on the top of the stairs or someone bumped into me from behind, resulting in the tipping of the wheelchair and sending Mutawo's frail figure down in a spin? I shuddered and decided to change my thoughts. I started worrying about getting my directions right on my way to the church. I could see that he was a popular figure in that building, particularly with women. They came giving him long hugs and sweet kisses, all of them calling him "husband!" Mutawo's hare-lipped mouth split open into a lusty bemused smile and I could not help but think of his health status and how he had acquired it. On the third floor, someone in a group of loud female associates came upon us like an evil wind. Grabbing the wheel-chair out of my hands, I discovered that it was Mutawo's nephew. From the look of things, he was flat broke and did not even know where his supper was going to come from that evening.

I was happy that my services to Mutawo were no longer wanted on that day and even beyond. Reason and con-science fought in my heart. To live in disharmony with rea-son and conscience for me is inhuman. Conscience is the hand stopping the other hand of the self from committing a terrible crime against all morality and God. Yet a kind of sadness for the man lingered in my heart. My survival in-stincts on edge, I groped my way out of Club Chambers and explored the block of darkness outside. I had the money Mutawo had paid me ensconced in the pocket of the shorts which I wore under my trousers. My eyes roved and groped the darkness for muggers. If they caught you, they would turn you head down and shake your body till all the contents of your pockets were emptied on the tarmac.

I darted through half-naked sex workers, flaunting their fleshy hips. Somewhere in the darkness, one of them purred, bargaining with a sex-starved drunken man who, reeling and pleading for a discount, could hardly stand. They never cared who they slept with in those abandoned, filthy crumbling buildings. Money talks in Joburg. My feet splashed through a foul stream of water gurgling into a drain. I had no time to check what it was. Sweating in my armpits, my weary hands grew clammy. My heart pounded. Fear sucked the moisture out of my throat. Walking that end of Joburg was like penetrating the chaotic belly of a volcano. Suddenly, caught in a web of surprise and abrupt relief, I lurched out into the familiar brightness and sur- roundings of neon signs and buildings with lighted win- dows. I recognized End Street. One can never fail to recog- nize it at that hour with the many women sex-workers parading themselves half naked, some sitting on empty beer crates with their feet cast wide astride and without wearing panties on the edge of the street.

*

Coming into Pritchard Street, I felt the voices in my head stir inside me what I had seen in that underbelly of inequity. Close to the church, I saw Dan talking to Matt. They were both smoking cigarettes under a street lamp. I greeted them with the joy of one who had longed for sanity for the whole day. Together, we drifted to a bar on Moi Street where we bought pap and beef bones for supper. We ate from the same plate sucking the marrow from the succulent bones. With our stomachs tightly packed, we trudged back to the church. We fetched our blankets from the storeroom and dumped them at our sleeping place. We used the mobile toilets which lined the street on the pavement in front of the church to relieve ourselves. There were some lawyers' chambers next to the church building and their cafeteria had a full view of the toilets which they did not find agreeable. Despite the fact that the toilets were emptied and cleaned every day, there was always a pervading mixture of human waste, urine and chemicals smelling around the toilets.

From the toilets, we headed for Shanty Town to buy some Joburg Beer. Each one of us had a shake-shake of Joburg Beer between his legs on the ground. We drowned our sorrows with the potent brew and shared anecdotes about our lives. Feeling light hearted, we whooped on top of our voices and some blocks of our stress dissolved. Our mouths flew open, burping into the night with our noses tingling. Then we weaved our legs back to our sleeping pavement buzzing politics. I told the story of how I became a hero and an enemy of the state overnight. I had just come from participating at a political rally and I walked the streets, the machine-gun of my intellect spitting out bullets that left holes in my enemies' arguments. Motorists hooted and waved at me when they saw my T-shirt. I waved back and everyone shouted for change. I went to the shops where I bought a Castle Pilsner from the liquor store and people grouped around me. I became the focus of attention. An elated man came by and said:

"You are one in a million."

I smiled and said:

"The one in a million gets his power from the million!"

All people loved it and soon everyone wanted to buy me a beer which gave me an idea. I said:

"Let each man buy the one next to him a beer for we are one and we shall all celebrate our power as one."

I shouted: "Everyone CHANGE your ways and remove the government of thieves!"

And the resounding echoes rippled into the distance :

"CHANGE!"

"CHANGE!"

"CHANGE!

Inhabitants of the neighbouring houses streamed out to witness our bold proclamation. Some repeated the declaration, waving their palms at us. And so I went home that day a hero and a man with a lot of enemies. The following day they stole under the darkness of the night and raised a gun to my fore-head. They did not shoot but they promised to come back and finish what they had begun. Then someone who loved me called on my cell-phone. He used a restricted number and said:

"We are coming to fetch you! I do not want your blood on my hands. Please leave now and never come back!"

"Who are you?"

"You don't need to know me. If they get to know that I have tipped you, I will be dead, too."

"Then why are you warning me?"

"You taught my child and he always speaks about you. He hated school, but you changed all that. You created him into something I am proud of this day. Your inspiration to him was more than what I, his father could do and I do not want to spend any day of my life regretting over your death. Please just go! Just go very far away! As long as you stay in this country, you are a walking dead man!"

The roads widened and narrowed through the eyes of Joburg Beer and soon we were at the pavement where we slept. We arranged our cardboards and spread the dog blankets on top. Slipping into the cold blankets, we lay talking to each other for a long time. Later I realised that Dan and Matt had dropped off to sleep and I was left talking alone.

Around midnight, my cell-phone vibrated. I hid my head away from the sight of the marauding robbers under the blanket and answered:

"The mother of my children!"

"The father of my children!"

"You sound different. Are you well?"

"I am not well."

"What happened?"

"I was nearly run over by a car."

I was shocked.

"You are injured!"

"A broken arm."

"Are you sure it's only a broken arm?"

"I just came from the x-rays."

"What are the doctors saying?"

"They are going to dress it with the plaster of paris."

"Who did it?"

"I don't know."

"Where is the person?"

"I don't know."

"What!"

"He sped his car away."

"Sped away?"

"I was walking on the roadside around seven o'clock this evening. I turned and saw a car swerve from the tarmac coming straight towards me. I tried to run into the gate of the nearby house and it struck me with its left fender."

"What!"

"The car swerved back onto the tarmac and without stopping it sped off."

"What kind of car was it?"

"Its headlamps flashed into my eyes. I couldn't see well."

"Did anyone see it?"

"A few people."

"What did they say?"

"No one recognised it."

"Stop wearing your Che Guevara beret."

"I'm wearing it now!"

"They'll kill you!"

"They've already killed my heart."

"They hate us."

"I hate their ways, too."

"Be careful my love!"

"I will."

My heart bled, I boiled with frustration and anger. We both paused, listening to each other breathing from the other end of the line. She was the first one to speak:

"You're angry my husband."

"I'm furious."

"They say you are in Mozambique."

"Doing what?"

"Training a dissident army."

"But I'm not even a soldier!"

"I know."

"I don't even know how to hold a gun."

"I know that your machine gun is your pen and you launch missiles out of your mouth."

"I love you my wife!"

"I love you my husband!"

"I miss you my wife!"

"I miss you, too, my husband!"

Then I cried and kissed the mouthpiece of my phone. I heard her kiss into her phone, too.

*

Insomnia kicked in. Lumps of un-dissolving sleep rolled in my eyes like pebbles. No thought could lubricate my weary body to rest. Like one sleeping on a bed of fish bones! My mind was in the hospital together with my wife. I was lying like that when I sensed, rather than saw, a silvery serpent flying above me and then falling like a giant whip on top of my blankets. I leapt onto my feet with everyone else. Our surprise turned to anger when we saw that it was only the new security guard setting loose the fire-hose upon our sleeping bodies. He shot at us purposefully as if we were burning targets. Fuming but powerless to fight him over his jurisdiction, we all gathered our half-wet blankets and moved away, cursing. Yet we could not find free space anywhere. The street was full of sleeping bodies of men and women. We had no choice but to get back to our pavement where we waited for the wind to dry it up. Then, again, we spread our cardboard and blankets. Dawn was already spreading in the sky and he was still laughing at us.

There is a saying which says that "you do not push a man already falling down the hill." This man was playing with fire. When he finished his shift, the refugees followed him. He did not see them. Somewhere in Hillbrow, he slithered into a public toilet. He was urinating when the men set upon him. They whipped him with *sjamboks* and he leaped pissing everywhere. He pissed on himself, on the floor, in the air, on other people in the toilet and the men who attacked him. The people he pissed on got mad and joined in punishing him. Someone punched him on the nose and blood sprouted like tomato sauce. Blows, kicks and whips stung all over his flesh. He howled in pain and tried to wriggle out but people blocked his way. The crowd heard him cry for his mother and they laughed. He scuttled into another compartment with a blocked drain and a toilet seat overflowing with human waste. It spread all over the floor like a soft carpet. He tried closing the door behind him but the angry force outside pushed it back open. He slipped, twisted, stiffly stretched backwards and flew on his back. Then he fell on top of the open toilet seat with his buttocks. Into the soft cushion of human excrement, his buttocks sank while his legs and hands flailed in the air like the useless legs of a fly accidentally stuck on a fly catcher. He tried to rise. Someone hit him again with the door. He skidded, twisted and lay sprawling. Like a giant he rolled, kneeled and rose to his feet. The refugees looked at the funny spectacle he made and all roared with laughter. They tore out of the building holding their noses.

After a long interval, the security guard like a confused Martian whose brain had been displaced to his stomach, staggered out of the toilet. Holding his cap heavily decorated with faeces he begged for mercy. There was no need for him to fear his attackers. With all the different kinds of human waste splattered on him like a camouflage, he was just untouchable. He ran into the public baths behind the toilet where a bad wind announced his arrival. The queue of people waiting for their baths broke up chaotically like a horde of flies, opening the way for him. Someone came hastily dragging a hose pipe behind him fireman style. He connected it and the water shot out on to the stubborn clinging faeces. It floated away into the drain. Laughing, the attackers boisterously drifted away, too. We never saw the security guard again.

PART 2

ONE

We placed our bags in the lockers lining the passage and took the keys with us. Ras Menzi directed us to a backroom in the library where we sat in a semi-circle. Ras Menzi chaired the meeting. Poet Nya, excited as ever, was there, his head always carrying his spectacles high as if he concentrated over something above our heads. His verse, the only thing that kept him sane, he seldom went to bed without reading some of his poems. Thandabantu quietly sat in his chair, holding a copy of his poem "The Unfinished Story of a Refugee." Two new members joined us, John and Toto. John was from Kenya and Toto was from the Democratic Republic of Congo. Smiling, Matt looked at everyone with his glasses askew. One arm of his glasses was broken and he improvised it with wire. With his poetic eye sometimes he saw everything double.

We had agreed in our first meeting to call our organization "Zimbabwe Writers in Exile" but in that meeting we changed the name to "African Writers Forum." This was to open the doors for members from other countries to come in. We agreed on a publication that would be called the

"African Wright-Us Forum Publication" and our preamble read as follows:

"We, The African Wright-Us Forum, believe in the potential and the importance of arts which is founded upon the craft of writing, that all inhabitants of our continent should have a way to express and tell their stories without fear because an outspoken nation is a free nation!"

Having agreed to start submitting works for our first publication, words tumbled out of the chalice of toasts and the meeting ended.

Diversity sprang out. The differences in our background experiences, tone and language wove a glittering tapestry. Thandabantu was the passionate trumpet of African Unity. To that, I said:

"I am all stamped with the blood of humanity, trampled, loved, abhorred, the face of covered histories smoking out through cracked surfaces."

John Wanjiku, a Kenyan who had been wandering through the mazes of Joburg said:

"At times I feel like my mind is gone, but I wonder where it might have gone, for I used to live in a place where another soul lives today. And I carry my home everywhere, for I am housed within!"

"Whatever! Life will always be life!" piped up Charmaine.

We all laughed gleefully and tumbled out of the building. These words said by everybody, breathed the first words into our African Writers' Magazine. Leaving Ras Menzi in the House of Movements where he was making his contribution to "destroy the brutal system which oppressed the people." These people gave me back my voice. My life.

In the passage a huge surprise blew a stunning blow in our eyes. Dan's locker yawned open. Bemused, we were all cast in stone and stared.

"WHAT?!" Dan croaked bewildered. A fly could have flown in and out of his mouth. His key dangled in his hand.

"Who did this?" The words tumbled out of our mouths like a stupid choir.

Dan's bag was gone. All his high school and degree certificates vanished. Who could have stolen them? None of us had an idea.

Dan lost all faculty of speech. I saw his shoulders sag and eyes lose their colour in an instant. His world tumbled into a chink of sorrow and helplessness. We did not know where to start. He walked out, eyes wide open and not seeing anything but his destruction and end. He just wanted to be alone. He was a mad bull. He could not think straight and I feared, in his blind dejection, he could be run over by a car on the street. All he wanted were his precious things back - his whole world. He eluded us and for some hours, roamed the streets of the Joburg CBD hoping to come across someone carrying the bag. But it all came to nothing. I walked with Matt, combing all the places we could think of until we got tired and went to the church. About three hours later, Dan arrived looking devastated and inconsolable. We perched on the stairs in the foyer. Our feet hurt and we all took off our broken shoes. We had no words for what had happened. Dan pointed at the Zambian guy, a backpacker who somewhere in his adversity had been eluded by all the zest for life. He spent most of his time plaiting his dreadlocks, creeping to plunder roadside dust-bins and laughing at his ingenuity. Dan said:

"Without my bag, my condition is worse than that man!"

It was a scary condemnation and we continued to sit in awe as if somebody had died. Then a young man of about twenty came and greeted us. He asked to speak to Dan alone in the sanctuary. Ten minutes ticked away. Then our senses were roused by something heavily dropping before our beleaguered feet like a dead body. It was the missing bag! We both looked up and saw Dan's thawing face.

"What!" I shrieked, leaping to my feet.

"That's your bag!" Cried Matt.

"Yes!"

"What happened?"

"Too complicated."

"Tell us."

"I don't even know."

"That's strange."

"Very strange."

Suddenly, we all felt hungry. We put on our shoes and streamed out. I went into one of the mobile toilets lining the street to relieve myself. While I crouched in there I heard the sound of a truck pulling by. Voices of men leaping from the back of the truck floated into my toilet. Then I felt the toilet being lifted with me inside. Pants down to my ankles, I struggled balancing on my feet and banged the fibre glass walls with my fist. The men put the toilet back on the pavement again and I quickly wiped my bottom. Hitching up my trousers, I tumbled out of the toilet fastening my belt. The crowd of people outside peeled in a huge explosion of laughter.

We crossed the street and sadly watched the men load the toilets onto the back of the truck. The lawyers at Pitjie

Chambers had secured a court order for the toilets to be removed. They were placed in front of their cafeteria. From that day, the two toilets in Pritchard Street and Von Brandis started operating twenty-four hours every day. They became ever busier than a McDonald restaurant on peak hour and the cleaners manning them, exhausted and failing to cope, suffered from burn-out!

Sadly commiserating on the removal of our mobile toilets, we limped to Shanty-Town. We bought three plates of pap and beef tripe mixed with casings and served with vegetables. Feeding upon it with a ravenous appetite like people from the land of the dead, we wiped the plates clean. Then, we ordered three shake-shakes of Joburg Beer. Smacking our dry lips, we began to drink our life back. It was, then, Dan told us what had happened.

"The young man and his two other friends had no passports. They jumped the Beit Bridge border into South Africa. Because they were not employed, they could not raise the money to go and apply for asylum papers at Marabastad, in Pretoria. It was, then, they decided to pick the locker room locks and steal the contents. They thought since rich people used the library, they were going to strike something big, a lap-top or something of that value. Unfortunately, they picked Dan's locker. They only realised whose bag they had stolen after they opened it and had gone through its contents. Feeling guilty, they decided to return the bag with all its contents."

Matt proposed a toast. We all raised our shake-shakes and piped-up:

"To the return of the bag!"

We took long savouring gulps of our beer. Then Dan said:

"There's something else."

"What!"

"My cell-phone."

"What's wrong with your phone?"

"It's gone."

"What happened?"

"I went to the herbalist."

"What?"

"He wanted R200 consultation fee, so, I went and sold my phone on the street!"

"Sorry man!"

"I had no choice. I wanted my bag. That bag is my whole life and that phone was nothing. So I sold it and went back to the herbalist. He asked me to remove my shoes. He said I was in a sacred place. And I did. He threw his bones and told me that the spirits wanted me to bring fresh lion's blood and fat in a bottle. Without that, I could kiss my bag good bye forever."

"Bastard!"

"I was very stupid!"

"You were desperate!"

"I didn't know who I was when I left that place."

"We will get your money back!"

"It doesn't matter anymore."

"What?"

"I have my bag. They can keep the money."

"A deal is a deal in Joburg, no one returns the money."

"True!"

"Then, let's drink, friends. I could have lost both my bag and my phone today. In my bag is my whole life! My future! I can work and buy another phone but nobody ever lost and bought the future."

We called the *shebeen* queen and ordered some more shake-shakes. Blinking in the darkness, we watched the *shebeen* prostitutes, awkwardly flaunting their miserable hips on the dance floor. The night was getting old and they were getting more young at heart. Yet there was something replete with broken dreams in their rhythm. The lip-stick glistened like blood on their lips. I said to Dan:

"There's your lion's blood."

Matt stood up and went to urinate somewhere in the darkness. His urine splashing on the ground made a horrible noise like water shooting out of a broken gutter in the roof. When he came back, he opened his note book, burying his nose in it. Time flowed whilst he thought and scribbled. His skewed spectacles started sliding down his nose-bridge. He was trapped in the fiery beauty of the words forming in his mind and before he knew what was happening, the spectacles splashed into his shake-shake. He fished them out and licked the beer off the lenses. We all laughed.

The night was getting cold. We downed our shake-shakes, smacked our lips and decided it was time we went back to the church. Winter was creeping in. Intoxicated and with the fermenting warmth of Joburg Beer inflating our tummies, our beleaguered legs wove like an old woman's knitting to the place where we slept. Shivering, we moved, half leaping, staggering and gesticulating like shadows in the semi-lit darkness. Walking up Von Weilleigh Street, an approaching car flashed its lights straight in our eyes. Dan stopped in front of me. I bumped into his swaying frame. Clutching his bag on his chest and standing in one spot he swayed, swung like a pendulum a couple of times, lifted his right leg, did a 360° mathematical turn on his left leg like a ballet dancer and coming down heavily on his buttocks, he lay gasping, still clutching his vastly treasured bag against his chest. We marvelled at his theatrical fall. Laughing, we pulled him up back to his feet before proceeding on our way to the church.

When we arrived, Chimwene was having a plateful of chicken skins and a mountain of pap. He sat at the top of the stairs leading to the Sanctuary and shouting at intervals:

"I am Chimwene! God's whip! Sent to punish all mad and greedy people like you!" then he would take a sip from a quart of Castle Lager sitting beside him. It was filled with water! "Next year's parliamentary and presidential elections results are already out! The Registrar General has them in his brief case!" He peeled into a paroxysm of laughter like ripping cardboard paper. People around him laughed emphatically. Yet in his madness we all knew an undisputable political truth prevailed.

We fetched our blankets, going straight to our bedroom on the street. We found it already littered with sleeping bodies.

"They're taking away my wife." Ncube mumbled, deep in his sleep. "I should have made her pregnant before I left!"

All his neighbours who were still awake laughed. There were many men like him, tortured in their minds and dreams with what could be happening to their wives and children. Men who were sick and tired of fighting their own minds. In that place, we sorely missed our loved ones and every benefit of keeping behind walls and a closed door.

Intoxicated and imagining all was well, we arranged our cardboard mattresses and spread the blankets. On top we lay a shield of plastic sheets, lest the rogue security guard should return and dazzle us again with the fire-hose. Satisfied, I slid under the blankets, wriggling out of my jeans. I folded the clothes neatly, depositing them painstakingly under my satchel which I used as my pillow. On the street, we lay marginally spaced out, unlike in the church where people slept like packed Vienna sausages. Before I closed my eyes, Matt floated his inebriate hand before my eyes. I read what he had penned at Shanty Town:

O' Sovereign one of dizzy heights!
Warp this bitter winter wind briefly etherized
From cracking our fragile being...

TWO

The following Saturday, we walked to the Hillbrow Community Theatre, our children rapidly chattering around us. Our school could not afford to hire a bus like other schools. Ajas meandered in and out of traffic across the street and did a jig on the other side laughing at us because we fussed about his safety. Child as he was, there was nothing we could teach him about moving around Joburg. He knew places we didn't know.

"This child!" Vimbai, a quiet pretty girl of about sixteen years old remarked holding my hand. "So much of the city already blazes in his heart."

"I fear with a fierce intensity."

"It's the streets, Daddy."

"The streets can never be a good place to raise a child."

"I lived on the streets for a year before I came to the church."

"I cannot imagine what you experienced, do you want to tell me any of it?"

"My mother died a couple of years ago. I was the only child and I don't know where my father is. He abandoned us a long time ago. What I recall of him is all embedded in mist. My aunts and uncles had enough troubles with their own families and I found myself on the streets. Then I came to South Africa where I stayed on the streets too. Until I met a man who told me about the church. Now I'm happy that I'm back in school and I want to forget what happened to me on the streets. I WILL BUILD MY FUTURE!" She spoke with unbridled fervour. In defiance of a past she sought to bury.

We were going to take part in the Inner City Schools Drama competitions. There were eight schools taking part in the contest. The theme of the contest was I AM AND I BELONG. Vimbai was not acting, but she loved the role of the mother whose child was the Albino. There were dazzling performances from schools and our children executed undeniably one of the most exhilarating show. The play centred on the story of an albino boy growing up in a prejudiced society with a law that all albino babies should be killed. The mother who could not bear losing her child decided to leave her village. After wandering through foreign lands, she finally came to settle on the outskirts of another village where the king had felt pity for her. Lonely, discriminated and ostracised, their life unfurled. Then the boy learned to play the mbira instrument and through his beautiful music, he managed to pull down the barriers of superstition, prejudice and hate. When the contest ended, our children won the "best act" production. They got two trophies and three other children, including the one who appeared in the role of the Albino boy's mother got awards for their supporting roles.

We walked back to the church fired up with currents of animation and pride surging through the group. Vimbai strolled elated beside me. Affectionately holding my hand.

"I have never had such a beautiful day, Daddy." The words tumbled out of her mouth. Then she stopped and looked in my face. Something she had never done with so much confidence. I smiled into her eyes.

"I can call you Dad?"

"You are my dear daughter!"

"There's something I need to tell you."

"Anything that is important to you is important to me, too."

"Yes, it is! If you're to accept me as your daughter."

"The moment you came into my life I accepted you."

"It's about my status. I take medication every day."

A moment of silence engulfed us. Then I opened my arms and hugged her! She hugged me back softly crying. This poignant episode became our first moment of connection.

"On Monday I will be going to collect my medication. May you accompany me?"

"I will my dear."

Then we walked after the other children. From that day, all her joys, her highs, her lows and her agonies became my own, too. These children never ceased to amaze me with their resilience and resourcefulness. Their remarkable stories of journeys replete with danger, pain, uncertainty, loneliness and sometimes breaking the law to make everything right in their lives, flashed through my mind like an odyssey...Yes, we were in the middle of an odyssey. A great odyssey! Proving that we did not simply roll out of the gutter.

When we arrived at the church, the celebrations erupted. Feeling the condition of our life a great accident, we were talking politics, Dan and Matt and I, when Ncube dejectedly plodded in. His face was hung low like a banana leaf on a hot October afternoon. Eyes glowing red as if two coals of fire had been planted in his eye sockets.

"Are you ok?"

"No!"

"What's wrong?"

"AK47 is dead!"

"What happened?"

"They burned him."

"Who?"

"The people."

"What people?"

"The local people."

"What did he do?"

"I don't know."

"Where did it happen?"

"In a park, outside Joburg."

The following morning the brutal snarl of xenophobia came stalking us at our doorstep. A group of cantankerous men armed with knobkerries, knives and whips approached the church, chanting songs of blood and war. War upon the foreigners! Shops clamped shut and people, all foreigners bolted themselves inside their houses. Those who lived in shacks were the most vulnerable. Fear bruited across the land like a hurricane. Word came to us that the men targeted the church. A flurry of activity and confusion reigned.

"We will not die like sheep led to slaughter! Everybody grab a weapon!" a voice, resolute and brave rose above the chaos.

"We will fight!"

"All women and children to the fifth floor!"

Instantly, the church assumed a state of preparedness for war. All kinds of weaponry sprouted from nowhere. Bricks, iron bars, knives, chains, screwdrivers, whips. And someone from the notorious basement room popularly known as Soweto even told people not to worry because they had guns. Nobody wanted to cross the path of any of the guys from Soweto and we all believed them in possession of such dangerous weaponry. The building, tense from the basement to the fifth floor, nervously waited for the attack. Never before was such a current of dread and apprehension ever felt in the church nor would it ever. Women and children sat trembling with fear. Sweat leaking out of their pores. Hearts fluttering against malnourished rib cages. Some prayed to God. Suddenly The Bishop surged in with the crowd of tenants parting in unison to give him way. Someone had alerted him in the middle of a very important synod meeting he was attending. He had to repeat several times to us to lay down our weapons. Grumbling, we reluctantly dropped our armaments. Thus bloodshed at the church was thwarted. The police came forcing the belligerent crowd to flow in another direction. And the pounding flood of panic receded. The media was rife with news of the xenophobia violence flaring up in pockets across the country. Our loving South African brothers hoisted their voices in unison condemning these acts of brutality.

A period of four days elapsed. Dan, Ncube, Matt and I decided to go to the park where our friend, AK47, had died. Our hearts cleaved in two and the other halves were with AK 47, wherever he had gone. Huge bursts of lava engulfed our hearts burning through the veins. Incensed with an incandescent rage that leaped in our eyes, we marched into the park up to the spot where his painful death took place. I felt a searing rage slither through my heart and gather like dynamite at the tips of my fingers. A rage if given its way brands one into a hater of mankind. But such I would not be for it equates one with those who pursued evil!

We stood surrounding the spot. The lawn had been scorched to the earth. The charred remains of the tyre which they had used to neck-lace him with still lay scattered around the spot. One of Nkosi's shoes roasted in that fire, agonizingly lay on its side. It was a defiant spectacle telling a cruel story of its master's death. It was the only remaining part of him left and holding all the volumes of his anguish. His protest against an ignominious execution by a heartless people. I went and stood towering above the shoe. It smelt of his sweat and burnt flesh! I sat down on the lawn feeling nausea and bile leaping to my throat. Yes! The smell of his roasted flesh still lingered in the air. With tears in our eyes, we looked very hard around the charred spot, inhaling the image of his death. We felt it on our skin, in our flesh, our bones and in the air that endlessly rasped down our throats for several months to come. My face contorted with rage, I dug the violence of my trembling fingers into the cold wet ground. I motioned with my hand and we all knelt on the soft carpet. In an angry rippling murmur, I prayed to God to bring rest to Nkosi's spirit. I asked God to look after his family wherever they were—they may never know of his death for he had come alone like me in this land of strangers. I prayed that God remember him in the great road of pain and suffering he had walked. I prayed that his family whom he had missed in his loving heart with tears of pain so much would find the strength to heal in their heart when they found out about his death. And then I asked God to severely punish the murderers that they should bear the cross of this heinous deed to their graves.

This was the hardest prayer I ever made in my life. Pain and sorrow ravaged through my soul like a volcano of iron filings. I felt hot in my mouth as if Coals of fire lodged themselves in my throat. Hot fumes I breathed out trapped in ripples of AK's anguish. A tight knot rose and exploded like a bomb in my gut. I thought my chest would burst open and that I would die, too.

A man who had been observing us from a bench now rose and slowly glided to us. He was Malawian.

"Greetings to you my brothers."

"Greetings to you, too," we echoed back together.

"You knew the man who died here?"

"He was a good friend of ours."

"I knew him briefly. He used to sit alone on that bench," he said pointing.

"What happened?"

"A crowd of people armed with clubs, sticks and whips came by. Proclaiming that all foreigners leave immediately. For they were taking their jobs, women and space. We did not stop to see what that meant. We ran away. Your friend could not escape because of his injured leg. We heard that they beat him with the *sjamboks*, knobkerries, sticks and stones. Blood poured out of his head where he sustained a deep cut. The blood seemed to make them mad. One of them brought a tyre. They tied his hands, fastening the tyre with wire around him like a necklace. Someone poured paraffin all over the tyre and his battered body. Then he struck a match…" The man's voice trailed off.

With our tongues paralysed we could not find any fitting words for this cruelty. We were shocked!

"What did they do with his crutches?"

"They grabbed one and bludgeoned him with it until it bent and broke on his head. The other crutch they used it to imitate him, how he had tried to escape."

"What about the police?"

"He was already dead when they arrived. They only took statements. No one was arrested. Then they shovelled his remains into a body-bag and placed them in the steel coffin. All the limbs were burnt out. One could not say whether it was a man that had been burnt. This whole park reeked with the smell of his burned flesh."

We stood up and the Malawian fellow said:

"I don't want to stay in this community anymore. I'm scared. I came here because I can't stop thinking about your murdered friend. It felt like that was my brother dying. I have no family in South Africa, too"

We all hugged him, turned and left. We did not look back. But the smell of Nkosi's roasted flesh walked with us for a long time, even stronger whenever the ugly head of xeno-phobia reared its head.

Each one of us troubled by his own thoughts, we floated along the road in silence. Dan had come to South Africa alone. I had come alone, too. So had Matt. Only Ncube had some relatives in the country. If this could happen to AK, who could stop it from happening to us?

The desire to deal with this atrocity took us by the throat and led us to the kingdom of Shanty-Town. We noticed that a wall of plastic sheeting, swishing in the wind had been erected around the shed. A gleaming steel pole planted almost in the middle of the shed on an improvised stage, firmly pointed into the sky. The makeshift stage decorated with chevron paintings and stains of human figures was made of rough bamboo and wood from broken pallets. The transformed bar hung with an air of ineluctable mischief brewing. The music howled out a bit louder. Its heavy bass rhythm threatening to swallow reason. More people than usual sat drinking and talking animatedly. Anticipating. We ordered pap and rough tripe and four shake-shakes. We ate and drank our Joburg Beer like ghosts in a tale of silence. Engulfed in our own troubles. The booming radio could not penetrate to us. It belonged to another world.

Then something ate into the silence. The music grew louder, rowdier and lustier. Three naked women, only wearing G-strings and bras burst into our presence from nowhere. Each held a fan in her hand, fanning herself. They all looked trim in their stilettos. Slowly and artistically they swung their long legs onto the stage. Murdering the men with every single voluptuous movement! One of them sat down on a stool. The other two started doing some slow and deliberately erotic gyrating thrusts with their hips. Tormented between their legs, some men howled. Others watched intently. Capturing every fraction of movement with leaking lips. The two women stood at various different angles with their feet wide apart, their breasts and buttocks thrust high in the air like wasps and slowly working their waists as if they were broken and they were trying to fix them. Regularly, between their voluptuous acts, they gave the audience some mischievous feline peeps with their slaughtering slit eyes.

The men cried with whistles and whooped like excited delinquents. Some wayward drifters with uncontrollable desire shooting in their pants leaped to their feet and ravished in their undisciplined bodies, rushed like insane pigs to the stage. They were not allowed onto the stage but they could touch the ladies. They could not reach the mocking ladies' trembling buttocks, so with saliva leaking from their mouths, they had to settle for kissing their thighs. Provided they paid for it. The lady who perched on the stool coolly collected the money. The two ladies continued to prance in their highly corporeal manner throwing daggers in the men's hearts with their naked buttocks and hips. Coins and notes rained like leaves on the stage. The two finished their act with an obscene full stop which sent the delinquents' mouth drivelling like rabid dogs. Then they exited the stage promising to come back later during the night. The music volume was lowered so that people could hear each other. Body temperatures cooled.

Matt beckoned to one of the dancing queens. She came and he made space for her beside him on the bench. She sat down.

"You are good at what you do! Gobsmacking good!" Matt said, a glint of pleasure. "Do you do some other kind of dance?"

"I once danced for a musician. Then he thought he owned me. Sweating for him on the dance floor and then after that his sex toy to satisfy his lust! After which he would throw me away like a rag. I became his means to an end, you see? I could never call him my man! And he would never allow me to see any other man! Yet, he had many other girls."

"Bastard!" Matt roared.

"Men are all the same!" she said without emotion.

"Do you have children?"

"Two kids! If you're thinking of marrying me, you'll have to drag this broken branch to your home together with its leaves." She said smiling. "You can't shake off the leaves and leave them where you found it!"

Silence.

"In fact I'm a sex worker!" she continued. "That means you'll have to embrace me together with my past! All my customers are nothing. I don't feel anything for them. I know after I give them my services they don't care about me. They make us do things we find hateful and they enjoy it. I don't care a fucking bit about them, too! Once we're over sometimes I even want to vomit! So, are we on or off Mr Joburg Beer?"

We were all gobsmacked!

"No," said Matt. "I did not call you for that," to which she clicked her tongue and said:

"Forgive my language but money talks in Joburg. And I'm kind of expensive to keep, too. Thanks, anyway, for wasting my time Mr Joburg Beer."

She rose, stared into Matt's eyes and like a hot air balloon brushed her bottom across his stunned face. Situations in life had hardened everything about her. For her, there existed no other way of seeing or responding to what life had allotted her.

We became more aware of the lowered music. That less din, thankfully for me provided the fake silence needed by my mind.

In that silence, vast, empty spaces bruited in my heart. The spaces expanded with the soft music into expectant vaults teeming with emotion. I longed for my children. I longed for my wife. I longed for a decent life. My mind spoke to itself about many things. Better days that must come to sweep away the debris of our contemptible life. Every sip of Joburg Beer was pregnant with a healing purpose and measure for the vast spaces and vaults created by grief. Ideas rose, fluctuated and receded into the subconscious. The tree stump of philosophical fruit was shooting out in the murky weather of experience. I did not shun experience in that place. I did not deign to escape the psychedelic beauty of going through life in denial. Bad and good made my life wholesome! I took long gulps of beer, smacked my lips and talked to myself:

"The Lord always speaks to us on the much dreaded road of irrepressible sorrow."

"If we listen, we'll never be empty!"

"If we look, the signs will be revealed!"

"The whole wide world is my home. I go everywhere in my mind….. I have struck the bottom of a thousand bottomless pits….."

"I am the one whose fear has been treated by HORROR."

"Darkness is an absence of light just as fear is an absence of will! Darkness deprives us of beautiful sights just as fear cheats us out of our right to be happy. Happiness is the light that gives form to everything in our life and sadness is the darkness that takes out the form of everything in our lives. To choose to live in eternal sadness is tantamount to a life of endless formlessness and fear. NO LIGHT! NO HAPPI-NESS! WITHOUT GOOD AND BAD THERE WILL BE NOTHING TO LIFE…"

Thus, I was preoccupied in my mind when someone said:

"It's time to go home now."

I stood up, took a step forward, knitted my legs like a marionette out of control, pulled my spine backwards, twisted and fell back hard on the bench. Everybody laughed. The second time I came right. I walked, yet still knitting my legs. Ncube hit a brick with his foot and fell sprawling on the street. He crawled on his knees to a street lamp which he used for support to get back to his feet. Matt walked holding his spectacles so that they wouldn't fall. Dan clung to his bag like gold. We weaved across each oth-er's paths nearly bringing each other down in drunken tack-les. The world spun around us and the cold tortured our souls that Matt lamented:

"I wish I'd stayed over at Shanty-Town."

"I wish I had a room with a door," Dan said.

"I wish I had pangolin or tortoise meat to eat," Ncube said.

"Only kings and princes are allowed to eat that," Matt said.

"And the president," Dan said.

"Now we are all beginning to sound like Chimwene!" I said. And we all laughed.

"Chimwene is like a king. He sleeps wherever he wants in this place," said Matt.

"We will sleep wherever we want too!" said Dan.

That night we fetched our blankets and went to sleep in the Sanctuary. Drunk and loaded with Dutch courage we challenged people for the unoccupied space we saw between the rows of seats, declaring it ours. We arranged our cardboard on the green carpet, spreading our blankets on top. There was endemic coughing in the church but that was no source of worry for us. There were other dangers to be fearful of. The proximate dangers to our life we had left them outside. The probability of being knifed to death was liberally higher outside than inside the church. Why then fear human coughing? Of course the church was full of tuberculosis patients but that did not make it less safe. That night, despite dozing fitfully as always, we had much better quality of sleep. We never slept outside on the street again. The only challenge was negotiating one's way to the toilet over the debris of sleeping bodies.

THREE

Thirty people were chosen to work with the unaccompanied minors at the Albert Street School. A rumour bruited that we were going to be paid more than the school teachers and we had a couple of them prepared to resign and join us. Nobody wanted to lose that chance. We all fiercely dug into our spirits in competition. And the number was narrowed down to twelve.

"Bishop, I was not chosen!" Jim complained.

"What are you talking about?"

"I did the course, but I was not chosen."

"Maybe you didn't do well."

"I went every day, Bishop."

"What does that mean?"

"I was supposed to be chosen."

"I can't help you. I'm not the one who did the selection."

"I must be chosen, too."

"Maybe you should approach those who conducted the course."

*

We became the children's parents, shepherded them to school and supervised their nutrition and feeding both at home and at school. The government wanted to formally place the children in shelters and there was a lot of manipulation behind the scenes that soon rumours were spread around that some caregivers were selling children. Dan and I were part of that targeted small group. Undermined and unaware of this betrayal we went about honestly doing our work as usual. Some staff at the school began to hate us. We were caught in the middle of a war that we did not know existed. Let alone understand anything.

The refugees came to his church. The Bishop opened the doors to them and all the indigent in the city. Never were those doors closed. Day and night! He took initiative to deal with the refugee crisis in Johannesburg by giving them shelter and opening that school, too. We scoured the streets of Johannesburg, picking up destitute unaccompanied minors we could find and steered them to the church. We took them to the fourth floor which was reserved for school-going children, only.

Unlike the few privileged care workers and not quite understanding the conflict between The Bishop, the church, some children's organisations which wanted to be involved, the Social Development and the City of Joburg, Dan and I basked in an opportunity that flourished our intellect. We were typically the first Care Workers up every morning on the fourth floor. It was one big room occupied by almost one hundred and eighty children. We fetched hot water from the fifth floor to bathe the young ones and supervised the older ones in the shower. We made sure that no adults came in while the children bathed. They had porridge, then, we took them all the way to the school. Lunch time we went to supervise the children being fed. After school we fetched them and assisted them with their home-work. It was challenging work and some pulled out because of the measly recompense.

One evening, two Child and Youth Care Workers came burping and smelling like mops dipped in and out of alcohol in the middle of the night. Deceiving themselves that they scared their troubles away! Swearing, they entered the room and fell on top of sleeping children. They were fired on the spot! The following morning I discovered both my cell-phones missing. One of them had stolen them whilst I slept safe as a Bible, before they melted away. Immersed in our work, Dan and I missed some of the coup plots and chicanery weaving around us.

One day I saw a smile split with the dazzling power of lightning and spread across a small chubby face with the inimitable warmth of sunshine. This was a four-year-old child who stayed with his granny on the fourth floor. Dazzled, maybe, because I missed my son of almost similar age, I hoisted him into my arms, throwing him into the air above my head a couple of times. Every day I used to make time to greet and play with him. On that special day, I steamrolled into the room high with the infectious spirit that had become part of my identity. Like a beam of light, he cut across the floor with his arms flung out, words gleefully tumbling out of his mouth:

"Dad! Dad! Dad!"

Everyone was astounded. This was the first time everyone heard him call anyone "Dad!" Aunty Dee who was sweeping stopped dead in her trajectory and flashing the seductive gap in her front teeth said:

"What a wonderful thing, Bloggs. That child never said that to any man. You bring out the best in that child and every one of us all. You are a blessed man."

Speechless, I turned to survey the occupants in the room and collided with Vimbai who shot from a chair in a missile of flesh and bursting energy. She engulfed and crushed me out of breath in an ardent hug flooding with infinite emotion. Like one struck by a thunderbolt, I knew something had altered in my spirit and personality. When I looked in the mirror a burning light gleamed in my eyes as if something was melting inside my body. My veins flowed with a mysterious pirouetting energy. I felt a powerful invisible force around me. It made me feel weightless. A feather! Sometimes I felt like the wind went through me. Other instances, stupefied, I did not know who I was. Sometimes I felt my scalp being pulled out and smoke coming out into the air above me, being redefined. And I felt no weight at all. The power and light of a positive attitude swept all darkness out of my life! The conviction that we are responsible for the way other people see and treat us and that it is by the change in our attitude and approach that we can reverse their prejudices against us became a branded thread weaving my life.

These were children I had never seen being born. Strangers, we had met on the great road of adversity. Thrown together, we joined hands and opened our hearts to each other like a family. A pen with the ink of fire ascended in the book of my life scaling a new script with an irrevocable might. I took out my worn out notebook and wrote:

If we all tried to know, understand and love people from the deep humanity in their souls, not only shall we be able to walk arm-in-arm with those in need but in their slighted states shall we help them recognize their worth and be a restorative mirror to their mettle and the best they might be!

FOUR

Connie was a sweet strong willed genial soul. She carried her heavily built stature not with fickle energy. So much grace flowed out of that baby elephant frame. We were doing the Child and Youth Care course together. One day when I was getting ready to leave for the training, I watched her softly tread to where I sat. I never spoke much to her, but she came straight to me and said:

"I don't know where to start."

"Where to start about what?"

"My dream."

"Your dream?"

"Yes! I have it all the time. It plays out my life and then my death."

"Tell me more, Connie."

*

The dividing veil is a thick labyrinth of transparent cobwebs. Whereas they cannot see through into my new mysterious world, I can peep into theirs without being seen. My spirit moves freely between the two worlds. I can see both my mother's sisters. Their cheeks are lined with the salt of their tears. They are wiping them away. But the disturbed fountains would rather run their mourning course. My mother's brother has come from Chiweshe, where he stays in the rural areas. I can see premature old age is mercilessly notching upon his features.

"It's unfortunate," I keep on muttering with my voice a thin smoke of vapour that nobody sees or hears.

My spirit keeps slipping back and forth through the invisible barrier of cobwebs. But, I can only watch and speak in my vaporous voice without reaching them at all. Relatives and friends, I can see them all heaving their breasts like poisoned toads as they force out their crocodile tears. My children—my two precious possessions—are there, standing nearest to where I lie in this condemning box. Their tormented eyes are bulging out like fiery tennis balls. Grief laden tears cascade down their cold-weather cracked faces like miniature streams. Forlorn, they stand marked out by their broken humanity, their skin white like tomato-less fish soup.

I would like to reach out my icy lifeless hand and comfort them in their neatly patched clothes but my time and work abused uncle lowers the handkerchief from his eyes. He breaks open his round hole of a mouth again. So, I can only listen, reposed on this fresh mound of soil waiting to swallow me and my box.

"Friends and relatives, I wish you knew the pain that I feel in my heart today." he says. "But the ailments of the heart cannot be fully communicated, and that's unfortunate."

"Yes that's unfortunate indeed," I can only echo in my agonized vaporous voice.

"It's unfortunate that she had to suffer alone with only her young children around her to this tragic end."

"A sad end for all you cared," I echo.

"But what grieves me most is that nobody brought her anguish to my knowledge."

"Does it touch your heart that much pretty, uncle?"

"Nevertheless, I shall take both her children and raise them just as my own," he says, his hollow voice kicking around my vapours.

"Let the promise hold and you shall not wrong the dead." I say.

The benevolent priest comes forward to bless my departed spirit on its pilgrimage to the deep unknown lands of mystery. He looks religiously honest, friend to one none ever thought about in their life. He throws some holy water all over my coffin and prays for me to rest in peace. Rest in peace or rot in peace?

He retreats into the background and now the shirtless men with yellow and dark tartar on their teeth come forward. Their faces masking several graveside stories. They grab their shovels betraying no emotion at all. Now they pick up my coffin and gently lower me into the dumb gaping hole. In single file, friends and relatives each pick up a handful of dust from the mound of soil and gently release it into the mocking depths where I lie. My uncle passes by and I reprimand him in my vaporous voice. He has not the slightest idea of what I have been through together with my children. Yet he pretends to understand. Spitting his stinking phlegm of commitment. Deceitful uncle! Now my anguish is over, he buys me this gaudy shimmering box. I wish I had departed without a coffin and the money used on my children.

The shovels eat into the mound spitting the soil all over my cold derelict body. And the murmuring surge above me bruits another song across the veld:

You who herd us all, Jehovah
Only you know her well
Father take care of her spirit
Bless her with the peace of saints
Our shepherd, Jehovah

How she journeys forth, Jehovah
Only you know the path
Where her spirit shall rest Jehovah
Only you have prepared the place
Let her rest in peace
Our shepherd, Jehovah

Throughout my happy and unhappy days, I never heard such kindly speeches made for me. Never such eloquence did my living heart ever receive. Coward hypocrites! Are you not ashamed? You all cry and say you feel pain for my death and my miserable children but what love is there when I could not get it whilst I lived? My useless vaporous voice strays and whispers in the wind:

"It matters no more! It matters no more."

The mound of earth toppling on the body of the one they held contemptible in life thickens. Shovels frequently exchange hands. But tirelessly Maidei does not spare her frugal ill-used body. She too, is a piece of that which lives every day despised, trodden and unnoticed. Rejected. The scum of the earth. Oh Maidei! If you could hear my sisterly voice spiralling over into the infinite oblivion speak:

> *"Rest friend your weary body*
> *Though spare not your love dear*
> *Rather your ailing body save*
> *For ahead battles bitter stalk."*

I see my children cry and call me back. But it is beyond my power to escape from this vault. Their eyes keep on swelling with grief and it pains me to see them shake like wretched mice in the talons of a ruthless monster. Powerless and reduced to desolate wrecks, I can only watch, my touch, my kiss, my love and my words caressing them in the cool breeze of the setting sun. I have no claim on anyone to look after them; I had none during my contemptible life; how can I have one now?

The singing becomes a murmuring trickle. To me the dreadful storm and its whipping horrors are past. My spirit only feels a hazy swimming pain for my children. A white, bright, soft light whose eye I cannot see washes all over my light muddled floating soul. My path, only one way, stretches out like a soft ribbon of chalk. It luminously winds deeper into the mist. I pass through a huge warm rainbow gate into an awesome brightness whose soft light breathes music beyond the measure of words. It is only music. And I feel my spirit being swallowed rather than going through that music...through the awesome brightness...being pulled out...

She was briefly immersed in a tortured ponderous silence. Then the words toppled over her large dark beautiful lips:

"Bloggs, can you please interpret my dream?"

"You sound desperate."

"I am."

"Tell me more."

"I've had the dream for many times."

"How do you feel each time you wake up?"

"Scared!"

"It's really scary to dream about your own funeral."

"It's like I don't belong to this world anymore."

"You think a lot about what it may mean!"

"Then I sometimes I think I'm being asked to choose between life and death."

"But what's your final thought?"

"I don't know. I feel numb. Like I'm being pulled out of something"

"What something?"

"I don't know! Maybe life! Maybe death!"

"It's torturing your mind."

"It is."

"What would you choose between the two?"

"Life! I mean, being pulled out of death."

"I believe you."

"Do you?"

"The fear in your face tells me you have good reasons. I wonder though."

"You're right! My two children!"

"You fear what might happen to them if you die?"

"Exactly! My parents died in a car accident when I was very young. I struggled growing up, abused by my uncles. They kept me at home whilst their children were in school. I did all the washing, foraged into the forest alone in search of firewood, herded the goats and cattle alone. And when they strayed, they whipped me with a rope of cattle hide. I did not eat with the other children. I ate alone and sometimes was fed on left-overs. I was the one to weed and water the garden. Connie was their slave. I was their child of hate. A dog that everybody wanted to give a bad name and enjoy hanging it."

"That's very cruel."

"I don't know if my heart will ever heal." Tears sprang in her eyes.

"Connie! You are carrying a huge wound in your heart. What can you do?"

"Yes, Bloggs. Sometimes, as a child I just wanted to die! It was a lonely miserable place."

"Do you think about completing suicide?"

"Sometimes. Death is the end of everything but who knows if it's not also the beginning of other worse things? Who really knows?"

I saw her growing up as a lonely pretty girl, abused and unsupported. Unattached and always dreading rejection! Defined by her anchorless existence of an unloved orphan! The wound in her heart silently exploded in her face and I felt humbled by her show of that vulnerability. She had never bared that side of her nature to anyone in her life. Maybe only to her husband. I felt the heaviness of her fear and the responsibility of her choices in the game of survival. Deeply I listened, trying to sense the shadows where her nightmares came from. Then I explored with her what kept her going. Time flew. That day, we turned up late for our lessons. Outside the training room Connie said:

"There's a loneliness that breathes into one a kind of peace and there's this other one that burns to the core of one's deprivation of human need; a thrown-ness into being only known and understood by the blighted spirit." She apologetically finished her speech looking into my eyes with an appealing softness that touched and confused my mind.

"I'm very sorry, Bloggs, for troubling you with my pain and making you late for the lessons. I just thought I could speak to you. I've never done anything like this, please forgive me," she concluded.

"No trouble at all, Connie. I thank you for trusting me with what you're going through. I feel deeply honoured. Can we talk about it again soon? I'll be there when you need me." My spirit was deeply moved.

She hugged me and in that irrevocable clinging posture, I felt it was something her huge provocative body had long pined for. The human need for love, respect and understanding. Then, we went into the training room where we briefly interrupted the lesson and everybody clapped their eyes on us with nosy mischievous looks.

*

That evening Dan, Matt and I had pap, roasted mackerel fish and green vegetables for supper at the church. We had our meal sitting on the roadside kerb. Supper time was always busy at the church. Even some local people came to buy pap or rice meals at the church. We were an interesting community to other local people who chose to care. Some who heard our galvanising stories and recognised the pool of diversity constituting us came to make friends with us. Then there was always drama of some kind every day that we always wanted to avoid. The drama of violence, marauding gangs of robbers and highly stressed people shouting obscenities. Most of these were our own disillusioned fellow countrymen. We had no water to wash our hands, so we cleaned our hands with newspapers that we picked up on the street. Then we went to Shanty-Town to buy Joburg Beer.

Life in Shanty-Town never changed. Things stayed the same. The more shacks people built in the compound the more its ambience stayed the same. Carefree, jocular and dramatic! Only the number of people grew but the activities never changed. We drank Joburg Beer sitting on swaying rough wooden benches, under a lop-sided shed that creaked and groaned with old age in the wind. It certainly was a happy-go-lucky place of mystery with its inhabitants coming from different backgrounds and different countries! One's mind would be boggled with someone staying in Shanty-Town and owning a nice car. But that was normal!

In the yard across the shebeen, rose stacks of cardboard, mountains of empty plastic containers, cans and beer bottles stacked by recyclers who rolled along the streets of Joburg day and night. People fetched their water in small containers and buckets from a mobile tank on the outskirts. Sometimes a certain white man drove into the settlement with a couple of huge plastic drums delivering free water to the people. Men and women washed their clothes at the same old concrete platform they had used for ages. They bought big dishes like tubs and bathed in their shacks. All people used the same mobile toilets, also planted on the fringes of the settlement. At times there was embarrassing drama between opposite members of the sex barging on each other's privacy in those toilets. Night time, we chose to urinate only covered by the wrapping walls of darkness. And sometimes we watched our urine streaming out touched by the soft gleaming colour of the silver moon!

We took long gulps of the beer which left a rich creamy froth on our dry mouths. We licked our lips and revved our minds with politics, literature and societal trends rocking the moments. The prostitutes we saw every day came dancing, wriggling their bottoms like heaps of worms and flaunting their assets with sex-suggestive thrusts. We never looked at them. We were downright dead inside from the way they wanted us to be alive! They got tired and gave up. Undisturbed, they went to dance for someone else. There was always a fellow dying for their services!

Sometimes the meandering network of dusty road strips only changed when somebody built his shack in the middle of the road or when it rained hard and they became small trenches. Then the road would shift through someone's yard and the affected person would have to erect a wall of mattress skeletons to protect his property from the tres- passers. There were no outside lamps in Shanty-Town so people stole electricity and bulbs from the nearby electric poles. At first, they stole from the neighbouring abandoned factory. But when the electricity supply authorities discon- nected the dangerous illegal connections, they climbed the nearby poles with ladders and continued to have electricity.

No one paid rent. No one paid any water or electricity bills. That was Shanty-Town. It had a sweet perilous rhythm of its own. A treacherous freedom!

FIVE

The morning arrived with a cold wind that seemed to go through the bone and flesh of my body. I shook it out with the defiant fire I had become. A fire that baffled everyone amidst the decay and frustrations permeating the whole church building. I hoisted my baggage of blankets, books and clothes onto my shoulder and flew to the storeroom where I burst upon everyone. My body ready to respond was fired up with a glowing flame of happiness. Poor as a church mouse as I was, I developed an amazing field of magnetism very few who came my way could escape. Perhaps this was now being caused by sleeping more safely like The Holy Bible between folded seats in the Sanctuary.

"The happy one," someone called out.

"I will always be the happy one."

"The one who does not have any trouble in his life," another one said.

"Sadness is the shadow of happiness!"

"How is that?"

"I wish you were not that ignorant. Your eyes are open but you do not see, you hear but you do not listen!"

"What?"

"Most people opt to spend their lives trapped in the shadow of life."

"He's mad!"

"The tragedy is not that they don't know but that they don't see happiness in their lives. And your happiness depends on your perception of the world. Your perception of the world is a mirror of the state of your consciousness."

"He thinks he knows."

"Life moves for those who see and try things. Those who never stop dreaming at all. For those who fall but always pick themselves up. For those who don't, it sucks! Life is what you make of it. If you see failure, you're doomed. But if you have hope, it means there should be a way of improving on things. And the possibility of a better life. But remember there's no perfect life."

"He thinks he's better than us."

"I have only discovered my own system to live life abundantly. Whether riches come or not, I will live and appreciate life in the present. Not affected by the past or worrying about the future. ALWAYS IN THE PRESENT. You can, too."

"Explain yourself."

"You walk along the street, see a shadow on the ground. What do you do? Turn of course to see whose shadow it is. Then you see the shadow belongs to a woman of exquisite beauty. You see all her well defined assets, beautiful clothes, unblemished complexion and graceful flow of motion. Now I ask you to compare this breathing form with the blunted smudge you saw on the ground. Which one of the two paints an admirable picture in your mind? The blur on the ground? Or the beautiful manifestation of life that casts the shadow? Which one excites your senses? Which one do you believe in?"

"Wow!" the word escaped from someone's mouth.

"What does that mean?"

"The negative things you are going through are only a shadow cast by the positive things. The choice is yours which one to live in—whether in the negative which is the reactive state full of frustration, self-pity, anxiety and depression or in the positive in which you are in the proactive state where you've hope and see opportunity for change and growth in your challenges?"

"He wants to twist our minds."

"That's philosophy," someone said.

"What?"

"Philosophy! You idiot."

"Whatever!" I laughed, bouncing up the stairs to wake up and get the children ready for school.

I saw Dan and Connie were already on the fourth floor. Connie greeted me with a smile. She slid into the girls' room to help Aunty Dee. Aunty Dee always slept with the girls. Dan was in the big room, calling on the boys to rise, pulling the blankets tucked under their heads. The morning winter air stung their faces. They twisted and folded their visages all over like statues tumbling into life. Their eyes bloodshot and heavy with sleep! The fact is no one ever really slept in the church and the morning always stole upon us like a thief. Some children just lay still, pretending not to be hearing him or asleep. Dan drew the blanket from one child's head. The boy grabbed his wrist violently and leaped up. He saw that it was Dan. He apologised.

"Are you well?"

"Yes. Thank you."

"Why did you wake up like that?"

"I thought a thief was trying to steal from me?"

"Why?"

"Someone tried it twice in my sleep."

"Who was that?"

"I don't know. Since then I've learned to sleep with only one eye closed and the other one open. Do you know that I was a soldier back home?" he bragged.

"You were in the militia?"

"Whatever you may want to call it but I was a soldier," he insisted. The militia wrought unimaginable havoc and crime in Zimbabwe. They raped, maimed, tortured and killed anyone, young or old, relative or stranger. As long as you criticised the ruling party and its government, you were an enemy.

I worked from the other end. There was hardly any space to stand. The floor was crammed with the children's mattresses and blankets. They woke up traces of blankets planted in their hair. Red, blue, grey, brown and green colours wedged in their hair. They sat up with bloodshot eyes, rubbing and wiping white stuff out of them. Then they began looking for their clothes and other treasured items before they folded their blankets. The big room, in a buzz, transformed into a hive of activity and voices.

"Where's my phone?"

"Who has taken my shoes?"

"Where's my shirt?"

"I can't find my boxer shorts, who took them?"

"Someone please return my sandals."

"I can see only one shoe."

"Me, too!"

"Who has taken my other shoe?"

"My phone! My phone!" the first boy shouted in desperation. We would help locate all the missing items. We started looking for the phone, searching everywhere. A fight broke out between the boy who had lost his phone and his suspect. Dan and I pulled them apart. A friend of the victim joined in the fight. Others joined in and we had almost ten people fighting each other. Fortunately, the other Care Workers had arrived. The fighting stopped. We searched everyone and their bags. There was no phone to be found anywhere.

"There are people who come here while we sleep."

"Who are they?" I asked.

"We don't know."

"Adult people?" Dan asked.

"Yes."

"Where do they come from?"

"We don't know."

"From today, we will have Youth Care Workers sleeping in the room. They will take turns to sleep at the door and no one will come in. They will open the door for you when you go to the toilet. Everybody must be safe."

We continued packing and searching for lost items. Vanishing items maybe. Some were established in rather very unlikely places from where their owners claimed they had left them. One shoe was found in the girls' room. Someone coming from downstairs brought John's shirt which had been picked up on the third floor. Temba's new shoes were never found. Temba and Wasu roasted chicken feet on a small braai stand in the street after school. They bought fancy gadgets and clothes with the money. Tindo's shirt was found in the dust bin minus the buttons. It had a huge black smudge on it. Someone had used it to polish his shoes. Tindo clicked his tongue, cursed the unknown culprit and stuffed it back into the bin. And so on the events unfolded.

"I saw your sandals," someone said.

"Where?"

"In the shower. Fungai is wearing them."

"That's ok."

Clothes went missing and when they turned up on a friend's body there would be no issue. Most of them were friends and they freely shared clothing items. Yet where grudges existed serious outbursts of anger and fights erupted. They took off their shirts, flexed their muscles and fought viciously. We all were aware that the fourth floor was a perilous place for a fight. The wall on that floor, overlooking Pritchard Street, was made of asbestos. If anyone impacted on it heavily, there was a danger of breaking through the fragile material. There was no balcony. One would travel through the air and the ultimate destination was either the paving or the tarmac. Then undoubtedly broken bones, being crushed by passing vehicles and death!

We asked them to tie up their blankets in single bundles in a way they would easily identify them. They rushed to the shower where they stood in a queue. They stood under the cold shower singing and yelling all the time to each other as they surged out shivering.

"My soap!" someone would shout. "Who stole my soap?"

"Here it is!"

"You don't steal. You ask for it."

"Where is my towel?"

"Here! I've got it."

"Why didn't you ask for it?"

"When you wear my shirt, do you ask for it?"

We saw that they were all spruced up clean, that their clothes were nicely ironed and directed them into another queue for porridge. There were not enough spoons. Those who could not get them ate with their fingers. Always rushing against time the porridge burned their fingers. They ate first and we would have the left-overs.

We took them down the stairs of the building into the street. Some quickly became attached to us and became our shadows on the street. We saw them to the school gate. Inside they turned waving to us. We waved back.

We moseyed back to the church where we did not have much business after that. We collected our bags from Aunty Dee in the girls' room. Briefly we perched on the few chairs on the fourth floor, made arrangements for the people who were going to supervise lunch that day at the school. Then Dan said:

"Now, what's the breakfast plan?"

"Park-Station."

"Bye, Connie!"

"Bye Bloggs!"

"Bye Connie!"

"Bye Dan!"

"Guys!" Connie called us back. "We've a new girl child. I want you to meet her." She was about fourteen years old.

"What's your name?" I asked.

"Patience Mushaya!"

There was something about her surname and age that raised a red flag in my mind. Then a place exploded out of my confusion. Marondera!

"What's your mother's name?"

"Mercy Mushaya!"

My mind spun, tripping in a cul-de-sac. Scouring her face with my eyes another face from almost fifteen years ago floated into my mind. A woman I had known. And dated! Just before I got married. Then she heard I got married. Without a word from her she evaporated out of my life. The last time I heard about her was when a friend came to me saying that he had seen her pregnant. She had told him not to worry me as I was married and surely starting a family. Could this be the child? And could she be my daughter? A profusion of pain. Regret! And panic.

"Where's your mother?"

"Dead!"

"Are you ok?" Connie asked me.

"Just a little bit dizzy. I just didn't eat well last night."

I could not fool anyone. Everybody knew I had eaten a full meal.

We plodded out of the room, meeting the nurse in the passage. Hands encumbered with medical instruments and linen, her dust coat flew behind her like a gigantic insect. She whacked the Home Based Care door with her stout shoulder, disappearing inside. Wondering, we went down the stairs, through the foyer, into the street where we saw an ambulance leaving without a patient and the Forensic Pathology Services van arriving. Someone had died! It happened often and we got used to it. After crossing a couple of robots we had forgotten about it. But I had not forgotten about a child called Patience. And the ugly hand of my sins now clawing back at me. Dan erroneously diagnosing my malaise started speaking:

"What's happening with Connie?"

"I don't know."

"You better find out."

"What do you mean?"

"Talk to her."

"Why don't you talk to her if you are concerned?"

"Bloggs! This is not about me. It's about you."

"What about me?"

"Everyone can see that you two have something between."

Once more the presentiment of discovering yet another shocking truth loomed large and ineluctable. Honestly, I thought Connie and I were just good friends. Only colleagues at work. Nothing else. What was it that other people saw that I was not seeing? Yet now I felt that on the previous day the stars had shifted between me and Connie. No doubt a connection had sprouted and I desired full comprehension that I could survive the new trajectory without stirring any trouble - that it was something not like the Biblical fall of man! I wanted it to be honest and true! I knew I had a youthful past stalked by the guilt of undisciplined amorous pursuits and temptations by beautiful women. Whilst my peers were having successes with their careers, I was inundated with belles who seemed to be falling around me like manna from heaven. Something that I realized too late with overwhelming regret and bitterness!

We had coffee and fat-cakes. My mind whirling with apprehension of the inexorable proof that waited to seal my proximate discoveries. I could understand Patience being my daughter. To meet her, without any introduction, for the first time in my life, under our both uprooted circumstances of our lives, thousands of kilometres away from home, was something I could never have dreamt of. Yet, I could not forego the bitter-sweet pleasure of acknowledging that she could be my own blood and flesh. Why had her mother kept her away from me? What did I do? Was I really that kind of a brute? What really happened? Why did she choose to keep it a secret to her grave? Why did she not inform the child whose child she was? My mind was swamped with a lot of questions which had no answers at all.

After having breakfast, we drifted to the House of Movements to read newspapers. We looked for news from home with an insatiable appetite. Almost two years had passed since I left home. The Global Political Agreement that had been signed on 15th September 2008 was a deadly poison to swallow for the democratic forces in the country. We all took it like Socrates drinking hemlock.

The 2008 elections arrived and exploded with a brutal awakening for the ruling party. It took them twenty-eight years to wake up from their looting enchanted slumber and that the opposition had sewed up the parting between their buttocks. They could not simply sit on the toilet seat and relieve themselves of their guilt. Even the shops they owned had no toilet paper. It was a mess! Their dubious friends floated in to hold their hands. Quiet diplomacy from big brother South Africa and pressure from SADCC conspired against the voices of reason in the country! The forced transition state was a sham and another crime against humanity. Either sham or shame for all who participated in it and both to some of them.

I read with infinite dismay and fury about the suffering in my country. The suffering that had driven a fourteen-year-old orphaned girl to embark on such a dangerous odyssey alone! Unloved! Broken! SHATTERED! A child I should have raised and protected for that matter! I did not understand why her mother never informed me about the pregnancy! I did not understand myself! This was not the man I knew! Putting down the newspaper I had been reading, I grabbed my satchel and plodded out of the library. I had no destination in mind. Just wandering around town. The afternoon sun shooting on my head through gaps between buildings. Glimpsing into shop windows full of merchandise but seeing nothing until I found myself at Shanty Town with a shake-shake of Joburg beer between my legs. Once perched on the bench I fished out my cell-phone and called my wife:

"My husband!"

"The mother of my children!"

"Are you well?"

"We are dying of hunger, my husband."

"What did you eat today?"

"Only vegetables, my husband."

"What!"

"Vegetables and water!"

"Why?"

"There's no mealie meal in the shops. Everywhere."

Tears of pain arrived in my eyes. Swamped with a ghastly shame! What was I doing? What had become of me? And my country? In my country I became dead. In my family life, a man lost in the confusion of the world. A strange world. An insane world! In my self-esteem I became less than the shadow of scum without a name. The scum that life spits out. Worthless. A heap of dog pooh.

I looked at the newspaper lying beside my hand. Its print danced like fishing worms in my eyes. The thin layer of my dignity peeled off the peripheries of my jumbled life into the burning spotlight of my consciousness. I was a man broken and trapped. SHATTERED! Sleep deserted me. My body crawled and I shivered with the dreadful thoughts of my life without ME. Brutally punishing myself with daggers of un-mitigating self-disdain. I deserved to face a firing squad.

SIX

Some three men mysteriously came to me and said:

"There're some people we want you to go with us and see. Won't you please come along?"

"Where?"

"To Johannesburg Hospital."

"We drove to the hospital. The three men were political activists of the political opposition back home and I knew them well. They told me the two men we were going to see had been abducted and tortured back home. They survived by sheer luck. And now they were recuperating in hospital. We were directed by a nurse to the side ward in which they were housed. There were only two beds in that ward. On the bedside of the first patient, leaning on a crutch, there stood a woman crying. She grotesquely dragged her legs around, wiped tears from her eyes and greeting us, painstakingly hobbled out of the room like a grasshopper on broken legs. Her feet stiffly and lewdly wide apart. I sat on the first man's bedside with one of the two activists and spoke to the torture victim:

"What happened?"

"They came in the middle of the night. They pounded the door, but I refused to open for them. The fury of their axes hacked away at the door until there was nothing left and we were dragged out. Our hands tied. The children came out. They beat them back and force marched us into the bush. They said I was growing too big in my pants and they wanted to reduce my size. They beat me with barbed wire, tied to a tree. One of them pulled my trousers down and tore away my underwear using a hunting knife. My wife screamed. They whipped her with the barbed wire on her back and bound her legs with rope. The one with the knife stood in front of me. He grabbed at my private parts and savagely pulled. One kicked them viciously. Another one came and pounded them with a claw hammer. I fainted. There was no water, so they urinated in my face to revive me. I was unconscious for some time. When I finally woke up my body was numb. The one with the knife held my male member in his hands. He started cutting into it as if he were peeling a banana. It was like a nightmare. My legs didn't feel like mine. All my private parts were numb. My voice left me and they argued amongst themselves:

"Why's he not crying?"

"If we cut it off, he'll know how to cry!"

"No! Leave it like that. He must see it like that for the rest of his life."

"Then they turned upon my wife where she lay. They lifted her skirts, tearing away her underwear. One of them brought a handful of ground hot chilli. He forced it into her private parts. Her screams were ringing in my mind when I fainted again. When I woke up they had a huge fire going. They took two steel rods out of it. The steel was red hot.

They burned her with the steel. They burned her buttocks. I can still smell her burning flesh. She was unconscious for a long time that I thought she was dead."

The man overwhelmed with emotion choked on his words. He trembled as if life was absconding him. His arms and body disfigured in a shocking maze of black welts, punctured flesh and gaping wounds. I offered him a glass of water which he gladly guzzled down. Gently holding his hand, I squeezed it. I said he could tell me everything next time if he so wished and he approved.

I stood up and plodded out of the ward, returning with the man's wife. I could not escape the acrid smell of rotting burned flesh! I enquired after her health and whether she was free to speak her ordeal. She was still in shock and preferred to tell her story to a woman. They had taken her dignity and womanhood away from her. Lamely she walked because of the burns on her buttocks. Broken, violated, battered and bruised.

Promising help, I asked for a hand from each one of them, telling them to hold each other's remaining hands. We formed a lame circle of three with the man in bed. Then I prayed. I thanked God for saving the couple. I prayed for their quick recovery, healing and restoration to good health. I asked God to be gentle with their minds and their bodies for the doctors only dressed the wounds and the process of healing and restoration was his miracle. I prayed for the couple's power to comfort each other in their brokenness and to find a path leading to growth despite their devastating trials. I prayed for God to open their adversaries' eyes and unlock their consciences out of the dungeons of inhumanity. I pleaded for befitting retribution and that like Paul on the road to Damascus, they be pulled into the righteous path so that they can live to tell of their callous deeds and be God's instruments in the fight against all such evil. I prayed for their lonely children and desolate homestead. I asked God that this violence be the precursor to the end of the cannibal regime savagely beating, maiming and slaying the people who put it into power. Then I proclaimed His will in all the couple's affairs and life.

I walked into the next side ward and saw another battered and disfigured man propped up with many pillows in bed.

"How're you feeling?"

"I don't know whether I still live or not. I can't believe it!"

"You're in shock."

"I'm still scared for myself and my children back home."

"Your life has been violated and you fear for your children's safety! May we go through it together?"

"I have a rural plot in Bindura. I had a good harvest last year. They came, assessed our harvest and forced us all to sell our maize to the Grain Marketing Board (GMB). Serious consequences would visit us if we didn't follow their orders. We hired a truck and took the grain to the GMB. When the time to be paid came, we got nothing. Our families suffered but nobody cared. We followed up for payment several times into another rain season. We got paid less than half the expenses we had for that crop. My children left school because I could not pay for their education. I foraged into another planting season with hunger on my doorstep and empty pockets. I borrowed some money from my relatives to buy seed and fertilizer.

"I had another good harvest. They came again and ordered us to sell to the GMB. With a lot of credit sitting on my shoulders, I didn't listen to them. I took my harvest to my house in Harare where I sold it to hungry people. The shops were empty and people queued in my yard. I went back to Bindura to fetch some more maize. Arriving in the evening, I found the militia waiting for me. They took all my family into the bedroom where they tied my hands and feet using wire. They pounded me with sticks and flogged me all over with ox-hide whips. I don't know why I never bled. Then they ordered my wife to take off all her clothes and lie naked on top of the bed. Fighting, she refused and they whipped her until her dress was ripped to shreds. Her body wept rivulets of blood. Then six of them, fighting amongst themselves raped her. Calling her all sorts of names in front of our children. They stopped assaulting her and she attacked them, provoking them to kill her. One of them asked for the storeroom keys. Still fighting, she was dragged in and locked up. Then they started interrogating me. One of them asked me:

"Which one do you want, a short sleeve or a long sleeve?"

I remained silent. I knew they were asking me to choose whether they should amputate my arm by the elbow or by the wrist. Then a cousin of mine who was there amongst them said:

"Let's take him to the river. We don't want his blood on our hands."

"Let the crocodiles do the work for us." Their voices echoed in unison.

"And then I'll have his wife again."

"She doesn't belong to you alone."

"She belongs to us."

"Everybody in the party."

"They carried me to the pool of crocodiles. Many people died in that river. No one who was thrown in there ever survived. With my hands tied they counted one, two, three, and sent me splashing in the water. Sinking to the bottom I wriggled and twisted like a giant worm. Then suddenly my hands felt free. I moved and felt my body shoot up to the surface. My head breaking the surface, I stroke the water with my arms whilst I kicked with all might like a demon possessed man. It was a dark moonless night. Someone threw a stick into the water and it missed my head by a few inches. Then another one shouted:

"It's the crocodiles fighting over him! Don't disturb them!"

"After breast-stroking and kicking like a mad cricket for twenty metres across the river, I rolled my body on the other side. I dragged myself out of the water and untied my legs. I could not believe I had survived. My right hand felt as if it had a million needles stuck in it. When I looked I saw the flesh of my hand had been peeled down in my struggle to free my hands of the wire. It looked like a guillotine had shaved off the skin. The other hand had a massive cut in the wrist and the wire, cold as death dangled on it. I liberated my hand from it and threw it into the river. I felt a stabbing pain in the side. Two of my ribs were broken. Then I walked to my cousin's compound that side of the river. I told him what had happened. He tore his clean shirt and bandaged my hands. Then he hid me in his granary.

"The following morning, news spread to my cousin's compound that my homestead had been looted and burned to the ground. I was declared dead and nourishing the alligators in the river. When the thugs returned to my compound, they had found my wife in her death throes. In that storeroom where they locked her up, there was a packet of highly concentrated rat poison. She took it all including another half bottle of pesticide which was lying in there as well. She died in the early hours of the morning at the hospital. Nothing could save her!

"I did not attend her funeral. When night came, I was fished out of my hideout and taken to Harare. From there, I was hid in a truck which smuggled me out of the country."

I looked the man in his broken eyes and saw the depths of his turbulent soul. I saw loss, devastation and dejection beyond measure. I asked him if he wanted to pray with me. I asked God to rest his wife's spirit and for justice. I asked God to give him strength to deal with the looming desolation and loneliness in his life without his beloved wife. I thanked God for saving his life and asked Him to lead his servant to the purpose of his life. I prayed for healing and everything that would bring restoration of hope and livelihood. I prayed for his family that it may be protected and be blessed with everything they needed.

I promised the man that I would come to visit him often and so did I promise the other couple.

"Will you visit them again?" One of the political activists asked.

"I will!"

"We won't be able to visit them often. There is a lot of intelligence people around. Sometimes we are followed by unknown people. We don't want them to be exposed."

"With me, they'll be safe."

On my third visit, I heard they were all going to be discharged on the following day. Coming from that visit, Matt met me at the church and said a lady we knew had died. She had long moved out of the church and now lived in a suburban house somewhere.

"People are preparing to go to the funeral parlour now. There'll be a service at the chapel and I've been sent to ask you to come and deliver the final speech and prayer."

"I can't do that!"

"There's no priest and no one else can."

"I'm not a priest."

"There's no one else who can do it better than you."

"I'll attend the memorial just like everyone else."

The body, after being washed and clothed was brought into the chapel. At the end the master of ceremony boomed out my name to give the closing speech and prayer. I stood at the head of the coffin. Words tumbled out. Then flowed out like cooking oil. I summarised the lady's life as I knew it and as recounted by friends and relatives. A vast empty space spread like a vault in my heart and the words I spoke filled it up. I felt the same happening with the gathering. An unadulterated silence descended in the awe and presence of death. Then my supplications to God sprang up from the heart of the deceased in the coffin, her mourning kith and kin and the road that waited to be travelled to her final destination. When I finished a benevolent flourish gurgled approvingly in the crowd and wafted throughout the chapel.

The vast spaces in the people's hearts filled up with a hymn caressing their lips. The mood became eager and purposeful. Coming forward, the pall bearers hoisted the coffin, marching towards the hearse. The vehicles were brought to life. Then gripped with the immutable fever from the chapel, they departed for the long journey to Zimbabwe.

Walking away from the chapel, my body belonged to a stranger. I was exhausted and hunger poked my stomach like a demon. Someone stole upon me and gently laid a warm hand upon the shoulder. It was Connie. In the middle of my tired smile the words softly tumbled out of her mouth. But those words arrived like daggers in my heart.

"Patience is gone."

"What do you mean?"

"All her bags are missing and she didn't report for school today."

"Does anybody know where she went?"

"Nobody."

"God! What've I done?"

"Done what?"

Utter sadness fell upon me. I swooned like a pregnant woman and said:

"Some water to drink, please, Connie."

SEVEN

Connie came to me and said:

"Bloggs, why are you avoiding me?"

"I'm not avoiding you, Connie."

"Where were you this last couple of days?"

"In the world."

"What were you doing in the world, Bloggs?"

"Mourning."

"How can you answer like that?"

"A friend of mine died."

"I'm sorry! Forgive me for my impetuosity. I thought it was about Patience."

"You've done nothing wrong. You're very correct."

"What happened to your friend?"

"They neck-laced him in the park."

"You mean the xenophobia victim who was burned in the park?"

"Yes! You knew him?"

"No! I heard about him. What a way to die."

"I wouldn't want to die like that. My spirit would never rest."

"Where did you know him from?"

"I met him in Joburg."

"May I buy you coffee, Bloggs? Do you mind if we go to Park-Station?"

"Not at all, Connie."

We sat opposite each other while we drank our coffee. We talked about small things like weather. I avoided any talk about Patience. Then we talked about our plans in Joburg and shared about where we came from.

"Are you married?"

"Yes, I am."

"How many children?"

"Three sons."

"And you, are you married?"

"My husband left me."

"I'm sorry about that."

"Any children?"

"Two daughters."

We both smiled at each other.

"Your wife is lucky to have you."

"I don't think so. Sometimes I frustrate her with the dangerous decisions that I randomly make. And then she says that I'm over-strict with the children. Especially our eldest son."

She tossed her beautiful mane back and laughed.

"Do you want your children to be like you?"

"Not exactly."

Again she laughed, her infectious mellowness raising devils under my skin. The realization struck me that I had always raised hell in my children's lives about their studies. I even offered extra lessons to school children at our house because my desire was to see bookish kids all over the place. I said:

"I think you're catching me somewhere I never suspected."

This time we laughed together. I was glad that I had breathed word of my living marriage to Connie. I did not want her trapped in a confusion of feelings and false expectations. Yet her voice was full of mirth and I noticed not the kind of degree I often heard her with other people. I feared the dangerous connection complex Dan had hinted. My moral and ethical dilemma had ruthlessly begun to rip my heart apart. Anchorless. Lonely. And unsupported.

Walking back to the church, she stopped at the corner of Bree Street and Von Brandis Street.

"Buy me some apples, please, Bloggs," I purchased a plate of apples which the vendor put in a plastic paper-bag.

Moving forward, crossing Jeppe Street, we bumped into a dirty man with a severely wounded leg, hobbling on one crutch. Swaying like a scarecrow, he begged for food. Connie took one of her apples, handing it over to him. It was then that I looked him in the face. Instantly recognizing him as the thug that had attempted to rob me along Bree Street, coming from Mashona Bar.

"What happened to your leg?"

"I was attacked by a gang of robbers at night."

"Liar! I know you. I suppose your luck has run out. May this dose of your own medicine be the permanent cure you so much deserved! Do you remember me?" I observed he had no clue what I was talking about. Or pretended rather. "You don't remember the man you tried to rob and shoot along Bree? Remember yourself nearly being run over by cars and leaving your gun behind when you dropped it? How many people did you kill with that gun?"

He was silent as a tomb. Connie tugged at my hand and I moved forward, surprised at the turn of the events. I did not wish him ill. Yet I desired that this should be a turning point in his life to pursue an honest living beneficent in some measure to one community or another. This man who once instilled nameless fear in people on the streets of Joburg had now been reduced to a piteous spectacle begging for food on the same streets! Soliciting for donations from the same people he callously robbed without showing any shred of remorse! A man could live many lives on the streets of Joburg! I would not be baffled the next day turning into another street corner and running into him acting the blind with a bowl in his hand.

*

I walk through a broken portal into a deathly quiet clearing. In the harsh glare of the attacking sun, my life leaps out of its marrow. Flapping like a messed-up beautiful ribbon rescued out of the garbage can. I feel like I just rolled out of sewage effluence whose faeces decorate the body forever. In my ears, a hymn creeps in like a maggot chewing into my eardrum. On the lawn before me and glinting in the sunlight, pops up a polished wooden coffin. The hymn showers around me like invisible soft teeth in a storm. Nibbling! And thick puss flows out of my ears. Tumbling to the ground.

I lift up my withered palm to shield my eyes from the sun and see the flashing barrels of police rifles. My heart pounds! Standing there, a kaleidoscope of weird tortured emotions whirl inside me. Swimming in a tumultuous ball of my future or maybe my ex-future dreams? It is more like I have only one eye left, blurred by the eye-scorching brightness of the coffin.

The scene changes. Drops into a shack. I am packing a small duffel bag. Like one packing for his last journey! Death! I shove in all my belongings—two pairs of trousers, three T-shirts, a shaving machine, a couple of underwear, my jersey, a piece of laundry soap and a copy of John Milton's Paradise Lost. Then a copy of my treasured poetry manuscript. The landlady, Mama Mokoena has already placed two blankets for me in the police truck.

A horrible scene keeps playing itself out again and again in front of my eyes—AK 47's death! It emerges from the back of the sunlight, playing havoc with my mind before deceptively receding into the darkness of the sunlight again.

"Don't you move or make a sound,"

"Why? What's going on?"

"Shhhh! They're here!"

"Who?"

"Those who hate foreigners," the landlady speaks in hushed urgent tones. "I will put a lock on your door from outside and tell them that you're not at home. Quick, close your window and draw the curtain! Quick!"

Fear and confusion are like a nuclear bomb gone off in my mind.

"Quick! Quick."

"Don't lock the door from inside. They may try to peep through and if they notice that the door is locked from inside they will know that you are here."

I shove myself in a dark corner. Trembling and sweating profusely like a hare chased in the veld by a pack of greyhounds. The mob outside is craving for blood. Like vampires. Someone comes forward and rattles the lock outside my door. My mouth runs dry and my tongue is like a stiff piece of rubber. Body and mind rupture apart. The wretched shack spins around, turning up-side down.

"He is not here!" someone shouts.

"What?"

"The Zimbabwean is not here."

"Mama Mokoena, where is the Zimbabwean?"

"He is still at work." responds the landlady.

"Let's go to the next shack."

"Yes, the Mozambican!"

"Pull down his shack!"

"Burn him, too!"

And I feel the evil cloud leave and move on to settle above Arumando's shack. A hail of stones and bricks rains upon it. Caught in a morbid spell, I creep to peep out through a hole in the galvanized steel wall of my shack. What an unmitigated frenzy! What a nameless hatred I see! A crow-bar is thrust between the flimsy door and the frame, snapping the rusted wire that was used as the hinge. Within a minute, one corner of the shack crumples in mangled surrender. Something callously ravishing, clutches, burns and drags heavily to the stripped bottom of my heart and stomach. The scourge of xenophobia pouring a river of molten wire through my body.

Five men disappear into the shack and re-emerge, pulling between them poor Arumando, still in his overalls. I see in his eyes the overwhelming fear of one sensing the end. They force him down to his knees. He begs for mercy. No one minds his pleas. He is the fly in their soup that must be taken out and crushed without any mercy. Bricks and sharp stones cut his body open. For a moment, he almost breaks free. But there is nowhere to run. With unimaginable brutality, his body is frayed into huge weeping wounds. Spitting vitriol a cantankerous woman brings a blanket from Arumando's shack and they wrap it around him. Another man appears brandishing a golf stick. The crowd parts to give him space. With all his evil might he swings! There is a cracking sound and flesh peels exposing white broken bone of his forehead. Blood gushes out like a broken water pipe, flowing into his eyes. Blinding him.

They tie his hands behind him and a man who is Arumando's neighbour comes forward. He places an old vehicle tyre around his neck. Chanting profanities and spitting at him. Then they pour two litres of paraffin all over his body. A burning match-stick leaps out of the crowd. Then I see a writhing blazing mass. A tortured voice whips, echoing into the red sunset skies above. His agony detonates, spreading in concentric circles, closing the eye of the bloodshot sun. I witness him fall, rise and tower like a macabre gigantic bat above their hate as they run away from their flaming sin.

Shaking, I scuttle under the bed like a sewer rat. My bladder loosens up. I slither out again, pee in a bucket and roll back into the tiny space between the floor and the bed.

Stomach and chest flattened against the rough floor, I lie there. Breathing dust and absolute fear.

The noise outside suddenly stops. The crowd vanishes. Only the choking quietness of death lingers. I walk out into the street. It is still littered with stones, bricks, pieces of iron and broken bottles, most of them where Arumando was neck-laced with the burning tyre. The debris from his looted shack lies strewn everywhere as if there has been a hurricane only in his shack. His mangled half-burnt shoe grisly stares upwards at the sky in piteous supplication for a verdict I cannot fathom. Nobody seems to be bothered at all. No one seems prepared to do any cleaning at all for the man who burned like an exploded gas tank.

Standing there, I want to make a prayer but a policeman grabs me by the hand, leading me to the back of the waiting vehicle. Before I climb into the back of the truck, my landlady comes forward to hand me a lunch box.

"They promised me that they will be coming to loot your shack because I hid you," she says.

"Thank you for saving my life mama, they can have everything."

"I will come to visit you at the camp and if you need anything, please, do not hesitate to call me."

"Yes mama!"

"When it is quiet again, you can come and stay with us, son, this is your home" she pauses, briefly looking at her two silent daughters standing in the yard. "You know I have a son no more," tears roll out of her motherly eyes. "Sipho went to Johannesburg and they killed him there. He died for the wrong reasons. Sandile went to work in the mines and they shot him like a dog at Marikana. This time it was the police. I thought God had given me back my good Sandile in you. But now they want you dead, too. Everything is futile, what is wrong with this world?"

The disinterested policeman flinches at the mentioning of the Marikana massacre and says that it is time to leave. I spread my open arms to her and we hug with tears streaming down her dimpled cheeks. I wipe them away with my handkerchief before the doors of the truck shut behind me. As the truck drives away, I put the handkerchief against my cheek and feel her cool loving tears. Her two daughters do not stop waving until the truck has disappeared round the bend.

What pain. What loneliness. So much despair! What desolation do I realize fill up the erased chapters of the book of this mother's life. The tears she leaves on my shoulders are for what happened at Marikana as well. The brutal killing of her son and other thirty-three miners for striking against poor wages and working conditions. A sad day for South Africa's new democracy! Something died in the bosoms of all South African mothers on that day. And something nasty was reborn in the citizens' minds. The spectre of apartheid!

My mind whirls in a flood around all the beautiful affectionate people and doting relationships I have found and lost in my search for freedom. Someone, sitting next to me in the back of the police van, tells me to forget about it but I ask him:

"How could I ever have inner peace without freedom? How could I sit properly with a thorn in the flesh of my buttock and bury my heard in the sand like an ostrich? How could I take my brokenness, my sickness, and celebrate it as the strength and pillar of my soul? How?"

I woke up sweating as if I had been pulled out of an oven. I wiped my cheek with the palm of my hand. Only sweat. I poked a finger in my ear. No puss. No Mama Mkoena. No burning bodies. No police around. No coffin. I was lying on my mattress as usual. Why did I dream about Mama Mkoena and her daughters? What was the cause of this dream? Had it been sparked by the recent xenophobic events? Was it my loneliness? The fear of a breaking mind or an anchorless mind? Lack of love in my physical life? Mama Mkoena was a member of The Methodist Church. We met at the church. Arumando was one of her tenants. Then one day her two daughters brought me a pair of jeans and a shirt. She invited me to her home. I got my first hugs in South Africa. It was a beautiful experience. Like being born again.

Then, my mind turned inwards into the man that I had become. Displaced in the tumult of exile, the whole wide world—detention camps, street pavements, forests, crocodile infested rivers, sleeping under bridges, skirmishes with thugs and haters, futility, frustration, loving and unloving strangers, all that fabricated my home - my life - and my wisdom. A battle to transcend beyond the borders of an uncaring humanity. When adversity relentlessly knocks you down, when no one loves you and when everything collapses around you, sometimes, the real purpose of your life begins. I opened my notebook and wrote:

"It is broken but it can be fixed. With a little heart we will all grow the wisdom that the tragedy is not that our humanity is broken but that not everyone is prepared to do the possible things we can do to mend it. That the multitude would rather all stand back and watch. From a distance.

Refusing to be accountable. Playing the same old hide-and-seek blind game where in our minds we choose to stay in a sterile circle of denial. THE CIRCLE OF SILENCE!"

EIGHT

We sat in the library at the House of Movements overflowing with excitement. Our eyes pouring over the first issue of the African Writers Forum magazine. Thobile floated in flashing everyone her cool blissful smile. Settling down she led us into a passionate discussion on The Role of The African Writer in an African Society. A part of something I had lost sprouted gay and exquisite in my mind. I no longer felt my life crouching on the murky banks of insanity. The fragmented self which I knew was Bloggs condensed like a pregnant cloud heavy with stories about to pour down. I wanted to live my purpose! I did not want to grapple with insignificant matters. I did not want to fear death! I craved to live! I knew my work was with people and I wanted something that separated me from the trite and self-condemning isolation often fed by the fear to speak out.

I was coming from a world that had been made wild and starving by bullies and liars called politicians whose debate weapons were murdering thugs. A president who held on to power by perverting the state organs, the police and the army to kill citizens. Whatever it was, I deigned not to be dominated by their horrible system. I determined to live by my own standards! To live out a set of values and ideals that conveyed the best my intentions might be! had to be my own man or else be made someone else's man!

One looking at the camouflage blend of people coming and going at the church could be easily duped by what one saw. We had no material means for them to judge us. We all stood in queues for charity food, blankets, clothes and medicine. We had all rolled out of the gutter of a broken country and found ourselves deposited on the rich alluvial soil that was the church. The church picked us up in our brokenness and healed us. Teachers, engineers, artisans, accountants, nurses, managers and administrators, we all looked the same in our semi-derelict status. Yet in that sanctuary of hope the spark that every person was re-ignited, restoring people to be masters of their own destiny! Some looked upon us as the scum of the city. Our existence a bottomless enigma. Some of us absolutely stateless and the jetsam of a revolution turned cannibal! All that made us unique.

That day a candle of unquestionable belief in the possibility of freedom ignited in my awakening mind. Every moment of my life became critical and urgent. When dusk came, I found my way to a street corner near the Oriental Plaza in Fordsburg where a doctor came in his car every Thursday to dish us out some meat and vegetable soup served with bread. After having our meal we would then consult with him about our health problems and get tablets for common ailments. When my stomach was full, I stood in the queue for a course of pain killers which I safely deposited in my satchel, before walking back into the Joburg

CBD under the glare of street lights and neon signs. I drifted up the steps entering the Virgin Bar on Pritchard Street and ordered:

"One Castle Milk Stout, please!"

With my quart of beer in my hand, I sought a quiet corner by the counter and perched myself on a stool, reflecting on my life. My mind exploring the road to my release from the cynical past! I thought very hard and it came to my mind that life was not what it was but what my mind made of it. It was the state of my mind that mattered. What I chose to believe in! I pulled my notebook out of my pocket and wrote:

"Land is life! My conviction about land is important. I can choose to dig a grave or a garden for myself. Or I could build a house on it. It is my choice."

A man with a protruding belly came in and ordered a beer. I wondered what he thought about land.

Three women sat at the counter chatting to the bar lady. I tried to reason in my thoughts what they thought about land too. I gave up. I did not want to judge.

Then two men came in talking in raucous voices. I winced as if I had been hit. Their noise jarring across the peace of the bar. Both had long scars, one on the right cheek and the other on the back of the head. Their ugly eyes swept over everything in the bar and came to rest on me. I ignored them. They bought one bottle of Black Label Beer and perched on a free table next to the counter. They started sharing the bottle. I finished my beer and ordered another one. The one with the big scar on the cheek turned and said to the bar-lady:

"What does that Malalapipe want in our bar?"

"Whose bar?"

"Our bar! We drink here."

"That doesn't make it your bar."

"Why?"

"Because he drinks here too."

Then Scarface jumped up to his feet and came to me. I slid off my stool and stood measuring him.

"Hey! Malalapipe! Who said you can drink here?"

"That's not my name."

"You sleep under the bridge."

"If you're so fond of giving people names why don't you find a woman and make some babies?"

Incensed by my insult, Scarface threw a punch. I was waiting for it. I ducked and his knuckles cracked against the wall behind me. Without hitting him, he fell over a chair, rotated in mid-air and with his bones creaking crashed onto the floor, twisting weirdly in a heap like a tyrannosaurus having fits. His friend plunged into the fight. I sidestepped and he flew past tripping over the coffee table. Hitting the floor with his head he lay sprawling on the floor, eyes bulging and working his mouth without sound like a grasshopper. A bag of alcohol spewing traces of vegetables, meat, pap and Joburg beer like a broken sewage pipe. The whole bar reeked. The doorman charged into the middle of the scene and the bar-lady pointed at the two thugs, shouting:

"Throw them out!"

The bouncer extricated a whip from under the counter. He whipped one and then the other. They both howled like castrated jackals. He did not stop whipping them until they sped out of the bar, leaving their beer half-downed. I did not stop drinking. Ordering another milk stout, I took a sip and smacked my lips, satisfied with the dosage of medicine I had doled out the thugs. I was Bloggs! The man who would not be dominated by any other man's system.

Somebody punched a coin into the jukebox music machine. The atmosphere vibrated with the heavy tunes of Lucky Dube's reggae song. Impelled by the music, I floated to my feet and performed a stylish jig. The drums and the heavy bass rhythms exploded in my heart like a living bomb, the spears arching from the slurring percussions and the lead guitar tearing through my blood. Flinging her arms forward, the bar-lady moved her legs fast gliding towards me. Gyrating we danced in a sparkling circle of red, green, blue and white flooding disco lights, her face thrown backwards in a cocktail of passion. The heat increased and I was soon a shimmering explosion of waves and flesh. I danced as if there was no tomorrow. The music stopped and I downed the last contents of my beer in one swig. The bar-lady saw that I was about to leave. She brought another beer and said:

"This one is on me."

Then she made a surprising toast:

"Here's to more dances!"

When I left the Virgin Bar, I was knitting my legs. Before stepping outside, I locked with the bar-lady in a swaying hug and we both felt the outburst of heated feeling pumping wildly beneath our ribs. She did not seem affected in any measure by my sweaty skin. Planting a kiss on my lips she said:

"See you tomorrow."

That even made me more intoxicated! I could not recover from my confusion until I arrived at the church where Connie gave me another hug and with pain in her eyes said:

"You are smelling of perfume! Another woman's perfume."

Then she confounded my befuddled senses by laying a plate of pap and beef rough tripe. Sadness stole the charming light from her face. Dispirited, she went to bed. A vapid desolation sneaked into my creaking bones! And when I finally dragged myself to bed between the folding seats in the sanctuary, it was with immense turbulence in the mind. Flashing pictures of a fourteen-year-old girl with a restless soul and a quiet, striking rectitude haunted my tired inebriate eyes. Connie's kindly cute face surfacing and dissolving in the cobwebs of my mind was torture in the holy places of my temple. Closing my eyes, I regretted not having kissed her. Her smooth dimpled cheeks. Those full plum lips. War had sneaked into my body! Far away, in my stupefied sleep I heard a voice repeat itself a couple of times:

"I am Chimwene! God's whip! Sent to punish all mad and greedy people like you."

I threw a fit of misery at the harrowing thought of what kind of whip God had in store for my sins.

NINE

My mind twirled and tripped in a bewildered daze from the previous day's hangover and amorous events. On the other hand, the fact that Patience had come to me and left without knowing that I was her real father ineffably harassed my conscience. Introspection prosecuted my courage and cowardice without any shred of pity. Why did I let her go? Why had Mercy never bothered to let me know even about the pregnancy? I just wanted to be alone to think about these matters. I was also avoiding Connie and I decided to go to the Park-Station alone. I was not sure how to explain myself to her lest I should end up weaving unalterable wrong messages in her mind. A dangerous force tore into our traumatized hearts with a burning magnetism. And the last thing I desired was to lead her onto a runaway train destined over the cliff-edge. She was a combination of exquisite humanity and we flowed into each other like milk and chocolate. We were both being eaten up by the same affliction. Loneliness. And tormented by the same hunger. LOVE! Yet I was not naïve to what it could do to both of us. I had no income. No pot. No plate. Not even a stove. I had no means by which I could provide for a woman. I could have space for her in my life that time but not forever. I was already taken.

I determined to triumph and to draw happiness out of the dismal situation but now a larger, sinister cost projected. Yet, despite the host of paradoxes encumbering me from living a full life, people saw something in me. A toddler who had never spoken the word "Dad" first managed to paste it on me! Vimbai who had never known the love of a father had surprised everyone by breaking out of the tomb interring her profound feelings and opening up to me. I was the only adult person she hugged besides her boyfriend Tim. They studied and went almost everywhere together like two peas in a pod. Then my most possible daughter had come and gone without getting any shred of recognition from me. Her father! Powerful and sometimes powerless in the face of challenges, my life seemed to roll out beyond control like an odyssey that escaped from the mythical world into real life.

My beleaguered mind was vacillating between these burgeoning matrices of my vast moral dilemma when a shadow fell beside me and said:

"Why are you avoiding me?"

"I'm not avoiding you." I felt like I had a fish bone stuck in my throat.

"You're going to Park-Station alone?"

I did not respond.

"Why?"

I looked in her eyes and saw she still stocked the pain she dragged with her to bed the previous day.

"What do you think of me, Connie?"

"Amazing. A rare good man. And me?"

"A generous soul. You deserve better from life."

"Really?"

"Really. From the bottom of my heart."

"May I come with you to Park-Station?"

"You're welcome."

I felt I had to sever a vein between us. I wanted us to walk further apart from each other. Yet on that day she walked much closer to me that even the hair on my arms was curiously startled by the warmth of her bursting body. I stumbled through my words like a man lost in a deep enchanting forest whose beautiful torment I was not ready to be saved from. And my heart melted.

When we finished eating breakfast, she said:

"Take me to the Zoo Lake."

I looked in her face and saw in her bliss something very fragile which I felt it would be evil of me to break it. With a mixture of delight and fear in the back of my mind, I said:

"That would be great fun!"

The public baths at Park-Station were open when we left our table. When we had money, we would frequent them for a hot tantalizing bath in the showers. We paid five rands for a bath. Carrying my satchel and my toiletries, I entered the male section and Connie slipped into the ladies berths. When she emerged, her soft light skin had the bewitching fragrance of a field of roses. My mind swivelling in a daze, we waltzed to the church where I slid into a clean set of jeans. She effortlessly slinked into a pretty bright yellow dress that transformed her large beautiful body into an angel. Teasing me, she laughed at how I never ironed my jeans. I always slept on top of them. Now I owned a mattress and slept together with the children on the fourth floor. I just laid them nicely beneath the mattress before sliding myself under the blanket. No stress. We hooked our arms together and something I had never felt in a long time erupted inside me with shocking poetry from my head to the toes. Battling to suppress the burgeoning knot in my heart, we flowed an invisible river of brawling ardent forces to the MTN Taxi Rank where we got the taxi to the Zoo Lake.

We drifted round the therapeutic environs of the Zoo Lake shoving down the torturing pleasure in our bodies. We gave each other more of our past lives, strolled round the lake and fed the ducks with bread broken by passionate hands that instead longed for the other person. We sat close to each other on a bench like two peas in a pod and drank orange juice with straws in the corners of our tight smiling mouths. The sparkle in her brown eyes gently reflected the magma tormenting her soul. Tired of the charade she touched my chin and I touched her on the cheek, too. The jail temporarily unlocked completely. Then we laughed like nervous teenagers and looked away from each other, somehow aware of our mischief and the proximate consequences. Lying on the flourishing green lawn on our stomachs, we fed each other with ice cream and smiled, oblivious of our defective lives. When it was time to go home, we locked our hands and waltzed to Jan Smuts Road. While we stood waiting for the taxi, Connie pensively said:

"I would like to ask you something. May I?"

"Permission granted."

"What's LOVE?"

I could not speak. I had not seen it coming! Then the unexpected happened. She leaned over and planted a kiss on my cheek. Her eyes glowing in the twilight. Dazzling! Harrowing!

"What's LOVE?"

She inclined her head to one side and waited. Serious. Listening. Breathing heavily.

The words fitfully scattered out of my mouth:

"Love is a sacred movement of zealous attention, longing and true feelings of honour. Love does not doubt. Love does not judge. Love is blind to any fault. It nurtures heart, spirit and body into one fluid release of unconditional acceptance and attachment to someone. REAL LOVE leads to BLISS, GROWTH and FULFILMENT. Love is an ultimate submission of trust between man and woman that cannot be shared with a third party for when that happens the pay-off can bring about a misery exceeding death......"

She pressed her finger against my mouth, placed the other arm around my shoulder, crushing my chest against her breast. She chirped:

"Shhhhhh! Say no more SUNSHINE!"

I turned into a vacillating block of fear and delight! The place where she kissed me ablaze with a profusion of ravishing urgency. Wanting to let go of her but chained in a bizarre transitory imprisonment. Her heart beating into my heart. Her rhythm becoming mine. And mine melting into hers! She tilted backwards. Perilously.

TEN

We had just finished observing break time at the school. The social workers pushed their haughty stomachs through the open gate. Leaving their cars parked on the street.

"All children staying at the church are not safe," their spokesman was saying. "We want to move you all to nice shelters with hot water and comfortable beds. You will have good food and television. There will be no adults to abuse you like at the church."

"Will there be schools?" one child asked.

"You will go to nearby schools. This school is not registered."

"Who will look after us?" Another child asked.

"There will be caregivers to cook and wash for you."

"What if we don't go?"

"You will have to go because this school will be closed."

The children spoke with one voice:

"We will not leave our school and our teachers and we will have no other caregivers besides our own."

Then they all ran, climbed over the walls, jumped into the neighbouring yard and melted into the heart of the city, leaving the social workers shocked and dejected. The children's torrential escape was a loud statement of their covenant to stay together. They could not see themselves separated in their struggles. Neither in their healing nor in the re-alignment of their lives. Their refusal to be moved stunned the social workers and their allies.

We did not even know where the children went. We soon understood that not everyone was to know. I spoke with Dan and we decided to go to Boxburg to see a labour broker we had heard of. I got a job in a factory where I learned spray painting and stayed in a former apartheid prison. We slept on bunk beds like prison inmates and we were forced to go to church every Sunday as if in a reformatory school. Two months into our new jobs, we heard that the labour broker was collecting a third of our wages and the spirit of freedom again rose within us that we wanted to leave that place.

"You can't move out."

"Why?"

"You owe the pastor that money."

"What money?"

"The money he's collecting."

"That's absurd!" I exploded.

"That's exploitation!" Dan roared. "We'll move out."

"Then you'll have to quit your jobs as well."

"We'll not surrender our jobs."

"That's not negotiable."

"We'll defy that."

"He's the one who got you that job. That's the deal."

"We signed no deal! Besides a third of our wages is just outrageous."

"Shape up or ship out!"

"He can't have the money deducted forever."

"And we'll not live in this prison forever."

"Whatever! The choice is yours."

Shaken but not defeated, we retired to our prison beds. A couple of weeks later, I got a phone call on my cell-phone:

"You are urgently wanted in Soweto."

"I'm wanted in Soweto?"

"Yes! You and Dan."

"For what?"

"To work with the children from the Central Methodist Church."

Dan and I kissed good bye our jobs in Boxburg and landed our ever probing brains on Soweto. We arrived in the middle of the night to thunderous shouts of welcome from the children:

"The intellectuals are here!" somebody shouted.

"Yes! Welcome to the intellectuals."

"Show then their room!"

"Show them their desks!"

Ironically, we were shown no room. Neither were there any desks for us. All the rooms were full. We were given a mattress each and shown the corridor for our bedroom. We both refused to sleep in there. In defiance, we floated downstairs to the Lecture Room where we threw down our mattresses and bags on the carpet and scratching our erudite heads, paced up and down the vast chamber of learning. We did not care for any room. The Lecture Room became an instant familiar territory to us. We loved it. And it did not surprise us when, later, Matt followed us from the church. He burst upon us all face lit up and beaming with the second publication of our writers' forum magazine in his hands. We all took to working and reading in that place like ducks took to water.

And so we were overwhelmed every day by the enthusiastic learners. Yet from our colleagues we earned a welcome not less than vapid. A great deal had changed since our temporary divorce with the children. The building would be frequently smothered by the oppressive smell of marijuana and cigarette smoke. Vulgar diatribe tumbling out of the children's mouths without any respect. There was an urgent need to calibrate some kind of basic order and modes of behaviour in the place. We discovered that Ajas was now sniffing glue. He would slouch around with a glazed look, smiling obscenely.

"What's wrong Ajas?"

"I'm a dunderhead!"

"Who told you that?"

"My caregiver."

"Why do you believe him?"

"Because I can't have good grades in school."

"Don't believe him! You are good at football! You can be a soccer star. Believe in yourself. You are a good runner. Believe in all those good things you can do. Don't throw everything away."

"My father, too, doesn't believe in me. He doesn't love me. Why did he abandon me in this place? I don't care anymore!"

Playing truant from school, smoking marijuana and sniffing glue Ajas continued with his life. Then one day he left and never came back. Dan and I went looking for him and found him in another children's home in Hillbrow. He stayed in that home for a while. Then he tumbled out onto the street. I was overwhelmed with this young person's loss of self-esteem and the subsequent downward spiral in his life. One day we visited his new home under the bridge on the street. He saw us from a distance and ran away. Yet Dan and I did not give up on the children. He gave them extra lessons in History and I taught them English. We assisted them with their homework in other subjects, too, whenever we could. And the vast spaces in our minds that came with an inquisitive disposition expanded in abundance in that environment. We affiliated ourselves with many organizations and enrolled on a Personal Growth and Counselling Course which irrevocably changed the course of my life.

Soon we noticed that these children were a promising walking business boom with various child organisations vying for strategic positions. They all wanted control of the children. The children suffered a great deal and sometimes went without food while well-fed social workers and these organizations wrangled. It was a dismaying game of politics. My heart bled when the children went to school without food. They would eat at the school only and sometimes went to bed without having supper at all. I felt sympathy for the girls who were the most vulnerable in that group. On some occasions, when they went for the whole day without having any meal, I bought the girls bread for supper from my own purse. We sat in several meetings with the government social workers from the beginning of the year until in its middle when I blew up a bomb in front of one of the social workers:

"You people are hypocrites!"

"What?"

"You're hypocrites!"

"Why?"

"I don't see any goodwill in all your presence in this place."

"Why are you saying that?"

"Because your talk-shops don't interest us anymore."

"We're working very hard to move things."

"Are you?"

"Yes! We are."

"Wait until we march on you with our children. Very soon, you'll see!"

"What!"

"We'll march from Constitution Hill holding our placards with our children in school uniform and then we'll come to your offices where we'll deliver our petition to your minister."

I saw fear spring in his eyes and I enjoyed it. That day, he did not stay for long at the centre when he heard the threat. About three days later, the social worker called me to a meeting with a United Nations (UN) director working together with the European Union (EU). Surprisingly, there were some funds meant for our project sitting which had already been partly diverted to other projects in Limpopo.

"How much are we talking about?"

"R5 000 000,00!"

"What figure are we working with now?"

"R2 400 000,00."

"What happened with the rest of the money?"

"I don't want to talk about it. I am only one month old in my job and I cannot account for what happened before my appointment."

It boggled my mind indeed. We then applied our minds to set up a plan of action with the remaining figure of R2 400 000,00. Then my colleague and I were strangely nudged out of that committee. It did not surprise me. They renovated the children's hostel and erected another building to cater for those studying at the University of Southern Africa (UNISA). The building was never completed.

We sat in countless meetings to develop the children's lives but nothing was ever done to upgrade the social welfare of the Child and Youth Care Workers. In one meeting when the caregivers complained of the R500,00 salary, they were earning at the time, they were threatened with dismissal. Then they requested to have their training completed but nothing ever happened. It was sad to see people working hard as they did without any meaningful change in their lives. A donor came to me and said:

"I can raise money to complete the building and for you to do the next level of your child and youth care course."

"That's very kind. Thank you!"

Four months down the line, I said to him:

"We're still waiting to complete our course."

"But I thought the money, together with the other funds to complete the unfinished building, were deposited in the church's bank account. That was about three months ago." Nothing ever happened. Disgusted, the donor left. He never came back.

The social workers were still determined to remove our children and place them in shelters. Owen asked for re-unification with his family members back home. They took him away to a shelter in Musina. Three months later, Samanyika also asked to be re-united with his family back home. Again they moved him from the centre to Musina. A full month later, Samanyika turned up in Soweto with broken shoes. He had walked back long distances until boils broke out in his feet. Then he saw a lorry loaded with sacks of oranges coming to Joburg and asked for a free ride in the back. He had grown as thin as a reed. We were ineffably shocked to see him in that deplorable state. We dished for him a meal for two people each time the children ate. My heart broke to pieces when he recounted that he had left Owen living on the streets in Musina. Owen was surviving by foraging the dust bins for groceries' receipts which he sold to people. His customers were cross-border shoppers who had different reasons for not having receipts for their groceries. The common motive was seeking to deflate the cost of their goods so as to avoid paying customs duty. I thought:

"What a strange way to survive for a kid!"

Then the children, incensed by the suffering of their two brothers had a fight with the social workers at the Sci-Bono where they were now attending school. One social worker had to scamper for his life like a mouse and flee in his government car. The swarm of children flew at him, the sleeves of their shirts rolled up and their fists itching to sting him black and blue. The incident overwhelmed the social workers with a nameless fear that they all forgot the centre ever existed. The social workers got under my skin like leeches, too. Once a sixteen-year-old girl attempted suicide by taking an overdose of tablets. She collapsed! One of the social workers was there. He simply leaped over her prostrate body, tore down the stairs and vanished in his government car as if nothing had happened. I was shocked by the social worker's conduct as we had no car at the centre. We had to call for an ambulance.

The hypocrisy and the interplay of politics amongst the authorities at the expense of the children ate into my heart like a river of napalm. I sensed greed, self and political interest. An absolute lack of genuine good will in the best interest of the vulnerable that I sometimes saw going to bed hungry! Because of food shortages at the centre, many girls were forced into sexual relationships with the boys. I caught them several times cuddling in dark places and on the stairs in the middle of the night. Young as they were, most of them already knew the anatomy of man and woman like they were forty years old. Because we had few girls in the centre, that breakfast and lunch were rarely served, the politics of the stomach dictated most of the relationships. Most of the girls were coerced into having multiple partners for the sake of survival.

*

One afternoon Dan came to me, his face heavily tortured. Sad words toppled on his quivering lips:

"Ajas is dead!"

"What?"

"Ajas is DEAD!" he repeated harshly.

"What happened?"

"He was run over by a refuse truck!"

Time locked in stillness. Dan's voice dragged out like a broken record in my ears.

"They said he was high on glue. The refuse truck came around the corner. He ran after it. Imitating what its crew does. He tried leaping on to it. He missed the handle and his footing. He spiralled in the air hitting the tarmac with his head. And the rear wheels came. There was a terrible explosion. The driver of the truck braked. Too late! Blood, bone, flesh, and brain fragments lay splattered all over the tarmac. Some stuck on the wheels and chassis of the vehicle. They say it was such a ghastly sight. Two women passing by who witnessed the accident collapsed with shock. They had to be revived by the paramedics."

I lost my mind. In my eyes, I saw Ajas reduced to a mere puddle of horror evaporating on the street. Nameless anger poured napalm all over my heart. An endless current of gagging self-blame seized me. I gasped like one drowning. My jaws locked! Teeth chattering with shock! Dan had to take me by the hand like a lost child. In a tortured silence exploding with sighs he led me to Shanty Town, where we drenched our shock and sorrow in shake-shakes of Joburg Beer.

ELEVEN

I saw myself float out of the gate of my house. I was looking for my children but the whole place breathed of desolation. The scene collapsed and I found myself in the belly of a musty grey forest that belonged to a long bygone era. I was an alien in that forest and then a stranger to myself. Stupefied by my own agility, spidery hold on boulders and balancing feats. I was walking. Then crawling like a gobsmacked ant. Scrabbling up and plummeting down from giant warped cob-webbed trees. One moment I would be looking for my family and the next I searched for myself. Then I came to a scary, expansive meandering river and saw my son. He stood knee-deep in the water, under a lush gargantuan tree with his back to me. He was setting a trap in the mouth of a bird's nest that hung at the tip of a gnarled bare branch.

I glided towards my son. Suddenly two diabolical loops slithered and convoluted up in front of him in evident conflict. They turned out to be snakes locked in fierce battle. A seething river of torrential fear burst in my heart like flooding lava. Shock jumped in his eyes like a firecracker. He dug his feet deeper into the mud and he was a spinning faulty kite, zigzagging in aborted ascension. Then he came down crashing on his back onto a log floating in the water. He held onto the log. It tore away, a bobbing carpet splitting into infinite writhing hairs. Then all the water around him, his clothes and hair turned alive with writhing white bean-like hairs. Maggots. The log became a mangled relic of a man. Tearing apart in large chunks, nodding and colliding with each other in the water. The maggots swam into my son's mouth, nose and ears. Horrified, I leapt into the river and started swimming towards him. Then my son disappeared in the black mud of the river. I could only see the dead man. I looked into the eyeless visage of the splitting corpse and recognised my face. I had stumbled into my own dead body! Frantically, I called out my son's name telling him that it was only me in the river. Then I got a glimpse of him standing on the bank, trembling and fearfully staring back at me. Something I could not tell glinted like half formed lightning in his eyes. He nearly toppled his head off his shoulders shaking it. And then he took off, a leaping shadow in the wind.

I came out of sleep my hands flailing in the wind. Fighting like an overturned mantis drowning in a pool. I had fallen asleep sitting on a chair in the sunshine. By the lawn outside the Lecture Room. I was sweating profusely that had someone said they had just fished me out of the river people would not have doubted it. The stench of my corpse in the dream was still stuck in my nostrils when Dan came to me. I declared:

"Very soon, I'll be going home."

"What?"

"I will be going home to see my family."

I saw Connie gliding by and I called out to her. She came to where we were sitting.

"I've got something for you."

"What's it?"

"A job opportunity."

I gave her the piece of paper I took out of my pocket. I had been holding onto it for two days.

"Call them now."

She called and was given an interview date. A couple of days later she went for the interview and got the job. It was a stay-in position. I felt relieved. I feared the irrevocable power of what was developing between us. She set off reluctantly. But it was a better paying job than the voluntary work we were doing. Yet, no sooner had she gone than she called and said:

"Hey Sunshine! I miss you with tears on my cheeks."

I did not know what to say. My heart pounded with a yearning rhythm that threw my mind into a giddy turmoil, knees melting like butter. I missed her dreadfully, too. Then after three weeks of inner turbulence, I felt rescued when a man came looking for her.

"Who're you?"

"I'm her husband."

"She's left this place."

"Do you know where she went?"

"Phone her."

"I don't have her number."

"I can get it for you."

I drifted away into another room and called her.

"Hi Connie."

"Hi Bloggs"

"Someone's here looking for you."

"Who's that?"

"Your husband. May you please talk to him?"

"No!"

"Please!"

"He walked out on me as if I were a worthless piece of rubbish."

Soon after speaking those words, she hung up. I felt sorry for that man. I went back to him and laying on the table in front of him a piece of paper with his wife's cell-phone number I said:

"Good luck!"

*

One day I sat in the Lecture Room reading a book. My phone rang and answering it I heard an unfamiliar hollow voice that spoke like the wind against the open mouth of a bottle.

"My friend gave me this number and said that I could call if I wanted to speak to someone."

"You can tell me what is bothering you."

"I want to talk to someone before I die."

"May you kindly tell me your name?"

"Melissa," she said, hesitating. He staccato voice reaching my ears in a tired cold whisper.

"What have you done, Melissa?"

"I've written my last letter to my siblings. I'm lying in a tub filled with hot water and I have cut my wrists with a razor blade. I just finished snorting my cocaine. I am feeling high. And I don't feel like living anymore. I'm a bloody loser!"

"A loser is a label that sits on your identity like a parasite. It becomes bigger by feeding on you. It sucks all the nutrients in your body leaving you thin. As you become thinner, it covers the bigger part of your body insinuating itself as part of your identity. But in reality it is not! Melissa is one big living thing and loser is another different thing that depends on you to survive. Melissa doesn't need Loser to survive but Loser can't survive without Melissa. You therefore are not a loser at all. Whatever it is, we can go through it together."

"You think so? Why?"

"Because this is very important for you and your life. Where are you?"

"In a hotel."

"Where is the hotel?"

"In Johannesburg."

"Which part of Johannesburg?"

"I don't know."

"What is the name of the hotel?"

"I don't know."

"May I have your telephone number?"

I wrote it down on a piece of paper.

"What is the address?"

"I don't know."

"What is the name of the street?"

"Commissioner."

"What is the other nearest street?"

"I don't know."

"Describe any other building you can see through your window."

"I can't see anything, I'm in the tub."

"Any other place you can remember?"

"Gandhi Square."

"Do you have the hotel numbers on your phone?"

"No."

"Can you get out of the tub?"

"No. It's cold outside."

"Listen carefully because we'll do this together, I want you to remove the plug from the drain, now. Okay?"

"I can try."

"May you please do that?"

"Yeah! It's coming out now."

"Did you lock your doors?"

"I think so."

"All of them?"

"Yeah."

"I am sending an emergency response team to the hotel. I want you to press the cuts on your wrist. Can you do that?"

"I feel very weak."

"Now I am going to disconnect this call to send the emergency response team. Keep your phone with you. Unlock all the doors. I'll call you back quite soon."

"Yeah!"

Immediately, I called the suicide emergency rescue team, the police and the fire brigade. When I was sure that help was on the way, I called her again.

"Hello Melissa! I am back."

"I didn't think you would call back."

"I like to keep my promises. I sent a team of people to fetch you."

"Thank you."

"This is important. I am wondering if you would like us to go through this together."

She spoke very slowly and her faint voice seemed trapped behind a thick screen. She sounded drowsy, distracted and exhausted!

"I'm sick and tired of this world. My father was a drug addict. My mother was a drug addict. So, you see this thing I was born with it in my blood. I lost my job because of drugs. Now I have sold all my property. I sold my computer two months ago and last week I sold my bed. Two days ago I was evicted from my flat because I owed the landlord a lot of money in arrears. I am broke and no one can save me from this wretched life. This world is too much for me. I can't cope and I'm done fighting a losing battle. I've always been miserably afraid of myself. People! Life! And failure! Since I was a child. I always wanted to be someone in life. Because I never got good grades in school, my achievements amounted to nothing. My life just a contemptible void. I couldn't get myself a job. Someone had to do it for me. I always have been this despicable weak bitch! Afraid even of my lily-livered self. The person I could be is only an ideal. I went to see a doctor about it. He called it the illusory fear of death. Death? I never feared death! I started using drugs to deal with it. My siblings could not understand me and at school people called me a freak…I felt like running away from them all. Angry, bitter, self-loathing and broken…I didn't know I was a spineless jerk harming myself and the people who loved me. Running away from the real world. My drugs all the time…"

She was in the middle of moaning her story and self-deprecation when I heard the sound of a breaking door, footsteps and voices. Someone grabbed the phone from her and said:

"Yes! We are the paramedics and now attending to her," then the line went dead. Fifteen minutes later the emergency rescue team called me back.

"We've booked her into Johannesburg hospital," the caller said.

I breathed a sigh of relief, fished out my notebook from the pocket and scribbled:

I'll live life in its impeccable beauty. I will be impervious to everything that tears the spirit apart and I will not live my life trapped in the shadows of life. Laughter will be my best medicine. Happiness my irrevocable choice. And reason be my drug.

*

Sometimes I feel my life is still a huge dislocation. My head spins like I have been turned into a pendulum and swinging up-side down with my head pointing to the ground. I wonder where my world has gone? Where my children's world is going? I still feel the despairing vestiges hanging on the hem of my life. Waiting to pounce with a shade of depression! I am resolved not to bow to any of it. All the scenes of my broken life that shudder like a blurred television channel that cannot hold. Then I feel it gone. My life gone. My life without me.

I have been going to sleep alone for a long time. The dreams come pouring. Nightmares that stick a blade into my sleep. I wake up. My mind flowing with the terror of the unknown. I feel like one tossing in the streets of a flooded city of skyscrapers. Each moment an eternity.

Sometimes I walk out into the night. My legs pumping like pistons. I feel the world beckoning to me. Calling me. Needing me. Needing you. Calling you. Asking for your life with you. Asking for my life with me.

The voice is speaking. Saying things that are palatable side by side with those that are unsayable. The truth about us that we deny is us.

The blood on the tomb of lies erected on the tarmac of life and reality screams an epitaph:

Here lies one
Who was us
That was never us

PART 3

ONE

I lay still on the mattress. A beam of sunlight arrived through the window and fell softly across my blankets. It came alongside the sounds of chirping birds, road traffic and voices of labourers working outside. The sounds of creation. Creation never stopped. People woke up every day and made journeys in the creation of a better life. The earth trembled with men's machines at work. Men excavating treasure from the bowels of the earth! Men eating into mountains, spaces and forests to create roads, build factories, houses and places of entertainment. Men never stopped dreaming. Men never stopped creating wealth. And I listened to everything without stopping. Ever listening to the new creation within myself. I was aware of my phone vibrating under the pillow. It was a message from Connie:

"Hi Sunshine! I miss you with a tearing hunger for your lips on my cheeks. I wish you were the first person I met."

"That's dangerous," I replied.

"Why?"

"The truth is painful."

"What does that mean?"

"Our vows are not with each other. We already have both pledged ourselves to other people."

"It is that terrible truth corrupting my happiness. Please spare me that pain for just this one moment. It's painful. A cruelty and an injustice to need. I hate to say it but not saying it will make it worse."

"If it's not painful for us, it'll be painful for other people."

"He's already left me three times."

"I'm sorry."

"I'd rather stay alone."

"That's a tough decision."

"The world won't stop greeting me because I don't have a husband."

"It's hard when one doesn't have a choice."

"You've made me happy. Though you still have your wife as a choice. The tragedy is not that I can't have you but that it cannot be changed."

"I'm sorry Connie," I did not know what to say.

"This conversation's killing my heart. Yet I must speak."

"We'll not deliberately feed lies to ourselves, Connie. We're two feeble moths magnetised by a fire whose bewitching heat beckons to a scorching fate."

Immediately my cell-phone buzzed. It was Connie, again.

"Hi Connie," I breathed into the phone.

"Hi Sunshine. I just want to let you know that I'm nothing away from you." Her syrupy bubbling voice thick with emotion. She hung up. What a shattering silence! I groaned. My bones creaked. And futility was a river of bile burning the bottom of my heart.

I rose and folded my blankets. I had come to an incontrovertible decision. My bags were already packed and waiting in the corner. An illusory life had not always been mine. From the time I had to stand alone in my thirteenth year when my father died. Summoned by ruthless fate to enter the scary school of Jurisprudence of Survival. Of which I embraced without reserve its full curriculum! It was a necessary evil that I had to brave through. With my father gone its ineluctable byways of gruelling sorrow, loneliness, financial bottlenecks and futility were an amalgam I had to accept. I learned to curb both my bitterness and desires. I learned life was not what it was but what I made of it. And to pursue my potential when I saw the floodgates loose and open! Through self-transformation, I was exceedingly altered into a creature of instinct.

Books became my best friends. Chased out of school because I had not paid my school fees, I would go and bury myself in books in the municipality library. Barred from entering the school gate because I had no school shoes, I went back home, wrapped my foot in bandages and for the whole term attended school like that. For three years I went to high school without a school jersey. When I finally got the money, it was not enough to buy one of my size. Loathed as much by any other boy I could only get a small girl's jersey. It was very tight and I had to keep pulling it down at least closest to my waist it could get. Then because the arms were awkwardly short, I would pull the cuffs up to my elbows. It looked as if I had stolen it from a first grader in primary school. Other school children made me a source of ridicule and laughter. I did not mind. My responses turned their damp wit into naught. Regularly I would strut up and down between the rows of desks acting like a clown. Choking girls with laughter and getting derisive comments from jealous boys who saw how my comic acts endeared me with the girls.

One day our English teacher glided into the classroom, her face cracking into a splendid smile, her big eyes beaming on me. She said something and raised my essay flashing all the pages for everyone to see. There was not even a single correction she had made in that essay. And she had written on top of it "Computer Work!" The essay was passed from envying hand to marvelling hand around the classroom. The teacher made me stand up with the waist of my jersey kissing the navel. I was still standing bemused like that when the girls rushed at me. Tearing away the jersey I was raping, they bombarded me with kisses and hugs. The whole class exploding with shouts of celebration and applause. Battering my ears. I staggered like a giant. Glimpses of my detractors sitting ineffectually with stunned faces swam in the air like goblins stripped of charm. Across them fitfully ripped with stupid grins of torture. I was overwhelmed and I did not know what to do with myself.

"You don't hug a jersey!" Rutendo shouted. Her glowing guileless slanted eyes burning holes in my heart. Subtly murdering my heart.

"You hug girls! Real skin and flesh!" Rudo tweeted. Her dark heart-shaped face perforating into two enchanting dimples in the centre of her cheeks.

Smiling at those nostalgic days of my invincibility I could not wind the clock back to, my love was roused. Thus on that morning, soon after exchanging those vastly

poignant messages with Connie, I took a decision unalterable as the love behind it. And unbending as its dangers.

I floated into the shower and had the water lick my body
with a stinging new life. I rubbed my skin with a revitalis-
ing lotion, combed my short hair and pulling my jeans from
under the mattress, wriggled into them. I never breathed a
word about where I was going. My gait sombrely unruffled,
I just left, the candle burning in the radical chamber of my
heart unwavering. At the Powerhouse Station, I selected a
bus and approached the driver.

"Hello driver!"

"Hello papa!"

"Do you accept passengers who don't have passports?"

"Where're you going?"

"Harare."

"Do you see that man holding a ticket book?"

"Yes."

"Go and buy your ticket from him. Also get your luggage
weighed and loaded onto the bus."

"What about the passport?

"You already have one," he said laughing like ripping
cardboard.

I bought a ticket, weighed in my luggage and glided to
the seat the conductor directed me. I whipped out my cell-
phone to send Dan a message.

"I have made up my mind. I am going home to see my
wife and my children."

"You must be joking."

"I am on the bus right now. Approaching the Musina
Border Post."

"What? You must be mad!"

"I have lived with madness to be happy. Without it, my sadness multiplies."

"They will murder you!"

"They have already stolen sunshine out of my life."

"Did you hear protesters burned a warehouse at the border?

"I'm no arsonist."

"They'll create something for you and you'll have a dog's chance squeezing out of it."

"I'll not spend my life in servile fear of thugs."

"Where will you stay?"

"Everywhere is my home."

*

I thought I should send a message my wife as well:

"I am coming home now but tell no one."

"Is that true?"

"I'm on the bus right now."

"Are you not afraid?"

"My children need me."

"Life has been rough without you my husband."

"I miss you all."

"Your children can hardly remember you my husband."

"I feel bad."

"You had to go away so that we can see you again."

"Remember, don't tell anyone of my homecoming."

"I won't my husband,"

"I love you all."

"We love you, too, my husband."

*

I tried thinking of what could become of me. Arrest and trumped-up charges. Poisoning. Hit and run accident. Torture. Abduction. And detention. The list could grow a tail. Yet my ruptured soul felt no other way. I craved to see my loved ones. If I were going to start healing in my life, I had to stop hugging my jersey like what Rutendo had said during the celebration of my essay. Nothing could wipe my convictions into the dust bin. The die was cast. I had to see my wife and my children. Even if the sky were to fall down. It had to be.

TWO

I arrived. My wife and children wrapped all over me. Their bodies bursting with happiness and warmth. They nearly tripped me at the gate with the power of their joy and inextricable hugs. Clinging to me like human figures made of glue, they poured their affection without end. One could be forgiven for thinking that it looked like they feared that if they did let go of me, I might disappear into the crisp morning air. But my last-born son stood alone. Confused, timid and hesitant. Not sure which one was his father between the driver of the truck I had hired and myself. He was just holding his hands together and smiling with ineffable happiness, for when I left him, he was only four years old. Now, he was twelve. I broke the distance between us and hugged him, pouring out all the love for him that had been trapped in my body. Slowly I let go of him. I cast glances around me. We had all grown into strangers. Yet tears of happiness glistened like miniature Christmas bulbs on every cheek. Tears of remembrance, aching sorrow and abandonment. Tears of physical reconnection and the coming to an end of drought. My heart exploding with emotions, I could not move.

With gigantic effort, I forced myself forward. Rusted, the gate reproached me on its broken hinges. The driveway had disappeared and the garden told the tragic story of my absence. Paint was peeling off the outside walls of the house. My throat bursting with burning emotion, I walked to the back of the house. The tap outside was broken. The earth all around it turned to mud with dripping water. Someone had tied it with a piece of bicycle tube to keep it from bursting out. I plodded into the house and lowered myself into a broken seat. The paint on the walls was peeling off, too. In the bedroom, the wardrobe doors hung precariously with two of them missing. I was depressed. In my forced absence, I had unkindly neglected my family. But it was lovely to see them in their home. Pleasant to observe that all my three sons were genially wild with happiness and so courteous. Thank God they had not become wild dissolute scoundrels without a name in my absence.

The curse of decay lay sprawling upon the country, the fetid breath of death and despair everywhere. The roads were tattered ribbons of tarmac with large gawking evil eyes taunting the traffic. The rule that people should drive on the left-hand side of the road no longer applied. Cars meandered on what was left of the road which looked like it had been bombed-out in a devastating war. The government was really in a state of war against its own people. When I passed through the city centre, I heard some people saying:

"This country must be closed."

"And be re-opened like it never existed."

"Yet it has fabulous people."

"Very peaceful and long-suffering."

"Cowards!"

"Maybe. But war dehumanizes people. Our government is bringing war to its people."

"It is breaking us and plundering our resources."

"We've gone through it already. We all saw it during the liberation struggle when they killed innocent people. They say that these were casualties of war which we all should forget. How could we just bury the truth like that?"

"How could we when the regime continues to murder all the voices of reason? People disappear and they treat them as if they've gone on holiday when they know that they've tortured and killed them."

"But we don't have to be like them."

"The Global Political Agreement didn't help anyone."

"It helped the politicians. Now they eat together and continue to buy expensive cars and properties, yet we have no medicines in the hospitals. When they're sick, they go to South Africa, Malaysia and China where they're building vast riches for themselves using public funds."

"Even the opposition has joined the gravy train."

"They both don't deserve to rule."

"It was a bad deal!"

"No bad deal is a good deal. People must claim their power back, they've ceded everything to the politicians who continue to deceive them."

I saw people selling the same things everywhere and I wondered who was buying from whom. They cast furtive glances over their shoulders all the time as if they were looking for someone to grab and force to make a purchase.

But it was the police that they were worried about. They would come and arrogantly deprive the vendors of their wares. They were actually robbing them and taking the goods to decorate and feed their children in their homes.

The following day, I was walking along the road with my wife when someone saw me and said:

"Oh! You're back!"

"Yes. I'm back."

"Now we know why the protests have started again."

"Sorry, I know nothing about that."

I couldn't believe my ears. I had arrived in the middle of the protests. On the previous day, sixteen people had been arrested in my area. Their eyes were everywhere looking out for people who spoke against them like me. Feeling unsafe, I walked away talking to my wife:

"He's mad."

"I don't like the look of this."

"Why?"

"Last time they came and broke our gate."

"What?"

"It was before the elections. They came and said that if they lost in this constituency, our house was going to be one of the first houses to burn."

"Bastards!"

"They are! And very proud of it. They don't look at us as people anymore."

"They wanted to make this country a one party state and when we voted no in the referendum, they started hating everyone."

"They started war against the people."

"And endorsed widespread looting for their comrades."

"I'm worried, my husband."

"What?"

"You heard that man. They haven't forgotten about you. And soon they'll be coming after you."

*

I said to my wife:

"I am going out to see the country."

"Be careful my husband," she admonished.

I had always wanted to cross the river of bitterness, this Harare's flood of hegemony and hate. I longed to rise above my broken heart with a confidence that soared on eagle-wings, to break free, celebrate the lives of my children and leave a legacy of my own. Yet they would not allow us to be happy without lowering ourselves into servile worship of their patronage. Dazed, I moved around the country. I was appalled with what I saw. I saw a woman sleeping under the eaves of a hut whose thatch was broken and threatening to collapse and bury her. I lifted one corner of the dirty gauze of a blanket covering what was left of her and said:

"How are you feeling?"

"I'm getting ready to die."

I held out my hand touching her forehead and said:

"Your body is very hot. You have a temperature."

"How can I not be? I have no food. The shops closed a long time ago. My husband died last year. My son went to South Africa a long time ago and we've had no news of him. Maybe he died in the xenophobic violence, too. Who knows? Everybody is fleeing the country because of the government. People are afraid to speak out because of fear. Many people who spoke the truth have been brutally killed, disappeared or have been maimed for life. The brazen emperor moves around like a demented naked witch. And the people just look. Afraid to lift a finger against him. Even to tell him that he is not wearing any clothes at all."

She paused, her body and breathing gripped in the throes of impending death. I poured some water into a cup from a clay-pot meekly keeping her company. I sat down in the dust. Her gourd of a head rolling on my legs. I tilted the contents into her foaming mouth.

"Did you go to the hospital?"

"I've been there countless times. They say there's no medicine. There's no use going there. I'll just spread my mat here every day and wait for death to come. I'm tired of fighting and there's no food. I don't want to live anymore. I wish I can die this very moment."

I saw piteously emaciated figures, consumed by illness, hunger and resentment for their own government. Skin without flesh clinging on fragile bones. They were forgotten souls preparing for total oblivion! Some of them did not know what their minds were saying anymore.

"I'm getting better now. I ate a whole goat last night."

"My wife came back from heaven. She brought me a plate of porridge this morning."

"Very soon I'll be okay. Then I'll go to the in-laws and ask for my wife. I'll ask her to forgive me. And we'll be happy together again."

In the shade of a mango tree, I saw a man lying on his back. There were some chickens pecking together in the dust. I came upon them so suddenly that the crunching sound of my approaching feet scattered them in all directions like popcorn. One of them ran over his collapsing chest and he cried out in a faint tortured reedy voice:

"Help! The cows are running over my chest."

I chased the chickens away and perched on the ground next to him.

"I don't know why they keep trampling all over me with their hoofs because I can't eat them anymore. Why don't they let me die in peace?"

"What's ailing you?"

"I'm HIV positive. A couple of weeks ago the doctors diagnosed me with tuberculosis."

"Are you taking any medication?"

"I got it two days ago. But I don't have any food."

"Whose chickens are those?"

"They're my brother's chickens. He has already given me one to pay for the drugs at the clinic."

"You paid with a chicken?"

"Yes. I paid with a chicken. Now I don't have money for food. I'm just taking drugs. There's fire all over in my body."

Having bought a chicken for the sick man from his brother, I let my woeful feet guide me elsewhere and left. I walked on through more barren lands and past derelict homesteads until coming into the forlorn shadow of a mountain that stretched out across the west. The dreadful silence was occasionally broken by very few birds poignantly chirping and flying around the dusty small bushes. All the big trees had been cut down for firewood. Everywhere I looked, the rhythm of nature had patently suffered a tremendous stroke from the desperate activities of man. Strangely, my ears could make out in low-spirited disharmony five or six different despairing choruses being sung. Curious, I hastened forward and stumbled upon a sprawling graveyard full of freshly dug and covered graves. The voices I heard were distraught groups of families and friends burying their dead. Their grim facial expressions replete with shadows of suffering, I saw in their eyes doomed broken souls, surrender, pain and a nameless terror. The shadow of a fearful silent question kept spreading and fading in their faces which seemed to say:

"Now, who's next?"

I turned to go with a part of the grief all those people were sharing. A cloud moved temporarily blocking the sun. I looked up and saw the handwriting in the sky:

"Lowest life expectancy in the world is here."

The imposing road of the people's suffering dropped me into a valley of scattered huts and tin shacks leaning in the whipping wind. I walked through a sea of grey sandy soil sparsely populated by dying malnourished maize plants, some of them already broken. A failed crop. Nothing to harvest at all. The wind picked the dust up in cruel gusts and tossed it into my face. I saw a woman rebuilding her broken shack alone. No doubt we had become a failed state. Absolutely.

"Where's your husband?"

"He went to a political rally and never came back."

"This land is not good. Did you harvest anything?"

"Something like a joke. They've grabbed all the good land for themselves and their friends. The emperor's wife took over all the citrus estates. She distributed some of them to her acolytes. Now she's taken over possession of the dam supplying water to all the surrounding estates. They've seized all the dairy cows that the milk we buy now comes from them. They want to own all the industries in the country. Next time they'll charge us for the air we breathe."

"When did you start staying here?"

"After Operation *Murambatsvina*[1] five years ago. My husband was a welder running an informal business. We were happy then. We had food, electricity and everything. Then they demolished our brick house and drove us into this heap of squalor. There are no toilets. No clean water. When it rains, we sleep standing up like cows in a muddy kraal. Our children don't go to school anymore. One died of pneumonia that winter when they demolished our home. I will never forget the harshness of that winter. The government promised us houses but after five years they have built only eighteen houses in a place where we have more than three thousand families. Those houses were given to loyal people in the militia, police and other law enforcement organs. We all have lost our livelihoods and hope. They've turned us into dirt."

"Now, what does your husband do?"

"*Anokiyakiya*."[2]

---

[1] Otherwise known as "Operation Clean up the Filth," was the government's crackdown on illegal structures in 2005. A move largely seen by the opposition and analysts as punishment meant for those who did not vote for the ruling party.

[2] Shona word for doing odd jobs and even illegal activities to survive.

"When he gets money we buy *marambaimakashinga*[3]."

*

The nation spun in an unending spiral of chicanery and power. The ruling party had painted its ghastly masterpiece of political ruin and despair! I saw the national skeleton of once an enterprising people. A nation of people who before their hardships had been looking even outside their country for better opportunities and trade. Informal traders went and sold their goods in South Africa, Zambia, Mozambique, Malawi, Namibia and Tanzania. Now our currency swallowed by inflation people traded with each other until it was wiped out of existence. Replaced by the South African Rand and the American dollar. It was sad seeing them broken, bruised and battered the way they were.

Once the whole nation basked in their creative glory. The country better known as "The Bread Basket of Africa." Its capital baptized "Sunshine City." Change murmured an amazing story in their communities. In their astonishing resourcefulness, the people moulded beauty out of the sludge of poverty. Then a tyrannical madness launched the blackest cloud of hatred and malice over their heads. Tired of the lies and looting the people voted against the arrogant gang stealing their wealth. For the first time the heartless looters were challenged and became schizophrenic.

---

[3]Shona word for maize half ground into chunks. Sarcastic euphemism coined after government's propaganda for people to persevere under the prevailing economic hardships.

Paranoid, denying and resenting the people's choice, they stepped out of the mist one wintry grey morning. They brought bulldozers and razed to the ground a burgeoning thrifty life out of existence! Women untimely gave birth in the cold and babies died. The unprotected were gang-raped. Some fragile elderly people were brought down by heart attacks. Unsupported and desperate, many scuttled back to their rural areas where the system condemned them to further incomprehensible persecution and torture. Because they came from the urban areas where the ruling party had been whipped in the elections, they were branded traitors and outcasts. Barred from the communities of their origin, they returned to the city where they became squatters.

Things took a wretched turn everywhere. Humiliated, tortured and displaced, people were dying. A horrid brood of nightmares tore out of darkness to torment the people in broad daylight. The United Nations sent its representative, Tibaijuka, to assess the situation. She was shocked by the devastation, the human degradation and the loss of livelihoods that confronted her. I looked down on the ground and saw a sad broken shadow of a nation lying on a bed of crime, chaos and corruption. The beautiful land had fallen! All joy and pride licked off by political saliva and greed. Tongue tied, I waded through the corridors of gagged up voices and usurped justice. Rule of Law, weeping and alienated, lay sprawled on a stretcher in the Intensive Care Unit. My heart spun in a perpetual metamorphosis, refusing to live in that misery. Refusing to be held complicit by keeping my silence. What abominable devastation. The ruling party had painted its masterpiece. And no piteous cry for mercy appealed to their conscience.

*

I returned home from my journey mourning. Appalled and fragmented in spirit. My son opened the door for me and said:

"They were here!"

"Who?"

"The men in dark suits and dark glasses."

"What did they say?"

"They asked if you're training dissidents in Mozambique."

"But I'm not even staying in Mozambique."

"We know that."

"Black-hearted bastards."

"They've already planned something for you. They don't come visiting for nothing, my husband. Judgement has already been passed in your case. You are now only waiting to meet your sentence."

"What do I do?" Fear thrust a fish bone in my throat.

"You've got to go away again so that we can see you again. If you don't we may never see you again, we'll bury you in the graveyard like the others."

"A scrap-yard! I saw a scrap-yard today. That was no graveyard but a scrap-yard."

"If they are courteous enough to allow us to see you again!"

There was the sound of a vehicle coming to a stop outside. My wife lifted the curtain's corner and peered through the veiled window. Her face a mask she turned and faced me, thrust her purse in my hand and dragged me like a doll outside, pointing to the wall. Once more I felt the towering strength and wise intellect of that comparatively calm and dauntless woman. That formidable quick thinking female power which convinces and saves without fail all men who heed it against a stupid act of bravery.

"Go my husband! Go!"

I sped forward, leapt into the air, grabbing the top of the wall. I scaled it like a frantic robber, landing like a cat in my neighbour's yard. I flew up another wall and then another one into a half-lit yard where I encountered a tawny starving dog that seemed least disturbed by my sudden appearance. Starving and too frail to bark, it saved my life by gawking at me in silence. As if it knew and conspired against those who sought to lay their bloody hands on me! Again, I scaled the wall and landed into the next street. Turning into a sanitary lane that piloted me into another street I flew through the maze of township streets commanded by fear.

I found the main road and took a taxi to the Masvingo Road round-about, where I hitch-hiked to the second restaurant en route to Beit Bridge. Two buses came and halted for recess. I made myself invisible by keeping in the shadows. Speaking to no-one! Then a heavy truck rumbled into the yard. Immediately I went and talked to the driver. He was keen to have a passenger like me on board. I was his contraband. He could smuggle me through the border and I was like honey from heaven trickling onto his mouth. I paid him handsomely. He drove on with me sitting in the dark shadows of the truck's cabin behind him. The spirit of death over my turbulent head. My path once more stretched out beckoning the way that once saved my skin. I prayed that the agents of death did not find it worthy to exercise their nefarious sport upon my children and my wife, too. What a tumultuous brief re-union. And what a futile poignant endeavour it had been. Shattered, my heart bled.

THREE

I crossed the border curled up like a foetus in a cold giant toolbox that smelt of grease, steel and oily spanners. It was already dawn. No one discovered me. Just entering the town of Musina, the truck broke down. The driver called his depot for a mechanic. He yanked the toolbox lid open and I came out carrying the smell of its contents! Grease, iron and steel! I surely had the odour of a garage! We rolled into a nearby restaurant for breakfast where we ordered coffee and tea. I had tea since I found coffee a catalyst to my depression and my mind was not in the best of state. I took my meal in a hurry, said goodbye to the truck driver and stepped out into the street where the police sprang upon me like a sudden whirlwind.

"Papers?"

I fished out of the pocket my asylum document. He scanned it with his eyes and then scrutinized me in the face.

"I think I've seen you before."

"That's true."

"What're you doing here?"

"A friend of mine died on a farm down that side. I came to arrange his funeral and now I'm going back to Joburg," I lied.

"We told you we don't want to see you within a hundred kilometres of the border."

"I'm leaving now."

"There's a taxi stopping for refreshments at the garage. We'll take you there."

Just then, a company of female soldiers passed by chattering. One of them looked up and in raucous excitement she exclaimed:

"Mr Teacher! Hey, look at Mr Teacher."

"Hey! Mr Teacher!" Two of her colleagues echoed with enthusiasm.

"Yes. Are you well?"

"Yeah, thank you. What're you doing here?"

"You promised me your gun, remember?"

"Now, what have the freaks done?"

"They're leaking their diarrhoea all over my body."

"Come to my station then and I'll give you my machine gun." She said, laughing and moving away.

The police, then, bundled me into the back of their van and took me to the garage. At the taxi one of them said to the driver:

"Take this man away with you. We don't want to see him here. He causes trouble for us." The last time I was in that place I met one of the chiefs from back home. He had come to buy groceries for his family because the shops in Zimbabwe were empty. He was wearing his chain of chieftaincy around his neck. I looked at it with awe. Flattering him I asked him to take it off and let me handle it. He did. I took it in my hands and thanked him. Then I walked away. I did not give it back. Instead I instructed him to take a bus back home or else face what they were doing to us, too. A police van suddenly appeared round the corner which he stopped and made his report. The police looked at him and their leader told him that they never meddled in his country's politics. Without another word they started their vehicle and drove away. Scared and without support, the chief left with his tail between his legs.

Now the taxi driver laughed and said:

"What did you do to get this special treatment?"

"I nearly stole their van and they decided to send me away to Joburg."

Everybody in the taxi laughed and I was a miserable hero all the way to Joburg. I had learned not to dwell on my sorrows or anguishes but to live life in the moment. The desire for material things had unequivocally slipped out of my mind. My happiness was always within and had ceased to be determined by the outside world!. When we arrived the taxi driver said:

"They sent you where the police vans are like sand. You can steal and never finish them."

"I've changed my mind, I now want to steal taxis!" so I said, gliding away with my wife's purse clutched in my hands and leaving behind me a small group of gently humoured folks. Laughing graciously like the untouchable James Bond, I carried myself forward. I was back in Joburg, walking in the cold shadows of the city's silhouetted buildings, with the afternoon sun casting yellow belts of warmth in patches across the street like a camouflage. Enigmatic Joburg. The city of gold. Vast landscapes of breath-taking mansions in juxtaposition with scattered shacks like acne on a beautiful face. Block mountains of sandy earth spewed out of the abandoned gold mines, where men born poor died poor breaking their backs, stand out like gigantic monuments of their wasted lives. Mausoleums of their gelded pride. Poor communities relegated to a miasma of unwholesome breathing air and the threat of acid water. The glittering flow of purring steel beetles resplendent in a million colours on the free-ways. Titanic steel millipedes slithering in and out of Park Station carrying scores of people. What a gigantic maze of concrete, steel and sprawling network of tarmac and looming buildings dressed up in vast sheets of colourful glass. What an unending creation and celebration of sprouting corridors of wealth, chicanery and power.

With the smell of grease and oil still lingering in my soiled clothes my mind gyrated searching for meaning. Great was the urge I felt to go on with life. Never quit but follow it through where it took me! Challenges were to be worked with. Not to be avoided. Whether towards death or life, I shoved myself forward. A few metres in front of me, the strolling crowd scattered and the unmistakable form of Chimwene emerged like a cracked elephant. Huge veins bulging like ropes under the creased rash of his neck and face! Sores bleeding puss. Staring in front of him as if in a trance and trumpeting hoarsely:

"I'm Chimwene! God's whip sent to punish all mad and greedy people like you. Get out of my way."

I could not believe that I had been home and back. The bitter-sweet re-union had unfurled like a bizarre dream. Like a punishment instead of being fulfilling. Dejectedly, I glided into the Main Library's precinct where I sought a quiet spot to temporarily sit down and meditate on the soft green lawn. I felt the phantom of my spirit rise and float above me. All the cargo of my life played out before me like a barge leaping on a turbulent river. What had I done with it? What was the purpose of all this humiliation? I had escaped burrowed in a giant tool box and came out of it smelling of grease, oil and steel. Then the truck broke down and ironically needed someone who smelt like me to fix it. What was the significance of these events? Was there any scheme of things in our lives? The revolution in my country was the river which turned into a farce in which people were ludicrously charged with crimes, tortured and executed as if they were no more than undesirable animals. And I decided to run away with my beliefs to escape from the Socratic deaths they prepared for people like me. My inner self had to die and be resurrected on the streets of Joburg. In a blossoming metamorphosis that coined a new form of existence for myself. I felt myself recklessly pitched into a new larger useful life. Locked in a clearer vision of my own ideals, purpose and meaning. And love for all people. Change developed the vast spaces I never knew abounded for people in my mind, heart and spirit. Change pushed me to grow in spirit, to relinquish fear and those safe but limiting beliefs that contributed very little or no reward at all to my existence. It led me to sever all relationships that had become redundant and meaningless. I was determined to keep moving on.

Emerging from my meditation, I collected myself and calmly floated towards the Carlton Centre Hotel. The Lone Ranger. Crossing Market Street my cell-phone pealed.

"Bloggs speaking, hello!"

"Thank God! I got hold of you. Your phone was off, where were you?" What a desperate sounding voice, I thought.

"Out of the country. Who am I speaking to?"

"Melissa! You saved my life some time ago. I need to see you. Urgently."

"Where are you?"

"Ghandi Square."

"You want me to come there?"

"If you may, please!"

I crossed Commissioner Street and strolled into Ghandi Square. Melissa saw me from the balcony of a restaurant. Again my phone rang. It was her. She directed me to the restaurant's balcony and described what she wore to make it easy for me to locate her. I settled into a chair on the opposite side of the table. Smiling into her beautiful quivering face. I guessed she was feeling nervous. Yet she was bravely smiling too. Her deportment sincerely craving forgiveness. And acceptance. Something vaguely familiar about her sprang in the back of my mind. It felt whimsical. She was having coffee and asked me what I would like to have. I settled down for tea. For a brief moment she stared at my wife's purse in my hands. Then her soft voice escaped in a staccato manner as she spoke:

"I'm sorry for encroaching upon your time like this."

"Never mind. Maybe it was meant to be….."

"But I think I owe you some gratitude for what you did."

"I would be gladly available for you again."

"This sounds weird. Your voice. It feels like I've heard it before. Even before that conversation on the phone several months ago."

"I'm sorry, I have spoken to many people on the phone. Maybe you can refresh me on that talk."

"I was in a hotel near this very square, in the process of committing suicide when I called.…"

"I think I remember something, too."

"I don't know," she spoke with confusion in her face. "But something haunts me about you. Something remotely familiar.…."

We were both silent for a moment, looking into each other's face. A scene enveloped in the mist of the past started forming in my mind. A ghostly face. Tears. Anger. Frustration. A frenzied fight. And the smudge of rouge like a smear of blood on pouting lips.

"You're right. We've met before."

"You remember? What? Where?"

"Some time ago, you came out of a restaurant, fighting with your boyfriend. I think it was about an affair he was having with another girl. You hit him with your bag and your purse tumbled out onto the tarmac. I picked it up and restored it to you."

Melissa's mouth flew open with disbelief. The smile faded away from her face replaced by an expression of profound confusion. Guilt. Shame. And amazement. She opened her mouth to speak, but it took her about half a minute to find her voice.

"I'm terribly sorry I treated you that way. I had no right. Actually you had much right to be angry with me. Even now."

"Don't!" I raised my hand. "Don't punish yourself. My life was on the edge, too. And I had no right to say the words I said to you."

"What words?" I don't remember hearing any bad words from you. All I remember was my callousness to you. Please, forgive me."

"I forgive you. And will you, please forgive me, too?"

"For what? I don't know what you said but whatever you feel was improper coming from you, it couldn't be worse than my conduct and I forgive you with all my heart."

She stood up from her seat and came over to my side. I rose and we embraced in a conciliatory hug. When we disengaged, she stood for some time looking in my face. Then she went back to her seat.

"Since that call, I've been haunted by your voice. It felt familiar. Yet I couldn't lay my finger on it. Honestly, it has always been torture upon my conscience ever since that day. That day when you saved my life."

"I think there's a reason why we meet the people we meet in life. I thank you for calling and requesting this meeting. It means more than you can imagine for me." I wished she knew where I was coming from, what complex extremity my life was mired in; that I once contemplated suicide too. But courage and what my children would have to go through is what served me from the ignominy of bringing my life to such an end. The river of razor-wire for a fraction of a second surged through my heart. I felt its transitory blaze instantly torching my eyes and if Melissa saw it, she could have transposed it as a concurrent response to her discourse, for she touched my hand and I found it impossible not to support her with mine. We connected in a moment of silence together. Then her face thawed into a dimpled smile. A glittering light sprang in her eyes. I felt relieved and happy for her.

"How's your boyfriend?"

"We broke up. Soon after that fight."

"I'm sorry."

"I took to drugs like an eagle takes to gliding in the sky. Trapped in their ecstasy and abuse all reason shrivelled. I lost my job. Myself. All my strength. I became weak—so weak that I didn't know myself anymore. Not even what was right and what was wrong. I didn't care. Then I hit rock-bottom. I felt my battered soul being squeezed out of my needle perforated body. It was, then, in what I consider as my last hour, that I had the chance to speak to someone like you. Lying in the bath tub. Water turning red with the blood spilling out of my sliced wrists. I thought that was my goodbye call to life. Instead, it became my welcome back to life call," she paused effecting a soft laugh before continuing. "My siblings came and booked me into a rehab. Now I have another job and I'm starting all over. I really felt that I would never experience any peace of mind until I have thanked you. And guess what? I just realized that everything happens for a reason, there's a purpose why we meet all people we meet in life, too."

"The universe is such one big thing. Isolated incidents, with the dots connected, can serve to show and instruct in life. What they uncover to us or how they instruct us will be arrived at by how our senses make meaning of it all. By taking things the way we choose to take them, we exaggerate, distort or seek to understand them. By matching reason with honest feeling, we confront reality. Adversity comes by and we find ourselves trapped in the darkest hours of our life. Yet in those bleakest moments of misery if we confront our darkest self, beneath that lies a deeper resource of infinite proportions. But human beings as social animals have choices to make, it is how far deeper one is willing to go that makes the difference. ONE BIG CHOICE THAT HAS ALWAYS BEEN DIFFICULT FOR PEOPLE TO MAKE IS TO BE HAPPY. AND HOW!"

"I've never known true happiness. I craved luxury and all sorts of comfort that other children had which I did not have growing up. Drugs gave me the biggest lie of happiness I had ever known. Yet they became the biggest enemy and threat to my life. Hash. Cocaine. Heroin. And crystal meth. I did them all. I stole. I lied and burned bridges with people who loved me because of my shameful behaviour. I crashed into parties where I was not invited, ruining other people's beautiful occasions without any remorse. Living only for myself. Little did I know that I was an accident waiting to happen. It took me the moments of that call to realise that all I was doing was chasing after the wind," she spoke with an intensity of a breaking dawn in her apologetic tearful eyes. Apologetic to herself for the abuse she had visited upon her body. Apologetic to the people she had hurt.

My heart went out to her. I looked into her agitated eyes and saw a soul with so much to give to a world yet ambivalent to her reaching out hunger and suffering. At that moment, I could only extend my hands to hold her scarred twitching arms. The burden she carried ultimately hers to accept and best make sense of it in her own way.

"It sounds like you you've just stumbled upon something new."

"I have, a new consciousness," she said, deeply sighing and pausing, "and I will never let anyone rob me. Not anything can take away from me what I have now. Never."

I smiled and said:

"True! The happiest people are not those who possess the best of everything but those who know how to make the best of everything they have. The highs and lows of our lives cannot be better known by anyone else except ourselves. It is good hearing that a new path has sprouted front of you. A way that will give you control and turn your experiences into power? Whatever it's, I sense a new perception whose consciousness creates the world in which it inhabits. Some kind of life situation you are prepared to accept and live by according to your own way? My best wishes to you then."

*

My mind wanders. Another anguished face leaps into my consciousness. Regret washing over my soul. And the guilt of letting her down. In her difficult moment she had come to me. Overwhelmed and crippled emotionally by a rape perpetrated upon her two years ago by a man she knew. Isolated, spurned by her family and thrown away like the brick that the builder rejects for his building. All this because she has opened a case against the highly esteemed friend of the family.

"I wish to speak to a woman," she says full of distrust in her eyes.

"I will find her, please come with me," I respond, leading her to the kitchen where I offer her something to drink. I show her around the kitchen and switch the kettle on. I see that she picks up the coffee jar.

"You sound depressed," I say to her.

"I don't even know how I got here," she says, groping for words.

"Feels like someone has stopped taking care of herself," I say. "Seeing there's caffeine in there how about, maybe, we start with making some tea?"

She stops and looks at me with sad forlorn eyes. A brief spark flares in her eyes.

"I care for what you do to yourself, too." I tell her, smiling.

I leave her alone to make her own tea whilst I go in search of a woman to counsel her. I find someone but she is busy! She can only set up an appointment for another day. I am sitting at my desk in my office when Lebo walks in and says:

"Kate wants to see you again."

I follow Lebo out of the room to where Kate is just finishing her cup of tea. I ask her to follow me into another room where I kindly offer her a seat.

"I think a woman would understand me better because of what I went through," she says, uncertain whether she should go ahead and I acknowledge her vulnerability.

"I hear you that a woman is the ideal listener for your story but what brings you here is very important to you. Because it is very important to you, it is very important to me too."

A softening comes into her grey feline eyes. Again I see another wavering light. Doubt. Then resolve.

"I thought I should talk to you because I do not know whether I will still be alive when I leave this place."

"Your life is under threat of death and I'm wondering if you could let me in so that we can go through it together. And whatever it is, please, I humbly ask a contract with you that you will let me know about what will be happening to you."

"I will spare you the details of the rape," she says and then bursts out her story in erratic morsels.

She was raped by a benevolent uncle whose saintly virtue everyone believed. And for two years, justice has failed her. The man is powerful. He's the owner of a church. And very rich. Now broken and struggling to move on she has been cast out of the family because of her decision to seek justice. Turned into a recluse, her social circle has closed its doors upon her. Her world constricted. Dark. Shattered!

"Kate, you've carried this brutal betrayal and humiliation, the bleeding wounds and the trauma with rage, bitterness and powerlessness alone. Your disappointment in the law system that is failing you is infinite. What they've done is to turn on a festering conflict in your breast, in your life. Wherever you go. Your spirit is broken, your body weary and your mind relentlessly tortured! Overwhelmed and exhausted, you cannot continue the fight for justice and the fight to reclaim your dignity. Not in this depressed state and despair. I'm wondering whether we can try another way for yourself of seeing this from an angle that truly speaks about you? It's true that you did not ask to be violated. Will you forgive yourself from a script that you never wrote but was written for you? Where in all this can you claim a place of your own, stand on it because it is the truth that you identify with? A journey you're prepared to take because in it lies your control and gives you your power back?"

She stares at me and when she opens her mouth, the session takes a turn:

"Wow! It seems as if you're seeing inside my heart. Wow! I never thought there could be another different way. I'll go and think about it."

I ask her to explore it with her counsellor in their sessions.

"I don't want to see anyone else!" she says.

"Maybe you should see your counsellor first," I suggest.

"I'll be happy to see you again," she insists.

"When you've finished your sessions with your counsellor, I can see you."

I can see a shade coming into her innocent cute face. Hurt? Disappointment? I do not know. Then she leaves. Reluctantly.

Days pass into weeks. Then Lebo comes to me and says:

"Kate called. She wanted to speak to you."

"Did she leave you her contact telephone number?"

"No! She said that she would call again."

"Please, make sure you get her contact details when she calls again. Thank you."

Again days passed into weeks, weeks into months but with no sign of her. She does not even come for her appointment. The realisation hits me like a thunderbolt. Desperate and suicidal, Kate reached out. I opened the door. She came in! She wanted to come in again. And I closed the door in her face. To her, that was another rejection.

God! What have I done? Where is she now? Could anything have happened to her?

*

It was the staccato voice that swept me back to reality:

"Can I ask you something?" she timidly said.

"Feel as free as air."

"There's still a lot of mist in my mind, I need you to clear it. I thought the person who picked up my purse and gave it back to me looked like someone staying on the street," her voice trailed off as if fearing to offend me.

I smiled and said:

"Do not doubt your senses about what you saw on that day. Truly, I was staying on the street. Yet on that day by twist of events and thought, I realized I was not living my life. That evening, I got my salvation, too."

She opened her eyes wide in wonder.

"Yes! THOUGHTS ARE VERY POWERFUL."

"You're right. And I'm convinced I've done the right thing looking for you."

Again she rose to her feet and came to my side. Again I rose and hugged her. I felt her solid small body talking. Expressing a world teeming with secrets and regret. Releasing. Settling. A monster dying in her past. And mounting anticipation. We went back to our seats again. But we did not sit down. I gulped down the last of my tea and when I put the cup down the dregs formed a star at the bottom before turning into a mere puddle. My eyes playing tricks? I removed my spectacles. Wiping them. It was then I felt the agitation in my eyes and I knew what it was. Sleep.

"May I call you again?"

"You're welcome, Melissa."

Then we parted and walked apart. I turned to see how she was going and saw that she had turned too. Our eyes met and I saw she carried a rapturous smile on her face. With every step I made, I tried to figure out what life was now like for an angel with scarred wrists where she had slashed herself. They were big scars and she had not been ashamed to show them to me. I could not help but wonder about the big scars in her heart, too. I am sure she got the faint odour from my clothes. But I did not tell her about the wounds discharging that deceptively placid smell of grease, oil and steel! I humoured myself that she could have imagined that my car suffered a breakdown and I was called upon to fix it which would account for that pungent perfume. Yet the truth was that I owned no car!

I went to the youth care centre in Soweto where I once volunteered. Vimbai who was now about to move out together with her boyfriend Tim sorrowfully drifted to me. Her face dark with incomprehensible sadness:

"I'm sorry, I disappointed you."

"Why, my child?"

"I slept with my caregiver for favours." She burst out crying. I held her hand. She dropped her head with shame and the tears flooded down her chubby cheeks.

"Did you report him?"

"No. I consented. Will you forgive me?"

"I forgive you, my child. But I want us to talk about it some more. This is very important." Her intelligible taut clipped words exploded in my ears and I felt the rush of a massive current such as one that breaks a dam wall. Humiliated, degraded, broken and her self-esteem trodden under the heel of a callous selfish man supposed to be her protector. I was shaking with anger when she finished.

"When did it happen?"

"Several months ago."

"We must do something about it."

"No! What will people say? I had no food and I was hungry. I am the one to blame because I agreed. And Tim was not working. I am ashamed. No-one must know about this. Especially my boyfriend because we are about to get married."

"I will not judge you. You may be just getting over eighteen years old now but in this place no one must take advantage of your needs and be allowed to exploit you! Not even your caregiver! That's a serious misconduct. Think about it carefully and come back to me. Something definitely must be done and I will be here for you!"

What could I do for her? I now knew her secret! Yet to divulge it would be to jeopardise her future with the man she loved. I was aware of the food shortages sometimes faced by the children at the centre and the thing I feared most had happened! Young girls looking for boyfriends and being abused in desperate times of hunger! And I had done nothing! Even though sometimes I took money out of my purse to buy the girls bread when there was no supper served. The tragedy was not the criminal act of violation but that what had been broken inside her would never be mended! The dent that she will carry forever simply because the system absolutely failed to protect her!

"Can I still call you Dad? I never knew what it means to have a father in my whole life." She asked timidly wiping the tears away.

"Yes my angel! You're my daughter! Always have been! And always will be!"

"Thank you, Dad!"

I hugged her in my arms. Tension escaped from her body. Then she floated away like an awakening spirit. And so awoke the pangs of regret that would sit upon my conscience throughout my life! The same day another nineteen-year-old student came to me holding her phone in her hands and said:

"These are the messages he sent me!"

"Who?"

"My caregiver."

She showed me the messages and the cell-phone number they were sent from. It belonged to her caregiver.

"Did you report him?"

"Yes!"

"What happened?"

"He was reprimanded."

"Only that?

I was furious! I vowed not to be part of this obscenely sadistic system where women were treated like rubbish. Every community is judged by the way it treats its women, children and elderly people! And this was an institution founded on a commitment to protect, heal and nurture vulnerable young people. Such an assault upon one defenceless, already struggling with loss of sense of oneself and threadbare feelings of belonging, to me, was tantamount to a crime against humanity. I felt my conscience challenged to action. My sin rose, too. Unveiling a priority I could not postpone. Patience. I HAD TO FIND MY DAUGHTER.

I took my cell-phone and logging on to my Facebook account wrote:

"A man who finds greatness and joy in the service of the poor and the broken hearted is a blessed man for he lives the world a light of God's purpose and creation."

Someone liked my status! I checked. It was the same caregiver! I was appalled. I thought I should add something to my status and again wrote:

"Virtue stands above knowledge. It towers above justice because it leads it. It is a cultivated extension of the humanity inside us. One finds it when one's heart and spirit sublimely submit to the sacred essence promoting the principles that honour and respect for human life are a commitment tasked upon us as something we should never fail."

Again the hypocrite liked my status.

Disgusted and in a seething rage, I logged out and took a taxi to Jabulani. My phone rang and I answered:

"Bloggs speaking, hello!"

"We urgently need your service! One of our supermarkets was robbed. A group of fifteen armed men stormed the shop. They shot dead the shift manager and one of the staff members fell from the first floor to the ground floor."

"May you, please, send me your physical address?"

When I arrived the people were still being further traumatised by police questioning. There was so much blood splashed everywhere in the cash office where the shift manager had been shot and on the floor where the lady staff member had fallen and died. She hit the concrete floor with the back of her head first, splitting her skull and dying on the spot. Some of them could barely speak. I walked their shaking frames into a safe, well ventilated room and asked for the management to provide them with something warm to drink. They could hardly think for themselves. Then I quickly went through their individual needs, made calls for their relatives to come and fetch them. I gave a brief talk on trauma, listening to what they were going through and asked them to take note of any emotional and physical changes they might be experiencing with the passage of time. I could only contain them and bring some kind of normalcy to what they were going through. They were still steeped in shock, so I set up an appointment to do proper trauma debriefing seventy-two hours after the incident. Then I left.

*

I walk alone. Cold. There is no fire that can keep me warm and alive than the fire of my children. The love of my wife. All that I left behind. I feel like someone has just pulled me out of my clothes. A furless rabbit. Blood rushes to my mind. Thoughts flow. Ideas explode. Screens tumble. I feel the world beckoning to me. Calling me. Asking me to live my life with me. To see myself in the broken multitude of the earth. Commanding me to appear from the dreaded spaces that the "us" do not wish to acknowledge. THE TRUTH that walks the streets like a vagrant while we see nothing of ourselves in the suffering being.

FOUR

When I arrived at the centre, I had the immutable dread of meeting with Connie in the passage. Where I stole the unctuous love charm that she now fell all over me, I never knew. I had looked in her eyes and seen the depths of her irrevocably tortured beautiful soul. It struck me with a nameless fear. I loved her but, truly, I could not give her what she needed. A husband. Yet I felt too the pain of having to let go of her. I felt smothered by the antagonistic feelings of falling in love on one hand and having the right thing to do on the other hand. I felt bad having to break her heart. I recalled her asking me what love was and how I abundantly experienced the flow of our feelings like two rivers approaching an unsparing confluence. Such a natural confluence desperately laboured against and diverted may still be painful, yet if allowed to merge the consequences can have lifelong devastating effects. I suffered a sweet burning pain which I decided to extinguish before it developed the consuming power of an unquenchable wildfire. Before I left, she had called me and said:

"Hi Sunshine! I'm nothing away from you."

I feared she was going to resign from her work and return, yet secretly I had a fiery longing for her warmth. There was a shadow in the doorway. My heart stopped. But only Dan appeared from the kitchen. I was a man relieved. And he was baffled.

"Already back?"

"There's somewhere I don't have a home. Ironically the place I left my heart."

"Sad! But good to have you back in one piece."

"I went to give my wife and my children what I had run away with! LOVE and CARE. Yet I came back without giving them even a shred of it. I feel empty and powerless."

"You sound depressed."

"You're right. But I won't go down that road again."

"We had to go through it so that we could be aware of the best of our shadow qualities! And how to befriend the shadow."

"Sadness is a necessary part of life. How would we know what happiness is without having tasted the pain of sadness and sorrow?"

"How did you find your family?"

"I don't know what to say. All I can say is that, at least, my presence washed away a flood of emotions that had been hurting them all along."

"That means you can still have a beautiful relationship together."

"I long for that! The landscape beckons us to turn towards instead of away. I will give everything time to grow. Only the politicians still remain a menace to the prosperity of our country."

"Still waters run deep?"

"Yes. The president and his garrulous wife overtly and covertly continue to run down the country, seizing properties, state enterprises, lands, dams and making mineral claims. Greedy scoundrels. The whole country now belongs to them. She even uses state funds to pay her workers. Chimwene is hitting the nail on the head when he says she is the fly in our soup."

"Bastards! But what about the coup?"

"What coup?"

"Oh! You haven't heard? The army staged a coup last night against the dictator."

"Really?" I thought Dan was joking.

"It's all over the news. The army has taken over the national radio station and all the police stations have been rendered inoperative. The two arms of the state are not working together in terrorising the citizens. At least for now. The army runs the show. They caught comrade Chamba with US10 million packed in bags which was hidden in his mansion. And the shocked president together with his family have been placed under house arrest. The army and the ruling party are seeking his resignation. But the president laughed brazenly saying that he will only hand over power to the opposition leader. Holding them complicit in all the elections he rigged. They all stole. Then he accused the army general of treason only punishable by death. Ironically it's the army general sharpening the guillotine blade. And he doesn't see it. After that he released a speech that he had spoken to his friends in other countries who had pledged to come and help him get back his presidency."

"What?" I was shocked. The moment I was crossing the border, a coup to oust the president had actually been in progress? There was no radio on the truck in which I had made my escape. I had been shut out in my own world. Inside the gigantic tools' box. Keeping as much less contact with people as possible.

"He still thinks he's the president. He's dreaming. And I'm sure his cantankerous wife is having a hard time flogging him back to his senses. They have to hatch an escape plan before the masses come to roast their insolent fat tails."

"Recently she sounded schizophrenic, making vulgar declarations that she will be the next president. Are you sure Dan?"

"As sure as my mother gave birth to me." Dan said laughing. He laughed exultantly like a toilet flushing diarrhea down the sewer pipes. "Tomorrow all the masses march to the state house and remove him permanently."

"They make my blood boil. I don't feel like talking about their shocking venal life for now. And their dissolute brood is downright disgusting." My mind was moseying up the insane wall and I decided to change the conversation to another subject proximate to my heart:

"Is Connie back?"

"Yes."

"Where's she?"

"She came and found you gone. What a holocaust I saw. Like a bombed-out mansion. I don't think she was thinking straight. She called her husband. He came flying. She packed her bags and they rolled away together like two stray ghosts that could not remember the location of their graves. I still see her walking as if about to collapse. And the merciless wind shoving her around like a distraught shadow or like a lamb being led to slaughter. It all happened in my eyes like a sad enduring movie."

"Sometimes the old that once seemed right ceases to be and one has to stick with the truth to do what is best. I'm sticking with the truth. I've no reason to break my marriage. Though I wonder about her reason to go with her husband, will she keep him?" I spoke more to myself.

*

Sighing bubbles of a searing pain on the margin of despair, I opened my satchel and fished out a bottle of Johnnie Walker Red Label Whisky. What a loss. Like a diamond one picks up and then discovers one cannot keep it. Yet there is a kind of treasure better lost forever before it can be enjoyed, for to keep it and experience its splendour would be embracing self-degradation and cosmetic bliss. I wondered whether the phenomenal deluge of losses and transient reprieves would ever trickle to an end. Dan disappeared back into the kitchen and brought a couple of glasses. He poured the whiskey into the glasses, mixing it with some Mazoe Orange Crush, diluted with water. I sent a lavish measure of it rippling down my arid commiserating throat. I did not know what I was celebrating. Connie's departure? Or the coup and no coup back home?

"You have a couple of silver hairs growing on your head." Dan observed.

"I fear getting old more than dying. I hate being dependent. Getting old and decrepit, alone in a foreign land is a scary idea to me."

"They say with age comes wisdom."

"I don't think you can say that about the American President. He just called our continent a 'shit-hole' in a tweet."

"If it's a shit-hole then what are we? Only maggots live in a shit-hole hole. That man is insulting us."

"I don't like becoming smaller and clumsy, which age makes us do but I think that man is very arrogant and deceitful. He's misleading his own country into kingdom hate."

My cell-phone vibrated showing a new message. It came from my beloved wife. I opened it. The screen blazed with her status:

"Loneliness is tearing my heart. I'm coming to where the cure is."

"MY LOVE?" I replied.

"Yes. I'm coming to you. I just boarded the bus now. And behind I leave a pitiful country celebrating a deposed president. Out of the tyrant's pan into the Military Junta's fire." I was overwhelmed with joy. Then she sent me a picture of our son standing high on an army tanker.

"But he's not even a soldier! What's he doing there?"

"In this country we now need everybody to be a soldier. The leaders and soldiers we have today don't represent the interests of the people. We cannot have land grabbers who chase away all the farmers because they think they can plough the land with guns. Not at all. Such people are dangerous to our nation. They must be weeded out. They only represent The Political Party of Thieves. And their selves."

"True! Come safely to me MY LOVE."

"I will, MY HUSBAND. Get ready to be drenched with LOVE."

FIVE

I have a new room at the centre. The storeroom. Things have taken a tumble at the centre. A pervasive attitude of selfishness, anger and manipulation prevails. I do not understand why but most of the children are happy to have me back. I am still volunteering but there are a few people I see not happy with my presence. I am minding my own business, so I do not pay them much attention. A child comes and knocks on my door. Half-awake I take time to respond. He knocks again and I struggle to my feet like an overturned beetle. Clumsy. Red eyed and tired because I have been typing on my computer the whole night.

"Who's it?"

"It's me, Mudhara," a timid voice floats into the room.

"Who answers to the name of It's Me? I didn't know we had someone with that name in this place." I respond unlocking the door, only to find Manasa standing there. He looks unsettled, glancing up and down the corridor as if he does not want to be seen by anyone coming to my room. I let him in.

"What's it? Are you all right?"

"Sorry to wake you up," he stutters.

"Don't worry! I have time any time," I smile back at him. "Sit down and tell me."

"Some big boys are bringing girls into the study-room. They sleep the whole night with them in there."

"What?"

"You can go and see for yourself right now."

I step into my slippers and tell Manasa to go away while I pay a visit to the study-room. It does not have a lock. I knock on it gently and ask to come in. I recognise the voice that answers me. I walk in. With respect. Tonde slips out of the blanket. He looks embarrassed.

"May you come with me?"

"Yes, Mudhara." he replies.

We go to my room where I ask him to sit down in my office chair.

"Who was with you in the blanket?"

"My girlfriend."

"Who?"

"Rute."

"Why're you sleeping with her in the study-room?"

"I'm protecting her."

"From what? From who?"

"A lot is happening here Mudhara. Even some of the young boys have been sexually abused."

"What?"

"I won't say much because it's useless to talk about it. In fact one gets targeted for complaining, here. I regret saying this but it's true. They don't want the police to know about it. They tell us that if the police gets to come, we'll be deported because we don't have papers."

I just sit on my bed. Frozen. Now I understand the secret meetings where I am not invited. Classified info that can bring the home into disrepute. Is that it? I'm going to rock the party.

*

"Where I am things happen." I say to myself, thinking about my old friend who had, upon seeing me, declared that I had something to do with the protests in which several people were arrested. And now the abuse of the young people at the centre.

"What do you mean?" Dan asks.

"Something happened when I visited home. Now I see that presence and participation in events are two different things. Change can never happen on its own. People have to stand up and kick the empty gourds sitting on the shoulders of our politicians. It's our choice to allow other people to carry our heads for us. I AM CONSCIOUS. Yes. I AM CONSCIOUS. I have lived my life without me for a long time. That's why I've always felt bored, restless and powerless with my life. Captured by all sorts of absurd emotions, anxiety and loneliness. Yes. Living without me! Longing for a living organism that can never be there without the spirit of its heart. A spirit of consciousness. All the citizens make the heart of the nation but it is their individual choice to be that spirit. Today I choose to be CONSCIOUS. To be ME." the words ripple past my lips punching into the air.

"But your ME is only a drop in the ocean. It makes no difference."

"Yes! What about your ME too? What about everyone's ME put together? Isn't that what makes an US? A NATION?"

"True. But you know the Military Junta kills. Remember the abductions, the short sleeves and the shootings on the streets of Harare. Joburg Beer boiling in your stomach?" Dan mocks my frustration.

He belches into the night. Joburg Beer! It smells like rotten things when you belch. Most men and women who take it do not have partners. If they do have, they both take it. Otherwise it is a punishment to sleep in the same blanket with one who has taken Joburg Beer. It makes one's body stink. We now only drink it when we are broke and frustrated. When nothing is suffocating our minds we prefer staying sober.

We like drinking Black Label a lot at Bizek's water-hole. Sometimes it is cheap brandy or gin and water at home, especially when we have to celebrate or spoil the brat in us. Bizek and his mother love us and protect us from bad toppers who come to their shebeen and want to harass us or share our purse.

"You didn't buy a beer Animal." she would shout at one particular topper who came to us most of the time we were there. "Make your way to Bizek and buy yours. That bottle has only one small outlet for one mouth. Go buy one for your mouth like everyone else."

But today we are drinking a distance away from home in Moletsane. Drinking Joburg Beer only. It is another shebeen we are trying. We are sitting on building blocks outside. I stare beyond the towering streetlights into the starry night. Feeling with pleasure the caged power within my body. Trying very hard to be in tune with it. And the pulsating life outside.

A woman screams, her shrill voice cutting through the night like a knife. There is a shack in the corner of the yard and that is where the scream comes from.

"Why do you light the stove all the time? Such blistering heat and you light the stove. What for?" her angry voice spills all over the yard.

"Now look what you've done to my dress." the woman charges out. There is a big hole in her new dress.

"I'm cold Lerato," stutters a frail man who limps out after her. He is holding his Joburg Beer in one hand. He stops in the middle of the yard to take a sip and then shivers like a cold dog.

"You've just ruined my dress now!" she roars stripping herself down to her panties in front of everyone. No petticoat under her dress. "There! Go ahead and burn it all. You idiot."

Before anyone else knows what is happening, she pounces upon him. We see a lioness. There is no Joburg Beer in the man's hand anymore. It is raining upon his small bald head and soon he is soaked in it. Smelling like a dirty bar he stands trembling in the middle of the yard.

"The cold will kill me Lerato," he says stumbling back into the shack and we all burst laughing.

"I'm tired of you Shakes! Too much *nyaope*."

She slaps him in the face and her face knit with anger, ripples back into the shack. The laughter dies into a murmur of voices. Dan gets up to go to the toilet. Matt still has not arrived from his school where he is now teaching in Joburg. I feel pity for this man reduced to a jerk by his girlfriend in front of everyone. I am happy my wife found me my life not messed up. He no longer shines like a star in the eyes of the one who, perhaps, once cried for his love. The *nyaope* drug has robbed him of all the fire. We are stars in our own right! Miles away and lost out of the galaxy. Shining in the wilderness that accepts and does not accept us. One day we will return to our place in the galaxy. Our beloved country. Our lustre restored. Back with all our loved ones where we will no longer be wasted tragic figures that look like bats.

The music starts playing. Lerato yelps from inside the shack. She forgets about looking for a clean dress to put on. Stoned or drunk I don't know what to call it for she is taking both weed and Joburg Beer! In a staggering waltz she comes to stop in front of the radio. Jerking and jerking her waist and butt with her back to the people. Then like one tripped she falls to the front taking the position of one doing press-ups. Her whole body trembles and people shout. She opens her legs, the left one bending down and the right one thrust upwards. She moves the right leg from her foot to the butt in rhythmic circles to the thundering music. She is doing the new dance craze known as the gwara-gwara. The howling crowd is obscenely infected with her gyrating waist. They go gwara-gwara wild and like frenzied frogs some trip to the ground on all fours.

A youthful group starts the fast paced, leg twisting and stomping pantsula dance on the other side. The bat-like figure of Shakes staggers into the midst of this group. Juggling his feet like the piston of an engine about to cease. Wheezing. Ghostly. And eyes glazed. He shuffles his legs, skinny arms flailing in the wind like writhing worms. No one notices his presence. His long feet glued to the ground. He feebly stretches out his hands and thrusts his tall arching body forward but nothing much actually happens. Then he reels backwards in slow motion, like a tree being felled or a huge scarecrow clutching at the wind, he hits the ground with the back of his head. Foaming at the mouth. Twisting and twitching, he lies. Then he becomes still. The music thunders on. Forgotten. And the people gather around the fallen Shakes. Lerato shrieks wildly. Something about Shakes not leaving her alone. His faded eyes staring into the sky show no recognition of anything at all. There is very little they can do. Shakes has departed!

*

"For how long shall we continue to be their marionettes, running around like mice whilst they pull the strings of fear? For how long shall we oscillate between hope and despair with the steering wheel of our destiny in their hands?" I blurt out.

"You left your loved ones so that you could see them again, remember?" says Dan, tucking in his shirt.

"We speak and condemn their evil, yet our actions dither between truth and the lies we choose to comfort ourselves with. How we choose like worms to wriggle in a place between nobility and cowardice."

"A single man does not take an army, Bloggs. Sometimes, even the strongest of armies has to retreat. Remember Napoleon? His mighty conquering army kept on advancing against the fleeing enemy. Seeking to annihilate the Russian army. Deeper and deeper he was led against his own better judgement to eventually defeat himself by following the Russians army all over vast Russia. Victory will prevail on the military junta's side, unless we fight with our minds."

"Right and wrong. This war can never be left for nature to decide. They can chase us all over the country but CONSCIOUS is the word - we all need to be CONSCIOUS. We'll have no power to liberate the country until everyone is CONSCIOUS."

The emaciated figures with caricatured human lineaments I have seen in my country leap back in a deluge, zooming like bats in my mind. Heartrending tormented souls. Figures such that one could never miss the sound of liquid cascading down the pipes of their bent skeletal bodies. The SHATTERED LIVES of a BRUTALIZED NATION. The meaning of their lives from sunrise to sunset and darkness making no difference at all. Vicious explosions of immense sadness and pain tear through my heart. What a holocaust.

The military junta, threatening all opposition with war, haunts the streets. Castrating men in front of their women. Their words like fish bones stab into our ear-drums. The crunching step of their march hammers fear into the people's hearts. Their brutal hands slapping the people's heads till the ears bleed out their wisdom and sense of humanity. Punching them in the face till their teeth are reduced to rubbery flesh whose words mean nothing. Stabbing their eyes till they explode in darkness and see no evil at all.

Meanwhile the emperor with no clothes on flashes his spear in front of the women's league and dusts his bottom over the nation. What posturing sabre toothed conmen. Bedfellows in stealing elections, crimes against humanity and the betrayal of the nation. Yet now denying their tribe they brazenly skin their kith and kin. Trading each other for political expediency. In a bid to keep the loot and fake show of rigorous justice. They strut in their starched army uniforms and shimmering suits like cockroaches, striving to brainwash the people's minds of the squalid dismal state they had plunged the country into. A cell version of the deposed president had usurped the throne. But the fury in the people's voice could be heard cracking like lightning:

"WE WILL PULL YOU OUT OF YOUR HIDE!"

They raise their fists and guns, roaring back feeble words that collapse like spaghetti in front of their eyes:

"WE WILL PULL YOU OUT OF THE IMPERIALIST CURSE."

People speak. Nothing changes. How ironic. A country without monetary currency. No exports. Surviving on imports only. Miniscule taxation revenues. Insane Gross Domestic Product ratios. An escalation in corruption and poverty. Emigration of highly skilled personnel. Scared investors - ENTER AT OWN RISK - the sign at the door reads. And then the countless broken homes…

Figures of people sleeping on the streets of Joburg surge out of the captured sea of human suffering in the back of my mind. The reel plays out in a jumbled mess. I cannot focus. Cross-eyed at the crossroads I stand. The clarity of an old experience seen in a new truth. The painful truth that we refuse to see and accept simply because there is no comfort in it. A cauldron of burning scenes telling an epic battle of survival by a people strung on borrowed time, false promises and hope.

Connie's large face, blazes out of a pocket of hope somewhere in my heart. Bursting like a flame lily she captures the passion and spirit of my thoughts. I have to blink my eyes several times and rub them to convince myself that she is not there in person. I am secretly craving for her voice again. Antagonistically waiting for her next call.

The slide passes on. Prostitutes in mini-skirts sit on doorsteps with their legs wide open. Pole-dancing in night clubs. Others getting their throats slit by marauding perverts and women haters afterwards. Cracked youth high on drugs, glue and cough-mixture! There is a new drug on the street. *Nyaope*. A merciless killer. They say it is made from Anti-Retroviral Drugs, rat poison, cough-mixture and other stuff. Gangs of men mugging distracted people in the street. Lost men who have forgotten their wives and children. Men and women using children to beg on the streets. Murder, rape and other things that burn one's eyes and cut to the brain like a blow-torch roll out in a frenzied kaleidoscope. The good and bad things. Soothed by the purr of sleek vehicles on freeways and music booming out of nearby drinking spots.

I take my phone out of my pocket to log onto my Facebook account. I cannot. With shock I realise that it has been hacked. God! And where are the ogres in dark glasses? I look around nervously. Their eyes are said to be everywhere. Like evil spirits.

The bitter-sweet manifestation in my burning mind glows in a pool of molten words. THEY DO NOT KNOW WHAT THEY HAVE DONE AND WE DO NOT KNOW WHAT WE HAVE DONE! We have made politicians our solutions and our solutions politicians. If only we could forget about all our politicians and start from the strength of what we are as a people. Realizing the treachery in the coup, a mercurial ripping thought detonates a bomb of iron filings that tears to my weary heart:

I have walked through fire without being burned and the wilderness that I wander is nothing but a wonder. Obeying my burden I will keep walking my journey. This ontological journey threatening to kill me if I stop. Joburg Beer and Johnnie Walker, stay with me all the way.

My cell-phone vibrates. There is a new message:

"Our bus just stopped in Pretoria. I can't wait to see you my husband."

Fifty minutes! That is all I have to get to Joburg from Soweto before she arrives at Powerhouse Station. I have to go. Right now!

About the Author

Thompson Charlie is a former school teacher turned writer and counsellor. He has published some of his poetry works online with Poetry Potion and Munyori.

He lives in exile in Johannesburg, South Africa where he spends most of his time travelling, doing charity work with local and foreign unaccompanied minors, orphans, and youth at risk. He also does voluntary counselling for Life-Line Johannesburg, a non-governmental organization based in Johannesburg.

Thompson Charlie is happily married to Margaret and they have been blessed with three sons. When he has taken care of serious business, he either sneaks into his magical world of poetical reveries with good music that shakes the body or just loses his mind to nature and appreciating the beauty of feeling alive in the universe.

Visit the website at +

Subscribe to the newsletter at

You can also follow the author on social media
Instagram:
Twitter:
FaceBook:

About the Publisher

Sulis International Press publishes select fiction and non-fiction in a variety of genres under four imprints: Riversong Books, Sulis Academic Press, Sulis Press, and Keledei Publications.

For more, visit the website at
https://sulisinternational.com

Subscribe to the newsletter at
https://sulisinternational.com/subscribe/

Follow on social media
https://www.facebook.com/SulisInternational
https://twitter.com/Sulis_Intl
https://www.pinterest.com/Sulis_Intl/
https://www.instagram.com/sulis_international/